LP M ROBINSON
Robinson, Steve (Novelist),
author.
The penmaker's wife

The Penmaker's Wife

Center Point
Large Print

**This Large Print Book carries the
Seal of Approval of N.A.V.H.**

The Penmaker's Wife

STEVE ROBINSON

CENTER POINT LARGE PRINT
THORNDIKE, MAINE

For my wife, Karen

PROLOGUE

London
1880

It was barely past daybreak, the gas lamps still cooling in the foggy half-light of what promised to be another fine summer's morning, yet the woman could already hear the city coming to life around her. Another hour and its busy thoroughfares would be crowded with hansom cabs and swaying omnibuses, the pavements loud with lively footfalls and the cries of the costermongers. But what did any of that matter to her? In another hour she would be floating in the Thames.

'Mummy, let go! You're hurting my hand.'

'You're five years old now, William. You must stop crying,' the woman said, her words conveying a good education and only the slightest hint of a French accent. 'I'm sorry, but we have to hurry.' She reasserted her grip on the boy's hand, their fates intertwined as they made their way along one of Southwark's dingier streets. It was strewn with straw, and rich with the stench of manure and other unsavoury odours that permeated the air from the open windows of a hundred overcrowded rooms.

'Where are we going?' the boy asked with a huff.

'To a better place. Now be patient and you'll see.'

'Is Daddy coming too?'

The woman gave no answer. Instead, she continued to pull the small boy along behind her, her pace quickening until she was almost dragging him. Every now and then she would look over her shoulder, not at the boy, but further back along the street, peering through the morning fog, watching for the man she was sure had seen her and was now coming after them. It didn't matter. Where they were going, no one in their right mind would follow.

They came to Tooley Street station and continued alongside the railway arches at a relentless pace, the boy growing heavier on her arm by the minute. The sudden clack of horses' hooves startled her as a hansom cab seemed to come out of nowhere, but she did not let up.

'Read all about it in *The Globe*!' a newspaper seller called as they turned the corner in the direction of London Bridge.

What good was a life without purpose or hope? she wondered.

Such thoughts had been her bedfellows on many a long night, but today she was resolved to silence them. If this was all her life had to offer then she was through with it. As the bridge came into view, she slowed her pace until they were level with the wharf gate. She stepped on to the bridge and stopped, momentarily mesmerised by the stone balustrade that spanned its length. She took another step and her eyes were drawn down to the murky green water of the River Thames, which was flowing fast on the ebb tide.

Then someone called her name.

'Angelica!'

She caught her breath. There was now no question that she was being followed. She pulled William onwards, brushing past an elderly match seller who was draped from head to toe in black, out early to catch the gentlemen on their way to work.

'Excuse me,' she called back, noting the growing number of people around her, some staring at her while others gave her a wide berth as she weaved between them. She supposed it was because of the sudden urgency in her step, the frantic look in her eyes, and the tatty clothes she and her son were wearing. They were out of place among all the fine frock coats, tall toppers and bowlers of the gentrified populace, but what did any of them know about her? She owned a beautiful turquoise gown as fine as any belonging to their wives, but she wasn't about to waste it on Old Father Thames.

When they reached the middle of the bridge, where the water was at its deepest, Angelica

9

stopped. Her heart began to pound harder, to the point where she thought she was going to be sick. She took a few slow breaths to help calm herself as she looked out over the balustrade at the various paddle steamers, barges and sail-boats on the river, which at this time of day were mostly moored at the banks. Then she looked further out towards the Tower, which, because of the fog, she was unable to make out. She thought that was good. With the current so strong, it would only be a matter of seconds before they were out of sight of anyone looking down at them from the bridge. Any waterman brave enough, or foolish enough, to attempt a rescue would not find them.

Without another moment's hesitation she turned back to William and picked him up, setting his small booted feet down on the top rail.

'Mummy?' he called to her, fear in his voice. 'I want to go home.'

'I've spoken to you about this, William,' Angelica said as she lifted the hem of her dress and climbed up after him. 'Now give me your hand. There isn't much time.'

William did not offer his hand, so Angelica took it, holding it so tightly she thought she might crush it.

'I say! Come down from there with that boy.'

Angelica spun around and saw a well-dressed man pointing a walking cane at her. Then, out of the corner of her eye, she saw the man who had been following them. He was running, as if to stop her, a squat bowler hat on his head and a limp that gave his approach a somewhat cumbersome gait. She turned back to her son and quickly lifted him into her arms.

'Don't cry, William,' she said, his small body trembling in her embrace. She smiled kindly at him. 'God is watching over us. Today we shall be born again.'

She felt a tug at the hem of her dress, but it came too late. As she finished speaking, she transferred the boy's weight to one arm, crossed her chest with the other, and jumped.

CHAPTER ONE

Winson Green, Birmingham
1896

As the Lord is my witness, what I am about to tell you is the truth of the matter, whatever the events that follow may lead you to believe, however dark and unimaginable they may appear. It should be noted that even now, after all the terrible things that have transpired, I do not regret falling in love with Angelica Chastain. Neither do I regret the circumstances in which I now find myself because of her. If I had known where our relationship would lead when we first met, I would do it all again in a heartbeat, such is the strength of my love for her. But all that is yet to come. For now, I must start at the beginning, from the events that led to that fateful day when we first met, and my life was changed forever.

You may in time come to question the authority of my account. You may find what I have to say too unpalatable to accept that it could possibly be true. I can offer no proof save that of my own eyes and my own ears, which you may therefore ascribe to nothing more than one word against another. You may not wish to believe it, but you must, if not for my sake then for the sake of all others who may yet come to know her and love her as I have.

I have been told much of what follows by Angelica herself, whom you may soon come to regard as an unreliable source, but when the time comes, consider this: why tell me at all? Perhaps she did so out of pity, although I choose to believe it was out of love, however unlikely that may seem once you have heard what I have to say. Either way, she did so knowing no one would believe me, but I implore you to do so, for I have nothing now to gain from lying.

I suspect the cause of it all really began long before I met Angelica, perhaps as long ago as her childhood in France, or her formative years living in the slums of London. But for the purposes of what I have to tell you, it began when Angelica first came to live in Birmingham with her son, William. That was sixteen years ago now, and I can honestly say that, to a point, they were the best sixteen years of my life. She and William arrived on a train one day with little more than the clothes on their backs. It was an inauspicious new beginning that augured failure even before it began, but despite the dangers and the dire circumstances they would soon face, Angelica was resolved to do whatever it took to succeed in making a better life for them both, particularly for William.

It was all for William.

London
1880

The London and North Western Railway train from Euston station was running almost ten minutes late, and with every passing second Angelica Chastain became more and more anxious. It was a quiet, mid-afternoon departure, and thankfully she and little William had their second-class compartment to themselves for now. She supposed that would soon change, though, if not by the time the train left, then further down the line as it made its scheduled stops.

She continued to stare out of the window, wondering what had caused the delay, seemingly transfixed by the large Pears soap advertisement on the platform opposite. It showed an elegant-looking woman at a washstand, and while Angelica was never so vain as to consider herself quite that elegant, she thought they shared many qualities: the pale slender neck and arms, the pinched smile and wide-set brown eyes. Even the woman's hair, which was loosely piled with a curled fringe, similar to hers, was the same shade of dark brown.

The advertisement promised healthy skin, a good complexion, and soft, white, beautiful hands. She thought a bar of Pears soap was just what she and William needed after their earlier encounter with the Thames. She turned away and looked across the compartment at William, sitting on his hands in his dark green knickerbocker suit and bow-tie. He looked quite lost.

'Are you absolutely sure you didn't swallow any of the water?' she asked him. She had been greatly concerned about the possibility of them both contracting cholera or typhoid, or some other deadly disease. 'Did you keep your mouth tightly closed after we jumped into the river, just like I said?'

William nodded emphatically but, for reasons Angelica was as yet unsure of, he avoided eye contact with her.

'Good,' she said. It was reassuring to have his confirmation again, but she would have to keep a close eye on him, and herself for that matter. 'I told you that sometimes one has to die to be born again,' she continued. 'Well, now it will at least appear that we have. Your hat will be found on the riverbank where we left it, and further down one of your old boots and my bonnet. Plenty of people saw us jump in, didn't they?'

William gave another nod, maintaining the silence he'd kept up since Angelica had pulled him out of the Thames with her and carried his wet, shivering body up from the south bank somewhere near Butler's Wharf. She had taken an unthinkable risk with both their lives, and she couldn't blame him for not wanting to talk to her, or look at her, but there had been no alternative.

16

As far as Angelica was concerned, it was better to be dead than to live their old lives a single day longer. And besides, she had no intention of staying to face the music after what she had done.

She reached across to the seat opposite and took William's hands in her own. She smiled at the boy, wishing his own mischievous smile would soon return. 'We have a new and better life ahead of us,' she told him. 'Isn't that exciting, William?'

William looked up from his lap at last, but he didn't speak.

'We're going to have a great adventure,' Angelica promised. 'Things are going to come good for us, you'll see. I'm going to build you a castle and keep you safe. No one will ever hurt you again, I promise.' She pulled him closer and continued to smile, almost to the point of laughing. 'And I swear I'll never ask you to jump in any more rivers with me. Now, can we be friends again?'

William's stolid expression cracked at last. He got to his feet and threw his arms around her. She felt him squeeze her as hard as she knew he could.

'There, that's better, isn't it?' she said. 'In a few hours we'll be far away from London, and everything that's happened will soon become a distant memory. Are you going to sit next to me now?'

She felt William's head rub against her ear as he nodded. Then he sat beside her and pushed himself up and back into the seat until his best Sunday boots were dangling in mid-air.

'Why do we have to leave London?' he asked, looking up at his mother with questioning, doleful eyes.

Angelica did not reply. She just gazed at his beautiful, innocent little face as she went over the reasons in her mind, finding none she could give voice to. How could she tell her son the truth of what had happened? What would he think of her if she did?

'Where's Daddy? Is he coming to live in our castle, too?'

Angelica sighed. She began to shake her head. Then she pulled William back into her arms, smothering his face in the folds of her best turquoise gown as she said, 'No, William. I'm afraid Daddy is dead.'

William had never been one to show his emotions, but Angelica felt him begin to sob into her bosom now. She began to stroke her hand over the back of his head to soothe him until she heard the train begin to get up steam, then she relaxed at last. They would soon be underway, and how she longed to be rid of London and everything it represented. She turned to the window again and stared up at the tangled framework of wrought iron supporting the train shed roof, wondering what lay ahead for them, until a tall policeman broke her concentration. She saw him striding purposefully along the platform in his blues, and she turned away from the window again to hide her face.

A moment later she heard the guard's whistle blow, and the train lurched forward with a jolt before settling into a slow and steady pace. She looked up again, and this time she caught her breath. The policeman had gone, but in his place she saw someone she wished she had not. Moreover, it was clear that he had seen her because he was now running directly towards her. It was the man in the squat bowler hat who had been following her through the streets of Southwark early that morning. His limp did little to slow him this time.

Angelica jumped to her feet, startling William. How had this man found her again? She rushed to the carriage door, meaning to stop him from opening it if she could. She pulled up on the handle just in time, but her strength was no match for his. The handle fell with a clunk. The door swung open, and just as it seemed that the train had picked up enough speed to thwart him, the man leapt inside, determination evident in his wild eyes. Angelica backed away. The door slammed shut. On the bench to her right, William, who had clearly recognised the man now that he was so close, pulled his knees up to his chest and cowered like the frightened child he was.

'Angelica Wren,' the man said in guttural tones, leering at her as he spoke. 'Well, well. Haven't you got some talking to do?'

'It's Chastain,' Angelica said. 'I no longer go by my married name.'

'Of course you don't,' the man said, stepping closer.

'Keep away from me!'

The man wore a tatty grey suit with a filthy collar at his neck. He pulled at it and scratched behind his ear as he stepped closer. 'Now, now, Angelica. That's no way to greet your old friend Tom, is it? I want to talk, that's all.'

'About what?'

'About a good many things.'

The man glanced down at the boy and caught William peering back at him through his fingers. 'Boo!' he shouted, thrusting his head forward and laughing as William whimpered and rolled on to his side.

Turning back to Angelica, he said, 'But there's no rush. We've got a nice little journey ahead of us. Where exactly is it you're off to? Birmingham?'

Angelica nodded.

'I figured as much, given the line you're on.' He pulled a face, as though considering their destination. 'Birmingham,' he repeated. 'I suppose it will do well enough, and along the way we have this fine compartment all to ourselves. I saw to that. I was standing outside, quietly turning people away so we could spend some time together in private.' He laughed to himself. 'Of course, I thought it best to make myself scarce when that peeler showed. Imagine my surprise when the train started pulling out. I had to run for it then. I thought I was going to lose you. I'm glad I didn't.'

'Why are you here?' Angelica asked. 'What do you want from me?'

A slow smile spread across the man's face. 'I think you know why I'm here,' he said. 'Reginald Price. Seen Reggie lately, have you?' When Angelica gave no reply, the man sneered and continued. 'As to what I want . . .' He left his words hanging as he eyed her up and down. 'I want you to work for me. A pretty penny you'll make, too. A man likes a bit of class, and you've got plenty. Look at you, all dressed up to the nines—a right treat on the eyes, and on the ears with that fancy French accent of yours.' He continued to study her, sucking spittle from the corners of his mouth as his imagination ran away with him. 'Yes, a pretty penny indeed.'

Angelica shook her head. 'You're insane!'

The man spat down at the seat beside him, then as he turned back to Angelica he stepped towards her so fast she had no time to react. He grabbed her by the throat, his coarse hands scratching like a hangman's rope around her neck. He threw her down beside William, sat uncomfortably close beside her and held her cheeks in his vice-like grip.

'I'm going to live like a king for a change,' he said, his eyes boring into hers. 'You're going to look after me in whatever manner I see fit. Do you understand? You see, I know what you did.'

Angelica's eyes widened.

The man began to nod. 'That's right,' he said, smiling again, revealing heavily stained teeth, of which several were missing. 'I was there,' he continued. 'I saw what happened all right, so I followed you. Your play-acting in the Thames didn't fool me. And how do you suppose to support yourself and your boy here without a husband anyway? Shop girl? Factory worker? I don't much fancy you for a servant in someone else's fancy house, scrubbing floors on your hands and knees all day. Those jobs don't pay well, either, and not half as much as what I have in mind.' With that, he shoved Angelica's head back into the headrest and got to his feet. 'So, you're going to do as I say, or your little game's up. You hear me?'

Angelica straightened her dress and sat up. She cast a glance at William, who remained curled into a tight ball beside her, as was often the case whenever Tom Blanchard and his cronies were around.

'How did you find me?' she asked, wondering how he could possibly have followed their course along the murky Thames in the fog. She and William might have gone ashore just about anywhere, on either side of the bank.

'That was easy,' Blanchard said, full of himself. 'I was following you, remember? After you left Reggie's place last night with the boy, I waited outside your house to see what you would do next. You had a large carpet bag with you when you set out this morning, just like that one there,' he added, pointing up to a floral woven bag on the overhead luggage rack. 'I saw where you put it. I took a quick look, and lo and behold, what did I see if it wasn't the clothes you're both wearing now.' He paused, and his dark features brightened. 'I saw something else in there, too. It was enough to make me think about letting you off the hook, but then I got to thinking. Why settle for that and let you go when I could have both?' He stepped towards the bag. 'Is it still there?'

Angelica began to stand up, but Blanchard shoved her back down into her seat again.

'Don't trouble yourself, Angelica,' he said. 'I can get it.'

With that, Blanchard lifted the bag down and opened it. A moment later he pulled out a black velvet drawstring purse, and his face lit up as he peered inside, the sovereign coins it contained casting a golden glow on to his face. 'There must be thirty pounds in there,' he said, weighing the purse in his hand. 'That's why I knew you didn't mean to kill yourself. That's how come I knew where to find you again. I knew you'd be back for your bag soon enough. All I had to do was wait.' He held the purse up by its drawstring and let it dangle in front of Angelica. 'Steal it, did you?'

Angelica reached for the purse. 'Give it to me! It's all we have.'

Blanchard snatched the purse away, smiling, clearly enjoying the torment he was causing. 'I think I'll hang on to it, if you don't mind.' His coarse laugh played in his throat again. He was clearly amused with himself. 'I was being what a fancy piece like you would call rhetorical. I'm keeping it whether you mind or not. And how far do think you and your boy would get without it? You'd be in the poorhouse within the week, working your fingers to the bone, your boy here sent up the chimneys and made to sweep. That's if I was kind-hearted enough to keep the peelers off your back, which I'm not. So, you see, my demands really are to everyone's mutual benefit.'

Angelica felt trapped. What choice did she have but to acquiesce? To protest would surely bring out the darkest in this man's temper, and she already knew first-hand just how dark it could be. Neither was she prepared to see her son suffer any further for her misdoings if it could be avoided—whatever the cost to her pride or person.

'Very well,' she said, her eyes locked on his, her already stern features sharpening further. 'As you leave me no choice, I will do as you say, but you must leave William alone. You're not to touch him—not one hair of his head. Do you understand?'

'You're in no position to make demands,' Blanchard said, 'but what do I care for the boy? As long as he keeps to himself and pulls his weight, he'll give me no reason to touch him. And as long as you continue to please the clients I find for you, why, we'll all get along handsomely.' He offered his hand as if to shake on their arrangement. 'Agreed,' he said. 'Now, give me that dainty little hand of yours.'

Angelica was hesitant, but she obliged. As soon as her hand was within reach, Blanchard grabbed it firmly and pulled her out of her seat, forcing them together. Then, in a low voice that was laced with menace, he said, 'I won't touch the boy, but I'll be keeping him very close. Cross me once and the deal's off. Then he'll feel more than the back of my hand. Do you understand?'

Angelica swallowed hard and quickly nodded. Then she felt his hands on her shoulders, pressing into them until she thought he intended to crush the life out of her. He didn't. Instead, he turned and threw her down on to the bench, away from the troubled boy. When Angelica looked up at Blanchard again she saw him loosening his belt. She began to shake her head.

'Come now, Angelica. I have to try the goods. How can I extol your many virtues to all those potential clients if I haven't experienced them for myself?'

He came closer, lascivious intent burning in his eyes, his crooked mouth drooling like a rabid dog.

'Please! Not in front of William.'

'Let him watch. The boy's got to learn sometime.'

CHAPTER TWO

Angelica and William spent the first week of their new lives in Birmingham living in a tiny, dank cellar in a small back-to-back terrace house in the slum area of Hockley. While Tom Blanchard sought more suitable accommodation for them, they were forced to share the single room with an unfortunate family from Ireland who, like so many, had flocked to the town and its booming industry in search of work, only to find that the reality fell woefully short of their expectations.

The house shared a yard, with its communal washhouses and filthy privies, with forty other houses and their occupants, far too many for the cramped, dimly lit and poorly ventilated rooms in which they were forced to live. As with the Irish family, this was a far, far cry from the new life Angelica had imagined for herself and William. She had previously been concerned that they might contract cholera or typhoid from their encounter with the River Thames, but it seemed all the more likely to her now that some deadly disease would find them here among the squalor of their neighbours' effluvia. Angelica dreaded each and every night they had to endure there, lying awake for the most part, listening to the night-men as they cleared the detritus from the yard and the stinking waste from the cesspit, which she was convinced had somehow leaked into the space beneath their floorboards, the smell was so bad.

It was with great relief, then, that on the evening of their seventh day in Hockley, Tom Blanchard returned, full of himself and a good amount of liquor too, judging from the reek of alcohol of his breath. Without saying a word, he began collecting up their things.

'Have you found somewhere?' Angelica asked, wondering whether there was enough money left in her purse to rent anywhere better than this after the man had spent so much of it on drink and the fat cigars he'd taken to smoking.

He had one in his mouth now, unlit and greasy with saliva from having sucked it more than smoked it, to make it last. 'Indeed I have,' Blanchard said, flashing his eyebrows at her. 'Now, wake that useless boy of yours and follow me.'

They walked and walked, following his crooked steps along countless streets in the early evening half-light, until the soles of Angelica's feet became sore and William began to cry and drag on her arm.

'Shut him up,' Blanchard told her. 'I'll not tolerate his whimpering. I don't care what we agreed. Keep him quiet, or I'll do it for you.'

William must have known what Blanchard meant to do if he didn't stop whining, because Angelica didn't need to ask him to be quiet. They continued on in silence. As they drew closer to the town centre, carriages and omnibuses began to pass them by. There was even a horse tram running alongside them at one point, and Angelica wished they could board any one of these vehicles just for the rest.

At length, she asked, 'Where are we going?'

'You'll see,' Blanchard said without turning around. 'It's not far now. I've got a gentleman coming to see you soon, so step it out. I don't want to disappoint him.'

Blanchard picked up the pace, and for all his awkwardness of gait, Angelica and William had difficulty keeping up with him. Neither had eaten a decent meal all week. Their faces were beginning to look gaunt, their bones more prominent through their pallid skin, especially Angelica's hands, which she thought had begun to look old before their time. She didn't know how either of them managed to keep going.

'You've arranged a client for me already?' she said, surprised to hear that Blanchard had been able to find them new lodgings and her first client on the very same day.

'Of course,' Blanchard said. 'We've already lost a week since we arrived, and this place doesn't come cheap.'

After fifteen minutes or so, they turned into another street and followed its narrow pavement for no more than twenty steps before Blanchard stopped. He put his hands on his hips and stared up at a house to their left.

'There,' he said, sounding proud of himself. 'A one-up-one-down on Kings Terrace. Right posh-sounding, that is. Should do us nicely until things pick up.'

Angelica gazed up at the terrace of houses, with their regimented chimney stacks and Welsh-slate roofs. She saw no broken windows anywhere, which was certainly an improvement.

'You'll have a room to work in while I keep an eye on the boy in the room below,' Blanchard continued. 'I want to see smiling faces coming down those stairs, you hear me?'

Angelica ignored the remark. 'Are you sure it's affordable?' she asked, stepping towards it and noticing the flower baskets beneath the windows. There were no flowers in them, just a few weeds.

Blanchard rolled his cigar back and forth in his mouth, sucking the warm evening air in through his teeth. 'As I've said, it wasn't cheap, but you've got to speculate to accumulate, haven't you? Any right-minded gentleman of position and wealth wouldn't go near a place like the one we've just come from. They don't want to do their business in squalor. They expect the likes of this, and more. If things go well, I aim to move us into even better accommodation so we can attract a higher class of gentleman still.' He laughed to himself. 'I'm sure you'd rather fuck for pounds than pennies, wouldn't you?'

Angelica didn't answer him. She wanted to earn neither in that way.

'And you're young and educated,' Blanchard continued, moving towards the front door. 'You're also more than a little pleasing to the eye. Why, your looks and my business acumen will keep the landlord from our door, don't you worry. Once we're nicely set up I'll see about getting you listed in the sporting guides. You could earn some serious sovs then—and a fine young courtesan you'll make, too.' He scrunched his brow. 'Exactly how old are you anyway?'

'I'm twenty-two.'

Blanchard sucked the air again. 'That's pushing it a bit. Still, I'm sure you could pass for nineteen right enough, so that's your age from now on, should anyone ask. Do you understand me? Because that's what I'll be telling them.'

Angelica nodded and Blanchard opened the front door, mumbling, 'It's a pity the boy isn't older. He won't be legal for some years yet, although I'm sure he can be passed off soon enough. Now, have a quick look around, then get out to the washhouse and clean yourself up. I don't want any complaints.'

. . .

Angelica's first client in Tom Blanchard's deplorable business venture was due to arrive at the house at eight o'clock that evening, and while Angelica longed for a quiet bed for the night, away from the heady stench of poor hygiene and the sanitary inadequacies of her previous abode, she had no intention of being there when the door knocker fell. As pleasant as the place seemed after her week in the slums of Hockley, she was leaving before anyone had the chance to so much as lay a hand on her knee.

But how to go about it?

On her brief look around the house when they first came in, she'd noticed that the clock on the mantelpiece in the downstairs room showed half past seven. That only gave her thirty minutes to come up with something, so when she left by the back door and crossed the yard to the washhouse under Blanchard's watchful eye, she wasted no time bothering to prepare herself for the gentleman who was coming to see her. Instead, she stood at one of the washbasins, gazing at her drawn and haggard face between the cracks in the mirror while she continued to think.

She had noticed that Blanchard was keeping William closer to him than ever, seemingly to ensure that she went to work for him without a fuss now that the time had arrived. How was she going to get William away from him long enough

32

during the limited time she had for them to make their escape? She began to wish they had fled sooner, while Blanchard was out procuring their new accommodation, but she no longer had any money. She wondered how much was left in her purse, and it angered her to think that Blanchard had probably squandered most of it by now. How on earth was she going to get that back from him, too? She was in no doubt that they would not last more than a few days on the streets without at least a few shillings to get by on.

When Angelica returned to the downstairs room, William was sitting in the corner, silently sobbing with his hands over his face. She went to him and saw that his little body was trembling.

'What is it, William?' she asked, kneeling before him. She began to rub his shoulders. 'What's wrong?'

William gave no answer.

Angelica gently lowered his hands from his face. One side glowed bright red. She turned and fixed Blanchard with a cold glare. He was sitting on a low stool on the other side of the sparsely furnished room, nonchalantly picking the dirt from under his fingernails. He glanced at her briefly, then chewed at one of his nails and spat at the floor.

'What have you done to my son?' Angelica demanded, getting to her feet.

'Nothing the brat didn't deserve,' Blanchard

said, sneering back at her as he spoke. 'He started making a proper fuss as soon as you left him—didn't want to be alone with his Uncle Tom while you were in the yard primping yourself.' He paused to study her. 'You've not brushed up too well, have you?' he added. 'Still, maybe the gentleman won't notice if you half draw the curtain and keep the lamp low.'

Angelica drew a deep breath. She looked down at William again, trying to calm herself. 'Don't cry, William,' she said. 'I'm here now.'

'Yes,' Blanchard cut in. He stood up. 'And you'd better get yourself upstairs, hadn't you? Your gentleman will be here in ten minutes.'

'We had a deal!' Angelica snapped.

'It was nothing. Just a slap, that's all.'

'I won't leave you alone with my son tonight. Not while he's like this.'

'You'll do as you're told, or maybe you'd like to feel the back of my hand, too.'

Angelica mocked him. 'What, and give your first customer spoiled goods?'

Blanchard came closer, withdrawing from his lapel pocket the stubby leftovers of his cigar, which he licked and set into the corner of his mouth. 'Then I'll come upstairs and sit with you until the gentleman arrives. The boy can stay in here by himself, safe and sound. While you're working upstairs, I'll wait out in the yard. How about that?'

Angelica gave a nod and made for the door.

Blanchard followed after her, and in a low voice, he added, 'And you'll be sure to give the gentleman his money's worth, won't you? If he doesn't come down smiling, or heaven forbid he comes down complaining and asking for his money back, I'll be after your boy with my belt. Do you hear me?'

Angelica ignored him. She had far more important things on her mind. She had managed to get Blanchard away from William. So far so good, but what now? She reminded herself then that even if they did manage to escape from him altogether, he knew she was still alive, and he knew what she had done in London the week before. She couldn't be sure whether or not he would follow through with his threats to go to the authorities and expose her, but it was not a risk she was prepared to take.

'Get up there with you!' Blanchard croaked. 'And be quick about it.'

As Angelica reached the foot of the narrow staircase in the equally narrow hallway, which was bereft of any ornament or furniture, she paused and invited Blanchard to go up ahead of her, thinking only that she had to end this nightmare if she could. If not for her sake, then for William's.

CHAPTER THREE

Winson Green, Birmingham
1896

It was indeed an inauspicious new beginning for Angelica and her son. There they were, having fled from one situation only to find that they must now flee from another, and who would choose otherwise given the unthinkable things Tom Blanchard would have them do for his own immoral gains? I did not learn the manner of their escape from Blanchard until some time after my relationship with Angelica had begun, once she had come to trust and confide in me, so I shall return to it at the appropriate time. Suffice it to say for now that they did manage to escape that night, and having heard what Blanchard had in mind for them both, I am glad of it, despite every terrible thing that followed.

Even now as I sit here, many years on from these events, I shudder to think of the life Angelica might have led—my Angelica. You may come to think it would have been for the best if Tom Blanchard had managed to keep her locked inside that little house for the rest of her days, and you would undoubtedly be right were it not for the sake of poor William. For my own sake,

I cannot hate her or wish that debased life upon her, because in doing so, as undoubtedly foolish as it may be to think it now, we would never have met.

I suppose it was fate that brought Angelica to Edgbaston, for I cannot believe our love was born of pure chance. She did not then know anything about Birmingham and its surrounding areas. She could not have known how affluent Edgbaston was, or that she would find charity there, but ours is a philanthropic society. Charity for those deemed worthy of salvation was every wealthy family's moral obligation, and there was no greater concentration of wealthy families in the Birmingham area than in Edgbaston. Hope for Angelica and William was therefore soon on the horizon, and it did not come a moment too soon.

Birmingham
1880

On the night Angelica ended her oppressive acquaintance with Tom Blanchard, and in doing so took control of her life again, she and William fled from that one-up-one-down house, heading south for most of the night until their feet could carry them no further. They slept rough on the streets until daybreak the following morning, thankful that it was summertime rather than winter. She had thought to head directly for the train station at New Street, to leave Birmingham again, but despite everything that had happened since they arrived, she was resolved to stay. There was, after all, great industry here, and where there was industry, there was opportunity.

It was on the evening of Angelica and William's second night sleeping rough, their bellies painful with hunger, that they were approached by an elderly, well-dressed man in a fine top hat.

'Good evening,' he said, removing his hat and peering down at them over the top of his round glasses as they sat huddled beside the bandstand steps in Cannon Hill Park. 'My name is Mr. Featherstone. I hope you won't think it presumptuous of me, but may I enquire as to your situation?'

Angelica noticed his eyes turn to William as he addressed them, and his frown spoke volumes. Here was a man who felt pain at the sight of a young boy living on the streets, with a mother who had clearly fallen on hard times and was no longer able to take proper care of either of them. When Angelica did not answer quickly enough, the man continued.

'Do you have somewhere to sleep? Has the boy eaten? He looks—' Featherstone paused. 'That is to say, you both look as if you could use a good meal and some proper rest. But what of the boy's father? Where is your husband, madam?'

'My husband is dead,' Angelica said. 'He left

us close to penniless. What little we have is almost gone.'

Featherstone began to shake his head. 'Dear, dear, this won't do,' he said, pushing his glasses higher up on his nose. 'It really won't do at all.' He leaned against his cane and extended his hand. 'Come along with me, won't you? I can offer you a clean bed to sleep in, and I'm sure we can find you something hearty for your supper.' He turned to William and raised his eyebrows. 'How does mutton suet sound?'

Angelica had learned to be wary of just about everyone she met, but this kind-faced man who had seemingly come upon them by chance in their hour of need appeared harmless enough. She looked for William's answer and saw a toothy smile on his face. It was the first she had seen since leaving London. In that moment she decided they would have to take a chance on this stranger, or risk dying of thirst and starvation. She took Mr. Featherstone's hand at once, accepting his generous offer for both of their sakes.

So it was that they came to live for a time in a small, single-storey mock Tudor almshouse in Edgbaston that formed part of a quadrangle of almshouses around a pretty, floral green with a clock tower at its centre. That night they ate and ate until their bellies were full, and they slept the most restful sleep Angelica had known in weeks.

On the morning of their second day at the almshouse, Angelica glanced up at the clock tower as she passed it, having been out all morning, and noted that it was almost eleven o'clock. She had a spring in her step and a smile on her face as she opened the gate and walked along the rose-lined path that led to their front door. Beneath her arm was a brown paper parcel, tied with string, and in her hand a large but light box dangled from a pale blue ribbon. She opened their door and stepped inside, her warm cheeks pink from the sun and the exercise.

'William!' she called.

Unlike the night before, when sheer exhaustion had taken him, William had suffered a fitful sleep. By morning, however, he could not be stirred, so Angelica had gone out without him, leaving him in his bed. Dear Mr. Featherstone, whom they had not seen again since their arrival, had been right about William's need for proper rest. No better tonic could have been prescribed to get him back to his usual self again, and she imagined it would not take long in such a pleasant environment. As for herself, she was already beginning to feel that life was once more something to look forward to, rather than to fear.

The almshouses each had a small sitting room that looked out from a leaded-light window on to the green. Angelica's was pleasantly furnished with bright colours and floral prints, although it contained little by way of anything ornamental. It

41

was, however, very comfortable, and more than enough for their needs. She paced across the rug, which almost entirely covered the floorboards, to look for William in case he was hiding from her, as he often used to. First she looked behind the armchairs, and then behind the clothes-horse by the fire where she had been drying their washing.

'William,' she called again, more softly this time, as she headed for the bedroom, expecting that he was still sound asleep, even at this late hour.

A second later she heard him scream. She dropped her parcels and rushed into the bedroom. William was sitting up in their shared brass bed, his forehead beaded with sweat, glistening in the sunlight from the window. His eyes were wide and staring.

'It's all right, William,' Angelica said. 'You've had a nightmare. That's all it is. I'm here now. You're perfectly safe.'

She went to him and sat on the bed, raising the palm of her hand to the boy's forehead. It felt cool and clammy.

William responded to her touch by throwing his arms around her as far as he could reach. 'Mummy! The bad man found me again.'

'There's no one else here,' Angelica assured him, stroking her hand over the back of his head to comfort him. 'It was just another dream. He won't hurt you again, I promise.'

As she held William in her arms and began to rock him gently back and forth, she silently cursed Tom Blanchard and the bitter memory of everything that had happened in London before it became necessary for them to leave. She reaffirmed to herself there and then to do everything in her power to ensure that from this day on William would enjoy a good and happy life, without want or fear, far away from the kind of people who inhabited his nightmares and caused him to cry in his sleep.

She smiled at William and pushed his hair to one side. 'I have something to show you. I bought it this morning. Would you like to see it?'

'Is it for me?'

Angelica laughed to herself. 'My darling little man,' she said. 'Everything I do is for you.'

With that, she pinched his nose and went back into the sitting room to retrieve her parcels. When she returned, William was on the edge of the bed, where she had been, his face beaming with anticipation.

'Now, close your eyes and promise not to peek,' Angelica said as she untied the string on the first of her parcels. She began to unfold the paper, but paused when she noticed that William was looking at her through his fingers. 'I said no peeking. Now, turn around so I can be sure you can't see me.'

William did as he was told, and Angelica

continued, excitedly tossing the paper and the string to the floor as she held up the contents and let it unfurl against her, hiding her now-shabby dress with another that was in a different class altogether. It was a princess-line walking dress in pale blue silk damask with gold lace detailing. With no waistline seam, the long, fitted panels accentuated her height and further slimmed her figure. It was a little heavy for summer, but that had afforded her a generous discount, and she would not have been able to buy the hat to go with it if she had opted for something better suited to the season. Combined, she thought they gave her the appearance of someone who was both elegant and refined.

In truth, Angelica had not really been able to afford either item from the money Blanchard had left in her purse, let alone the parasol she had bought to complete the look, not in the moral sense. Her purchases had left her purse close to empty. But for all his faults, Blanchard had been right about one thing: she had to speculate to accumulate. She had to dress for the life she wanted for her and William, not for the wretched lives they already had.

'You can look now,' she said, her face beaming as she began to envisage that life. When William turned around, she twirled in circles for him, still holding the dress to her frame. She imagined she was dancing at a royal ball. 'How well do you like it?' she asked him. 'Am I not as pretty as a princess?'

William began to laugh. It was a joy to see. He jumped off the bed and began to dance with his mother, turning and turning until they were both so dizzy that they fell back on to the bed together.

Angelica was now laughing so hard herself that she had to catch her breath. 'Hurry and wash the sleep from your eyes, William,' she said. 'If you're well enough, and I can see that you are, we'll go to the park.' She eyed him questioningly. 'You are well enough, aren't you?'

William gave her an enthusiastic nod.

'Then hurry along. As soon as you're dressed we'll be on our way.'

CHAPTER FOUR

Any other woman as finely attired as Angelica Chastain now was would likely have used some form of transport to travel the short distance from her accommodation to the public park at Cannon Hill, be it in her own carriage or a hansom cab. But then most women who looked as Angelica now did had sufficient means to travel in such style and comfort, and they did not do so from a charitable home for the poor. Not that she minded. Mr. Featherstone's almshouse was only a twenty-minute walk away.

A week had passed since she had bought her new dress, and she and William had been making the journey to the park every day since, sometimes going as often as twice a day. While Angelica looked forward to it, the novelty had worn off for William.

'Do we have to go into the park again?' he said with a sigh as they reached the main gate.

'Don't you want to see the swans on the lake?'

'I saw them yesterday, and the day before.'

Angelica laughed to herself. 'Then they'll miss you all the more if you don't go and see them today.'

William sighed again, and hand in hand they entered the park. It was another fine morning.

The Edgbaston nannies were out in force as usual, perambulating in their black gowns and white lace aprons, but Angelica was not there for any of them, despite their standing in life being rather better than hers at that moment. What good was making the acquaintance of a mistress's nanny when it was the mistress herself that Angelica aspired to be?

They took their usual route towards the boating lake, ambling clockwise through the park in the dappled shade of the trees that were to one side of the path. The other was lined with deep and colourful summer flower beds. Everyone she passed offered her a smile and a polite bow of their head—nannies and the occasional gentleman alike—and she would smile and nod back at them, feeling every bit the lady she purported to be.

When at length they came to the boating lake and William at last stopped protesting, Angelica let go of his hand and watched him run towards the swans and ducks that were gathered at the water's edge. There was another boy there of around William's age, tossing small pieces of bread into the water. It was causing a cacophony of quacking and hissing from the fowl that had gone there to feed.

'Remember, William!' Angelica called after him. 'Don't stand too close to the edge.'

She watched him stop beside the other boy, who was dressed in a skirted sailor's suit, which surprised her. He was a good two inches taller than William and clearly of school age, yet he was not in knickerbockers, not today at least. She approached them, wondering where the boy's guardian was. Surely he couldn't have come to the park all by himself? She looked along the path and saw two nannies rocking their perambulators as they stopped to talk to one another in passing. Then she noticed a figure dressed all in white stepping so quickly towards them that she was almost running.

'Alexander!' the woman called. 'You mustn't run off like that.' As she arrived, panting slightly, her otherwise pale cheeks flushing crimson, she turned to Angelica and added, 'I do hope my son hasn't been bothering you.'

'Not at all,' Angelica said, mindful to pronounce her words correctly as she studied the woman. She took in the high collar of her dress, which set her chin proud and made her look all the more elegant, and the fine strands of fair hair that teased out from beneath the brim of her wide sun hat. It positively dwarfed Angelica's hat, causing her to wish she had bought something bigger, although she had her parasol to shelter her from the sun. 'We had only just arrived,' she added. 'Your son has been no bother, I assure you.'

The woman, no more than a few years older than Angelica, glanced at the two boys and smiled. 'They appear to have taken a liking to one another already,' she said. She gave a small laugh that was as soft as the summer breeze. 'Alexander never usually shares his bread with anyone, not even me. I'm Georgina, by the way, Georgina Hampton.'

She extended a dainty, gloved hand, and Angelica took it. Her fingers felt cold through the lace, despite the warmth of the day. 'Angelica Chastain,' she said. 'My son is called William.'

'A good strong name,' Georgina said. 'And yours is quite beautiful, as is that lovely dress. You must let me have the name of your dressmaker.'

Angelica had no idea who made the dress. It had certainly not been made for her at the price she paid for it. She had tried on several. This one just happened to fit. She didn't know what to say in reply, so she simply smiled and changed the subject. 'It's unusual to see a mother out in the park with her son in the middle of the day.'

'Yes, and my husband frowns on it, of course, but I insist on spending every Wednesday with Alexander while he's young. He'll be sent away to school soon enough. Until then he's being tutored at home. My husband and I spend a social hour together with him each evening, but it isn't nearly enough.' She paused and laughed to herself. 'You must excuse my modern values. I'm sure the idea must seem quite irrational to you.' She looked over at William, who by now had run out of bread and was trying to sneak up on one of the ducks that had wandered up on to the bank. 'And yet here you are with your son also.'

'We're new to the area,' Angelica said. 'We're from London.'

'London! Well, that explains your lovely dress. Has your husband's business brought you here?'

Angelica thought on her answer. It would be the easiest of lies to simply nod her head, and by doing so further her pretence, but she felt suddenly uncomfortable at the idea. It would just lead to more questions. What line of business was her husband in? What did Birmingham have to offer such a man that London did not? She imagined her lie would soon be undone, so instead of nodding her head, she told Georgina what she had told Mr. Featherstone. 'My husband is dead.'

On hearing that, Georgina stepped close to Angelica and placed a hand on her forearm, which Angelica felt no more than if a butterfly had landed there. Georgina's eyes were full of concern. 'You poor thing,' she said. 'How frightful. But don't worry, I shan't pry.'

At that moment, laughter drew their attention to the water's edge. Alexander was bent over with one hand on his knee, pointing at something that had clearly amused both him and William.

'They really are getting along well,' Georgina said. 'Alexander is usually such a shy boy. He has very few friends as a result.'

'Due to our situation,' Angelica said, sounding almost tearful, 'my William now has no friends at all.'

'Then we must do all we can to encourage their friendship,' Georgina said. 'How would you and William like to come to tea tomorrow afternoon? I'm sure I can prise Alexander away from his tutor for an hour or so, and my other ladies will simply adore William.'

Angelica did not answer straight away. In her mind she had accepted the offer that instant, but she did not wish to appear too eager.

'Oh, please say you'll come,' Georgina persisted. 'I've rarely seen Alexander so happy.'

Angelica smiled. 'Then of course we'll come,' she said. 'Thank you. We'd be delighted.'

A carriage was sent for Angelica the following afternoon. By a quarter to four, she and William were gazing out of the windows, trying to get an early peek at the house as they were conveyed along the tree-lined carriage drive towards it. This was just what Angelica had hoped for, and yet she was surprised by how nervous she felt. Her palms began to feel clammy inside her gloves, and she supposed it was because she was worried about how Georgina and her circle of friends would receive her. She could still picture Georgina's face in the park the day before as she gave her their temporary address. Mr. Featherstone's almshouse was clearly well known in the area, and while Georgina had said nothing of it at the time, her raised eyebrows spoke volumes.

Nevertheless, she had not retracted her invitation. If anything, the revelation that Angelica and William were living by the charity of others seemed only to further pique Georgina's curiosity, which was just as well; since Mr. Featherstone had called on Angelica that morning bearing ill news, she was all the more anxious to further her acquaintance with Georgina and make a good impression.

As the house came into view, Angelica drew a deep breath to help calm herself. 'Isn't it a fine-looking house, William?' she said as she took in the red-brick building with its many tall chimney stacks and pointed iron-framed windows that were typical of the Gothic architectural style. 'Would you like to live in a house like that someday?'

William's face was so close to the carriage window that the glass had all but steamed up. He wiped it with his hand so he could see better. 'It's very big,' he said, blinking to shield his eyes from the strong afternoon sunlight.

They arrived at the front of the house, where the carriage slowly turned around a central stone fountain before coming to a stop. The carriage rocked as the driver climbed down, and a moment later he appeared outside the door and opened it. He was a jolly-looking man with a round face and wiry sideburns. His sincere smile immediately put Angelica at ease.

'Here we are, miss,' he said. 'Welcome to Priory House.'

'Thank you,' Angelica said, taking the driver's hand.

Over the man's shoulder as she was helped down, Angelica saw someone who, judging from her unadorned black attire, was another member of the household staff. She was standing in the shadows beneath a pointed archway that stood at the centre of the house, above which spread a tidy tangle of ivy leaves. As William jumped down from the carriage, scattering the gravel, the woman came to meet them.

'I'm Missus Redmond, the housekeeper,' she said with a suitably authoritative tone. 'You must be Mrs Chastain and the young Master William. If you'd care to follow me, Mrs Hampton's expecting you in the orangery.'

Missus Redmond, whom Angelica put in her late forties, had a quick step that was at times difficult to keep up with. She led them through a dark, Jacobean panelled hallway to the back of the house, where they were shown into a large and far brighter room full of plants, with windows that looked out on to a colourful formal garden. Most of the windows were open, drawing a pleasant afternoon breeze.

'Mrs Chastain, madam,' Redmond announced,

stepping aside and inviting Angelica and William through.

Georgina Hampton was seated in the middle of the room at a round table that was set with starched white linen and glistening silverware, ready for afternoon tea. She was already accompanied at the table by two other guests, one in pale apricot, the other in bold mauve and black stripes. Georgina was all in white again, with a frilled and beribboned cap. It was a different dress from the one she had been wearing the day before and Angelica wished she had arrived wearing something different herself, but her only other gown was now far too shabby for company such as this. She approached, smiling at her hostess as she walked towards her as gracefully as she could manage while William tried to hide behind her back.

'I told you he was adorable,' Georgina said to her other guests, almost laughing as she spoke and trying to get a peek at William, who was doing his best to stay hidden. She stood up as Angelica arrived at the table, and the other two ladies followed suit. 'I'm so glad you came, Angelica. And you too, William,' she added, smiling at the boy as he clung to his mother's side as if for dear life.

'We've been looking forward to it,' Angelica said. 'Haven't we, William?' she added, stroking the boy's hair back off his forehead.

William nodded, saying nothing.

'Splendid,' Georgina said. 'Now, before I forget my manners, let me introduce you to my good friends, Effie Wilmington-Reed and Violet Cosgrove. Effie is the youngest daughter of the Warwickshire Wilmington-Reeds. I'm sure I need say no more.'

'I'm very pleased to meet you,' Angelica said, gently shaking Effie's hand as she took in the full rolls of chestnut-brown hair beneath her bonnet and the pink blush of her cheeks against her pale skin.

'Violet's family is in the silver industry,' Georgina said. 'I have them to thank for this lovely silverware,' she added, picking up a fork and turning it slowly to show off the fine engraving.

'How do you do?' Violet said, her smile off-setting her brusque tone.

While Effie was clearly the youngest there, a few years Angelica's junior by her estimation, Violet was the senior lady by a good many years. Her hair was black and un-primped beneath her bonnet, and her eyes were full of scrutiny as she held out her hand. Angelica soon discovered it to be as firm as her tone.

'It's a pleasure to meet you,' Angelica said, not yet convinced that she meant it, or whether the feeling was mutual.

'Georgina tells us your husband died,' Violet

said. 'We have that in common. I lost mine two years ago.'

'I'm sorry to hear that.'

'Don't be. We barely saw one another. He worked himself to death, and I shan't marry again. I'm considering a dog instead—one of those miniature breeds. They're very fashionable.'

Angelica gave her an awkward smile. She had no idea what to say next, but thankfully one of the maids saved her. Angelica hadn't noticed her at first because she had been so still and so quiet, standing among the plants. She suddenly came forward and pulled out one of the cane bergère chairs.

'Thank you,' Angelica said, as everyone sat down.

Tea was served promptly at four o'clock, by which time Alexander had been brought in. He was dressed as a pirate, and William's eyes lit up as soon as he saw him. He let go of his mother at last and ran to Alexander, wide-eyed as he took the costume in.

'Do you want to play?' Alexander said, his own face beaming at the sight of his new friend.

William nodded his head several times. 'Can I dress up, too?'

'Yes, but you'll have to be a cowboy or a soldier.'

'A soldier,' William said. 'Then I can try to catch you.'

They were led away together for a special afternoon tea of their own, and it was as if no one else was in the room. William didn't even turn back to his mother, although her eyes never left him.

'So adorable,' Georgina said. 'Young William must come and play with Alexander often. I'm sure they're destined to become the best of friends.'

'I hope so,' Angelica said, thinking back to what Mr. Featherstone had told her that morning, hoping it wouldn't stand in the way of things.

Angelica had taken afternoon tea before, but not in a while, and never quite like this. There was an assortment of delicate colourful cakes on a tiered stand, and another for all manner of dainty sandwiches. There was fresh fruit with a variety of berries, as well as pastries, jellies and cream. The crockery felt so fine that she was constantly afraid of breaking it, but she thought afternoon tea was something she could easily become accustomed to.

'Georgina tells us you've come up from London,' Effie said with enthusiasm.

Angelica smiled politely and nodded as she sipped her tea.

'I've not been to London in years,' Effie continued. 'Not since my parents took me to the opera at Covent Garden on my sixteenth birthday. I love opera, don't you?'

'I'm afraid I've never been,' Angelica said, beginning to feel a little out of place in such refined company.

Georgina set her teacup down on its saucer with a musical tinkle. 'Tell me, Angelica, you're clearly not from London, though, are you? Were you born in France? You have the most charming accent.'

'Yes, in Normandy,' Angelica said. 'I was raised by my grandparents in a village near Rouen.'

'Your grandparents?' Violet said with raised eyebrows.

Angelica nodded. 'My parents died when I was very young.'

'You poor thing,' Effie said. 'How terrible for you.'

'It wasn't so bad for me,' Angelica said. 'I have no memory of my parents, and my grandparents were very kind.'

'So how is it that you came to England?' Georgina asked. 'Marriage, I suppose.'

Angelica wanted to pluck another cake from the stand, but she supposed she would be allowed no time to savour it and she didn't want to embarrass herself by speaking with her mouth full or, heaven forbid, spraying crumbs everywhere. 'No, I married after I came to England,' she said. 'Although I met my husband in Rouen. He was an Englishman there on business. There was nothing for me in our little village. I was young and he swept me off my feet with the promise of a grand future together in London, but it was not to be.'

'What happened, Angelica?' Effie asked, sounding genuinely concerned.

'What business was he in?' Violet asked, reaching for the cake stand.

'He was a leather-case maker. His work was very fine, and he had great ambition. He borrowed money to expand his business, but he had no head for finance. He'd overreached and soon fell into overwhelming debt, of which I had no knowledge at the time. It was only after he took his life that I learned the truth. William and I were suddenly left without a home, and little money with which to make a fresh start.'

'That really is dreadful,' Georgina said, then she clutched her stomach and winced. She put her cup and saucer down with a clatter. 'Do excuse me,' she added, her cheeks flushing.

'Are you well?' Angelica asked. 'Has something disagreed with you?'

Georgina gave a small laugh that was quickly accompanied by further titters from the other ladies. 'No, my dear, I'm going to have another baby. I should have given Alexander a little brother or sister to play with long before now.'

'Not for the want of trying,' Violet said, suggesting to Angelica that they had been close friends for some time.

'No,' Georgina agreed, 'and now I'm afraid

he or she will make no suitable companion for Alexander at all.'

'My own boys are all away at Harrow now,' Violet said. 'Were I a younger woman I would have provided a companion for Alexander.'

'I know you would, Violet,' Georgina said. 'You really are too kind.'

Angelica was glad the conversation had turned away from her for the time being, or she feared she might have had to explain how she came to meet Mr. Featherstone. She did not wish to relive the events that had led to her and William sleeping rough on the streets, or a single moment of the time she had spent in the company of Tom Blanchard.

She noticed that Effie was staring at her from across the table. 'Do you have any children, Effie?' she asked, attempting to keep the conversation going.

Effie seemed to wake as if from a daydream. 'No,' she said, 'I have not yet been blessed.'

'I should hope not!' Violet said. 'You are not yet married.'

'Not married?' Angelica said. 'But you're very pretty, and coming from such a prestigious family I'm sure you could have your pick of eligible gentlemen.'

Effie blushed and delicately bit into a sandwich.

Violet gave a low harrumph. 'I think your father must be scaring them off with that ridiculous gun collection of his. It's not sensible for any man to be so obsessed with firearms. I've heard he has close to a hundred pieces.'

'At least,' Effie said. 'He used to show them to me all the time, but I no longer have any interest in such things.'

'Yes, well, we're doing our utmost to find Effie a suitable match, aren't we, Georgina?'

Georgina had been playing with her high collar since she put her teacup down, as if uncomfortable with it. She finally loosened it and seemed to relax again at last. 'You're far too fussy, Effie. That's the trouble,' she said. 'You don't want to become an old maid, do you?'

Before Effie could reply, the door opened and a tall, slim man in a black frock coat and grey trousers entered. He had a claret-red puff tie at his neck and a top hat beneath his arm.

'Stanley!' Georgina said, getting to her feet. 'What a pleasant surprise. Will you be joining us?'

'No, no, I can't stop,' Stanley said, straightening his moustache with the side of his forefinger. 'I'm meeting Alfred at five. Good afternoon, ladies.'

'Alfred?' Georgina said, sitting down again. 'Whatever for?'

'I expect he wants to bore me with money matters as usual, and I want to show him this.'

There was notable excitement in Stanley's voice. He reached inside his coat and produced a flat leather case from which he withdrew a plain black fountain pen. He removed the cap and handed it to Georgina, who studied it briefly before turning it in her hands and studying it some more.

'Don't you see it?' Stanley said, smiling and shaking his head.

Georgina looked bemused. 'It's just another of your pens—and a very plain-looking pen at that.'

Stanley drew an impatient breath. 'The nib!' he said. 'Look closely at the nib. It's the first to be pressed by Hampton and Moore in our very own factory. Now we no longer have to buy our nibs from Josiah Mason, and that means we can not only create our own designs and save money, which is sure to please our partner when I tell him, but more to the point, it means we can now manufacture our handcrafted fountain pens and dip pens in their entirety.'

'I see,' Georgina said, her attention now focused on the nib.

'The confounded thing still leaks,' Stanley continued, 'but I've yet to see a fountain pen that doesn't.' He held out his hand and Georgina returned the pen to him. 'Well, I have to be going. I just wanted to share the news with you first.'

Georgina's eyes were suddenly on Angelica. 'You must let me introduce you to our new friend before you go,' she said. 'This is the lady I met in the park yesterday, with the little boy I told you about. Angelica Chastain, my husband Stanley Hampton.'

When Stanley turned to Angelica she thought he seemed to notice her as if for the first time. 'Your humble servant, madam,' he said with a smile and a bow of his head.

For all his excitement, he was a softly spoken man. Angelica put him in his mid-thirties, perhaps ten years older than Georgina. 'I'm delighted to meet you, Mr. Hampton,' she said, returning his smile. She noticed his ears prick up at the sound of her subtle French accent, but he gave it no mention. She saw an endearing blush rise in his cheeks as he retreated.

'I bid you all enjoy your afternoon,' he said, before leaving as quickly as he had arrived.

Violet was full of smiles. 'Such a charming man,' she said. 'And a most handsome gentleman indeed.' She turned to Effie and rekindled their earlier conversation. 'A man like Stanley Hampton would suit you very well, my dear.'

'As long as it's a man *like* Stanley Hampton,' Georgina said with a grin, 'and not the man himself.'

Everyone except Effie laughed.

'My husband studied metallurgy before he went into the production of pens,' Georgina said. 'He says that a pen is an extension of the mind, and would like nothing more than to put one in the hands of every man, woman and child, whatever their class or occupation.'

'It's a noble thought,' Angelica said.

'And a profitable one,' Violet added.

Georgina laughed to herself. 'Must you always be so direct, Violet? I'm sure my husband's interests are as much for education and communication as they are for profit. It's fair to say, though, that he and Alfred are keen to grow the business, and if that means greater profit, then it will certainly keep Alfred happy.' She turned to Angelica. 'Alfred is my husband's business partner. He takes care of the finances while Stanley looks after production and just about everything else.' She paused. 'But enough of business. Won't you tell us some more about yourself, or shall we save it for another day?'

In exchange for another fine afternoon tea in their company, Angelica would gladly have told them more. Here was a circle of friends she very much wished to be a part of, but since Mr. Featherstone's visit that morning, she feared it was not to be.

'I had better tell you all there is to know now,' she said, her voice rising in distress as she recalled what Mr. Featherstone had said. 'If not now, then I'm afraid I shall not have the opportunity to do so.'

'Whatever do you mean?' Georgina asked.

'I mean I must leave the area,' Angelica said. 'When it was reported to Mr. Featherstone that I had been coming and going with parcels under my arms and wearing such fine clothes as these, as if I were a lady of means, I suppose, I was told I had to leave the almshouse—that it was not intended for the likes of me. The truth is that I spent what little money we had left on appearances.' She flicked at her sleeve. 'That's all this is.'

'You wanted to feel like a lady again,' Violet said. 'We can understand that.'

'It was sheer vanity,' Angelica said. 'I would not even use the money to put food in our mouths. My poor William. How will I ever forgive myself? Now, of course, we have nothing, but we are not without hope. I recently met a man who told me he could feed and shelter us. He has work for William, too, if not for me.'

There were sudden gasps from everyone around the table as they imagined the kind of work a young boy William's age would be put to.

'Work for William?' Georgina said, looking as horrified as she sounded. 'That sweet little boy? He's so young. I won't hear of it. I've been thinking about your situation since we met in the park yesterday. In light of what you've just said, I have a proposition for you that I'm sure will be advantageous to both of us.'

CHAPTER FIVE

Winson Green, Birmingham
1896

It was the first time I had seen Angelica Chastain, and how I hoped it would not be the last. Something inside me yearned for her from the very moment our eyes met. A connection had been made, I was sure of it. Was it love, even then? If love can be defined simply by the desire, the need, to be with someone, then yes, with all my heart, it was love. I swear it was the happiest day of my life, and shall forever be. Her dark eyes enchanted me. Her lips invited me. Her pale, slender neck demanded my touch. I have led a privileged life. Until that day I had wanted for nothing. Only when I saw Angelica did I truly understand thirst and hunger. I had to have her in my life, and it was my profound hope that Georgina would find a way to keep her close to us.

Imagine my delight when she did.

Angelica had been offered the position of governess at Priory House, which she accepted with gratitude, and yet she was like no ordinary governess. She also became a good friend to

Georgina, and she was treated as such. Gone, though, were her designs on fancy dresses for the time being—her beautiful princess-line dress never saw the light of day again. At least, I had not seen her wearing it. But who was she to mind? To all intents and purposes she and William were now living the new life she had sought for them, in a grand house far nicer than any she had known, with plentiful good food and invitations to afternoon tea.

It was a wonderful summer, made all the better for having Angelica with us. There were dinner parties and picnics in the park, and even the occasional sojourn to the seaside, which Alexander and William naturally adored, but there was darkness on the horizon. The autumn of 1880 brought with it such tragedy that the summer was all too quickly forgotten.

Birmingham
1880

It was a pleasant if cool afternoon in the middle of October. Georgina had kept up her practice of spending Wednesdays with her son, and so had accompanied Angelica and the two boys into the town centre. Georgina had wanted to visit the fashionable new emporium that had recently opened, and Angelica had been promised a new governess's gown so that she no longer had to wear black, which she thought made her look too much like the housekeeper. She had come away from the emporium with a dress made of deep blue satin, which had a white collar that fell in a broad V to her waist. It was otherwise quite plain, as befitted her position, but it was nevertheless a step in the right direction as far as Angelica was concerned.

Georgina had treated the boys to a hoop and stick each, which they were both understandably keen to play with. Because of the ongoing protest over their use in the busy areas of town, however—having been cited as a nuisance to others and especially to horses—they had been told they could only play with them in the park or in the grounds at home. Alexander and William were a few paces ahead, carrying their hoops in their hands, every now and then letting them roll along the ground through their fingers without letting go, as they progressed along Bull Street, with its many shopfronts and awnings.

Although bright, it was chilly enough to warrant shawls. Georgina pulled hers tighter as they turned the corner at the Reece Brothers tobacconists on to the High Street and the wind got up. 'Shall we take some refreshment before we head back?' she said. 'I know a nice little place not far from here, but do tell me if your feet are hurting and you'd rather not. I know you've been on them all day.'

'I'm fine if you are,' Angelica said, looking down at Georgina's belly, thinking that she was now some months into her pregnancy and was barely showing. She was clearly still wearing her corset, and Angelica supposed that was why. Anyone who didn't know Georgina well would have been hard pushed to know she was pregnant at all.

'Splendid,' Georgina said. She called ahead to the two boys, 'Stay close and keep a tight hold on those hoops! It's very busy here.'

Angelica placed a hand on Georgina's arm and their pace slowed. 'I know I've said it before,' she said, 'but thank you for everything you've done for us.'

'Not at all,' Georgina said, smiling. 'I have to confess that offering you the position of governess was in truth rather selfish of me.'

'However do you mean?'

'I mean I did so as much for my own sake, or rather for Alexander's, as for yours. Alexander is so much happier when he's with William. That by itself was reason enough to want you both in our lives, but you are evidently well educated, and French governesses are so desirable, being known to teach correct elocution. And who is better qualified when it comes to tutoring Alexander in your native language?'

'I see,' Angelica said, smiling back. 'Then we are good for one another.'

'Yes, we are. Just as our fine boys are good for one another, and shall continue to be. I've spoken to Stanley. He's also become rather fond of you and William. We're both in agreement that William will be taught alongside Alexander. He'll receive the finest education.'

'That's too much to ask,' Angelica said, her eyes back on Georgina's, questioning whether it could really be true.

'There's nothing for you to ask,' Georgina said. 'The matter is already decided. You shall continue to tutor both boys in English and French, while the tutors currently teaching Alexander in other subjects will also teach William. When the boys are eight they will both be sent away to school together, as close as any brothers. When they are older still, Alexander will become a penmaker, like his father. There will be a role at the factory for William, too, both boys working side by side together as men. At least, that is my hope, if you will allow it.'

Angelica didn't know what to say. Such an education would cost a fortune and was far beyond her means, even with the generous allowance she was now receiving as governess along with her room and board at Priory House. And to be offered a position in the family business . . . Georgina seemed to have William's life all mapped out for him.

Several seconds passed before Georgina gave a

small laugh and said, 'Shall I take your silence as agreement in the matter?'

'Yes,' Angelica said without hesitation. 'Thank you so very much.'

They continued slowly along the High Street, taking in the shop windows—a hosiery and draper here, a greengrocer there—and Angelica became lost in her thoughts of the future.

'Is everything all right?' Georgina asked.

'I was just wondering,' Angelica said. 'What will happen when the boys are eight and Alexander no longer requires a governess?'

'When the boys are eight, my dear Angelica, I shall have a new charge for you, and perhaps several more in time.' Georgina ran a hand over her belly. 'Until he or she is old enough, I shall of course employ a nursery maid, but it's my sincere hope that, while you are under no obligation to do so, you shall stay on as governess. That is, unless you've found another husband by then, with an income sufficient to draw you away. Either way, William's education is secure.'

They caught up with the boys, who were still pretending to roll their ash hoops along the gutter. Every now and then Angelica would see William let go of his momentarily, just for a few seconds to watch it roll, his hand hovering above it, ready to catch it again. Then he would look back at his mother with a mischievous grin on his face.

'Oh, look at that,' Georgina said, drawing

Angelica's attention to one of the shops as they passed. It was a milliner's colourful window, displaying hats on stands like cakes in a patisserie.

Angelica turned to look, but as she did so, out of the corner of her eye, she saw William's hoop begin to roll across the street. Everything that followed happened so fast that Angelica was powerless to prevent it. Perhaps out of friendship or plain chivalry, Alexander had dropped his hoop and was going after William's. Angelica's eyes flashed briefly over at the hansom cab coming the other way and then back at the hoop that was rolling directly towards it.

'Alexander!'

She caught hold of William as he went to follow after his friend, then she saw Georgina suddenly running into the street, a look of horror on her face as the hoop and Alexander drew closer to the oncoming horse. What Angelica saw next made her shield William's eyes with her hand as she, too, was forced to look away. Another carriage had turned the corner out of Bull Street as they had. It had come up behind them just as Georgina ran out after Alexander. There were cries from the driver sitting up on his box as the horses began to whinny and rear up. When Angelica looked again, she saw that the carriage had not been able to stop in time, and Georgina was now lying lifeless in the street.

● ● ●

Later that evening, Angelica was sitting in the drawing room at Priory House, gazing at the flames in the fireplace and quietly sobbing into her handkerchief, inconsolable. The two boys had by now been sent to their beds, tearful and confused, but she was not alone. Stanley Hampton was standing over by the grand piano, his shoulders slumped, his dark eyes gazing down at the empty stool as if he could still see his Georgina sitting there. Effie and Violet had come as soon as they heard the news, and were sitting either side of Angelica, wiping the tears from their eyes and shaking their heads from time to time, as though unable to make any sense of what had happened. Georgina Hampton was dead, and what sense was there to make of death?

Everyone had been quiet for several minutes now, and the silence, punctuated only by the tick-tick-tick of the grandfather clock, was overbearing. The fire, though blazing a merry dance to ward off the autumn evening's chill, could do nothing to combat the mournful mood that was reflected in every black window, where all the drapes had been left open, the servants who usually drew them for the night having been told not to enter the room unless called for.

When at last someone spoke, it was Angelica.

74

She stood up, turning towards Stanley as she rose, and with staring eyes said, 'It was my fault! I killed your wife, and your unborn child.'

Her words seemed to wake Stanley from his trance-like state. He looked at Angelica, and her words caught up with him. He rushed over to her and took her by the shoulders.

'You must not blame yourself for this,' he insisted. 'You've explained what happened. Others who witnessed the accident have given the same account. It was no more your fault than it was young William's for letting his hoop get away from him, or Alexander's for that matter, for looking out for his friend and going after the blessed hoop in the first place. What could you have done to stay a mother's instinct to protect her child?'

'I should have seen the carriage sooner,' Angelica said. 'I should have warned poor Georgina in time to save her.' She sat down again and continued to sob into her hands.

Effie stroked her arm to soothe her and offered her a clean handkerchief to replace her own. 'You cannot blame yourself for what you did not see,' she said. 'You were looking at Alexander, just as Georgina was when she ran out after him.'

'Then I should have gone after Alexander myself. I was first to see the danger. I was selfish, concerned only that William was safe.'

'Nonsense, nonsense,' Stanley said. 'You're

his mother. You did exactly what any child's mother would have done.' He fell quiet. 'And so did Georgina, only she died doing so.' He could barely finish the sentence. He turned sharply away and wiped his eyes with his shirtsleeve. 'Now, I'll hear no more of it,' he added as he retreated back to the piano with his thoughts.

Angelica finished dabbing her eyes and held Effie's handkerchief out to her. 'Thank you,' she said in a quiet voice. 'My own was quite soaked through.'

'Keep it,' Effie said. 'In case you have further need of it. It must be terrible for you.'

'I'm the lucky one, aren't I?' Angelica said, sniffing back her tears. She studied the handkerchief, reading Effie's embroidered monogram on one of the crumpled corners. 'A keepsake then. I don't suppose I'll see much of either of you now that Georgina's gone.'

'Why ever not?' Violet asked, fussing distractedly with her own handkerchief, which she had been doing since she first sat down. 'I should think Stanley all the more in need of a governess for young Master Alexander now that the poor boy is without his mother.'

'Do you really think so?'

'I'm sure of it,' Violet said. 'Just give it time.'

Effie nodded. 'I expect Stanley would think it too hard entirely on Alexander to lose both his mother and his governess at the same time. I'm sure Alexander has become quite fond of you, and of William, of course.'

'From what I've seen, those two boys are inseparable,' Violet said. 'To split them up now would be tantamount to the most heinous cruelty.'

'Yes, I suppose it would,' Angelica said, wondering what life at Priory House would be like without Georgina. She would miss their conversations and their strolls in the park together on Wednesdays, and she supposed that if she were allowed to stay on as governess, then her role would have to be taken far more seriously. Mr. Hampton would surely expect nothing less. Time would tell how the coming years would turn out, she supposed, as her eyes drifted over to the piano. What indeed would life at Priory House be like now that its master was, at least for the foreseeable future, left a widower?

CHAPTER SIX

Winson Green, Birmingham
1896

Looking back on these events fills me with such mixed emotions. Georgina was dead, and yet her death was the very catalyst that brought Angelica and I closer together. Or was our love always meant to be? Perhaps it would ultimately have prevailed whether Georgina had died that day or not. I have tried to convince myself of this many times, for it is painfully difficult to accept your own happiness at the expense of another, especially when that person was close to you. I have tried to believe this, but I cannot deny that it was from our shared grief that our love began to flourish.

The seasons came and went, and with each passing year our friendship grew stronger. Perhaps Georgina's death had left such a void in our hearts that we sought to fill it with one another's companionship, and with the boys soon away at school there was little to distract us. We laughed together and we cried together. Angelica became as a sister to me, and we might have gone on living like that forever had I not yearned for more.

It was in 1883, almost three years after Georgina died, that I realised I could not go on like this. Seeing Angelica as often as I did, yet never being able to hold her longer than befits a welcome embrace, or to kiss her anywhere other than on the cheek, as friends might, had become quite painful to me. We were friends, yes, but was it merely friendship that had flowered within us, or did Angelica return my deeper feelings?

I had to know.

It was also at this time that I learned the shocking truth of why Angelica had to flee from London. She told me what she had done for William's sake, and what she had later done to rid them both of Tom Blanchard. She must have been terrified, but as I learned from Georgina's death, there can be no greater source of courage than a mother's fear for the life of her own child. As I have said before, under the circumstances I cannot condemn Angelica for her actions, however monstrous they may appear at face value. I can only hope that I would find such nerve in her situation.

But I digress.

How did Angelica feel about me? Was she ready to take our friendship further? I had to know what was in her heart—and soon, as it turned out, because there was upset on the horizon, forcing my hand, or perhaps guiding it. Either way, it quickly became clear that if I did not tell Angelica how I felt about her, I would risk losing her forever.

Birmingham
1883

It was a fine midsummer's morning. Stanley Hampton had invited Angelica and Effie on a tour of Hampton and Moore's new and expanded pen factory in the Jewellery Quarter to mark its opening, and not having had the opportunity to visit Stanley's place of business before, Angelica was keen to go. Violet had also been invited, but she was unable to attend due to a recent spate of ill health. As for Effie, she arrived early at Priory House with yet another new dress for Angelica. Over the past year she had showered Angelica with so many gifts that she had lost count of all the gowns and undergarments she now owned, very few of which had required the attention of the seamstress's needle, because Angelica and Effie were so similar in size.

It had crossed Angelica's mind once or twice that, after a suitable amount of time had passed, Stanley might let her have some of Georgina's things. He had kept everything just as it was for some time, as if unsure what to do with it all, or perhaps because he was unable to part with it. But then, exactly one year after Georgina's death, having drunk himself into a rare stupor, Stanley had ordered all Georgina's clothing to be piled on the lawn, where he set such a blaze to it that the flames could likely be seen from Wales. Angelica could barely bring herself to watch as all those bright and pretty things quickly turned to ash, but she understood that Stanley did not wish to see any other woman wearing his late wife's clothes. Angelica was, therefore, all the more grateful for Effie's charity.

Angelica was standing on a footstool in her room while one of the maids fussed with her bustle, which according to Effie was making something of a comeback. Effie had been sitting over by the window since she arrived, studying Angelica with great intensity, quietly smiling to herself as she watched the maid dress her, as if keen to see her old things brought to life again on Angelica's curvaceous frame.

'The dress is going to look wonderful on you, Angelica,' Effie said, as Angelica stepped down from the stool.

'We have such similar tastes that I don't doubt it for a minute,' Angelica said, poking at her frizzled fringe, which was another of Effie's fashionable suggestions.

The maid, a young girl who had not long been in service at Priory House, offered up the petticoat and began to help Angelica into it. 'Thank you, Rose,' she said, thinking that while it was not the first time a maid had helped her into such fine clothing, it was nonetheless extraordinary, given where she had come from.

The dress was next to go on. It was made of striped maroon satin with a bow on the bustle, and the reason Effie had said she no longer wanted it was because she felt it was too bold a colour for her. Her eyes lit up as soon as she saw it on Angelica, suggesting she thought it none too bold for her.

'Why do you stare so, Effie?' Angelica asked with a laugh. 'If you don't close your mouth soon you might catch a fly.'

'Was I staring?' Effie said. 'I'm sorry. The dress just looks so beautiful on you. I could never do it justice, but it complements you very well. I'm surprised you've not yet taken another husband.'

'I'm afraid my experience of men has not been good.'

'It hasn't?' Effie said, sitting up as though keen to find out why.

'No. My husband was kind enough, I suppose, but he never had time for me. Once we were married he only cared for his work, not that it amounted to anything. We never had any money to spare.'

'He sounds just like Violet's husband,' Effie said. 'Apart from the money of course. How did you meet him?'

Angelica smiled to herself as she recalled the

occasion. 'He came to Rouen with a cart full of leather cases to sell, and my grandfather, who happened to be in Rouen at the time, bought one from him. It was for his ear trumpet, to protect it whenever he left home. He didn't have it with him, of course, and when he arrived home with the case he found it was too small, so I offered to take it back, along with his ear trumpet, to exchange it for one that would fit. I ended up taking more back to our little village that day than I'd bargained for.'

Effie gave a small laugh. 'Did you love him?'

'I suppose I did,' Angelica said, 'but it didn't last. I was young and I didn't really know what I wanted—a happy future and someone to share it with, I suppose.'

'He doesn't sound so bad,' Effie said. 'I'm sure he's not the only reason your experience of men hasn't been good. Have there been others?'

Angelica's thoughts turned to Reggie Price and she decided she had talked enough about her past for now. 'You're beginning to sound like Violet,' she said. 'She's always asking questions about my life before I came here.'

'Am I?' Effie said. 'I'm sorry. I didn't mean to pry.' A moment later she fidgeted and added, 'It's a pity Violet can't come with us today. I'm sure she would have enjoyed it. I do hope she's feeling better soon.'

'I hope so, too,' Angelica said, 'but I'm glad

it's just the two of us today. Violet hasn't really taken to me, has she?'

'Let's not talk about Violet any more,' Effie said. 'A moment ago you told me that when you married you just wanted a happy future and someone to share it with. Do you still feel that way?'

'Yes, and if society didn't frown so on unmarried women, I could quite happily spend the remainder of my days in company such as yours.'

'You could?'

Angelica nodded. 'Although I must confess to finding Mr. Hampton quite different from the type of man who has so blackened my opinion of their sex. He's very caring.'

'Yes, he is,' Effie said, casting her eyes to the window, away from Angelica for the first time all morning.

'Now, with the boys away at school,' Angelica continued, 'I suppose I must turn my thoughts to leaving Priory House, before Stanley politely asks me to.'

'I can't imagine he would ever do that. I've seen how he looks at you.'

'How do you mean?'

'Oh, come now, Angelica. You must have seen it. It's become so obvious since Georgina died. I think that's perhaps why Violet seems a little cool towards you lately. She sees the way Stanley is around you. She often talks about it.'

'She does? What does she say?'

'Only that she doesn't think it right that Stanley should have so quickly forgotten his Georgina. Violet and Georgina really were the best of friends.'

'It's been three years,' Angelica said. 'I'm surprised Stanley hasn't found another wife by now.'

'Yes, well, he did love Georgina very much.' Effie smiled to herself. 'It's a good thing Violet wasn't able to come to dinner the other evening. Stanley was openly flirting with you from the moment we sat down. I shudder to think how far he'd have gone had I not been there.'

'He'd had too much wine, that's all.'

'I'm sure he had, but he wasn't flirting with me. In fact, he barely seemed to notice I was there. He's very fond of you, I tell you. He won't ask you to leave.'

'Perhaps, but I should not wish to remain with no greater purpose than to play écarté with him of an evening, as Georgina used to.'

'I'm sure he takes great comfort from it.'

'Just the same, playing cards is not enough. I have a small amount of money saved. Now that I no longer have to concern myself with William's well-being, I think it would be prudent to seek a governess position elsewhere.'

'Will you remain close by so that we may continue our friendship?' Effie said, looking out of the window again. 'Or must I be content with the occasional letter?' She turned back to Angelica with a smile. 'You know you could always come and live with me. I'm sure Father wouldn't mind. We can become old spinsters together.'

Angelica laughed. 'I'm sure society would frown all the more on that!'

'Who cares about society?' Effie said, scowling. 'We should be allowed to do whatever we please.'

'Yes, perhaps we should,' Angelica said. To Rose, she added, 'Pass me the hat, would you?'

Before Rose could oblige, Effie sprang to her feet. 'It's all right, Rose,' she said. 'Thank you. You can leave us now.'

'Very good, miss,' Rose said with a small curtsey.

Once Rose had gone, Effie offered up the hat, which was also maroon to match the dress. It had a narrow oval brim and was lavishly trimmed with red and black feathers and ribbons. She stepped close to Angelica and set it on her head, placing it just so before reaching her arms around Angelica's neck and slowly tying the ribbons beneath her chignon. The back of Angelica's neck began to tingle at her touch. As Effie withdrew her hands, biting her lower lip ever so slightly, their eyes met and neither looked away. For reasons Angelica could not explain, she felt a curious heat rise within her, flushing her cheeks. It was like nothing she had ever felt before.

'You really are quite beautiful,' Effie said, remaining close. She reached in and slowly tucked a few loose strands of Angelica's hair behind her ear, and Angelica could see that Effie's cheeks were also flushed.

Before Effie could take her hand away, Angelica held it close to her neck, and as she suspected, Effie made no attempt to withdraw it. Instead, their eyes met again and their gazes lingered as an unspoken understanding was exchanged between them. Then came a knock at the door and Effie pulled away with a gasp.

'Come in!' Angelica called.

When the door opened, the housekeeper came in. 'The carriage is ready for you now.'

'Very good, Missus Redmond,' Angelica replied, still looking at Effie, although by now Effie had turned away to the window again.

CHAPTER SEVEN

The Jewellery Quarter was home to many trades beyond the manufacture of jewellery. Among the factories and workshops were those dedicated to the production of gilt buttons and pins, cap badges and metal toys, and fountain pens. The jewellery trade was in decline, but thanks to the inventions of free-flowing ink, hard rubber and iridium-tipped gold nibs, the penmaking industry was thriving. This was how Hampton and Moore had been able to establish their new and expanded business in a former jewellery factory on Legge Lane.

As the carriage conveying Angelica and Effie to the pen factory pulled up in the street outside the main factory gate, which was busy with passers-by, Angelica gazed out at the building's three tightly spaced rows of tall arched windows with a degree of apprehension. She was unsure how she felt about being back in Hockley again. She had such terrible memories from her short time in the company of Tom Blanchard not far from here, that she would rather she never came near its streets again, but she had to remind herself that she wasn't there to live this time, and certainly not by Blanchard's unthinkable rules. Much had changed since then, and she had now become so ensconced in her new life in Edgbaston that she was starting to believe at last that she would never again have to return to the dark days she had left behind.

Two men were standing by the factory gate, waiting to meet the ladies off their carriage. One was Stanley Hampton, dressed as finely as ever, Angelica thought, in a top hat, grey pin-stripe trousers and a deep blue frock coat that shimmered as he walked towards them. The other man appeared to be of similar age, but there all comparison ended. The plain black suit that hung without structure on his frame had clearly not been made for him, and it had just as clearly seen far too much wear, suggesting that he was not a man of particularly good income. His presence alongside Stanley, however, and the bowler hat on his head, told Angelica that he was likely a man of position within the business.

'Welcome! Welcome!' Stanley said, full of smiles as he approached them. 'I trust you've both had an agreeable morning?'

Effie spoke first. 'We've had a delightful morning, haven't we, Angelica?'

'Yes,' Angelica agreed, 'and such a fine morning it is.'

'Quite,' Stanley said. 'Which makes it more the pity that we shall all be cooped up inside for the next hour or so.' He laughed to himself. 'It might just as well be raining. Drive on, Childers!' he called up to the carriage driver, who responded quickly with a flick of his reins.

Turning back to the factory gate, Stanley escorted Angelica and Effie towards it, one on each arm, his smile still fixed. When they came to the gate he stopped and the other man removed his hat.

'This is our invaluable foreman, Mr. Jack Hardy,' Stanley said. 'He keeps everything running like clockwork.' He winked at Hardy. 'Although we shall have to see how he does now that Hampton and Moore has quite literally doubled in size.'

He laughed and Hardy laughed with him, and as he bowed his head the foreman said in a husky voice, 'I'm very pleased to make your acquaintances. I'd shake you by the hand, only I wouldn't want to get any grease on those pretty lace gloves of yours.' He held his own calloused hands up, revealing numerous dark stains. 'I'm afraid it's something of an occupational hazard.'

'Yes,' Stanley said, grinning at him, 'even though I'm continually reminding you that you no longer work on the shop floor!'

Hardy shrugged. 'You know me, sir. I can't help myself when it comes to getting my hands dirty.'

'And you set a fine example by doing so,' Stanley said. 'Now, lead on, Jack, lead on. I'm sure our guests would rather be out strolling in the park. A woman's patience cannot be expected to last long in a stuffy factory full of machinery.' He paused and turned first to Effie and then to Angelica, before adding in a lower voice, 'Although I do have something to show you before you leave that I'm sure will delight your senses.'

They were about to go through the gate when a man in rolled-up shirtsleeves and a waistcoat interrupted them, drawing their attention with a cough as he removed his bowler. He held up his other hand towards Angelica, drawing her eye.

'Excuse m-my interruption,' the man said with a stutter, 'but have we m-met before?'

The man's features startled Angelica. On first seeing him she drew away, shocked by his appearance. The hand he had extended towards her was attached to a withered arm, and she thought his face nothing short of grotesque. It was crooked and disfigured, lacking any kind of symmetry. His mouth was twisted, his nose bent, and his left eye drooped lower than his right. His head was bald on top, his scalp red and flaking, although he had a thick crop of dark hair at the back of his head, which fell on to his shoulders in long, greasy strands. She put him in his mid-forties, although it was difficult to be sure on account of his appearance.

'We have not met, sir, no,' she said, looking to her companions with a wavering smile. She thought Effie looked as shocked to see this wretched-looking man as she was, although Stanley's expression, which was mirrored by Mr. Hardy, was more one of concern for their safety.

'What is it you want?' Stanley said, his tone firm as he moved protectively closer.

The man's head snapped around to Stanley now, as if he had only just noticed that he, or anyone other than Angelica, was there. Until now, he had been staring solely at her, presumably trying to recall where he might have seen her before.

'W-want?' the man said, his eyes back on Angelica. 'N-nothing. I merely wished to understand where we had met.'

'I have already told you,' Angelica said, losing her smile and her patience. 'We have not met. I'm sure I would recall you if we had.'

'Oh, b-but we have met,' the man insisted. 'I'm convinced of it. I rarely forget a face, and could never forget one as b-beautiful as yours.'

Stanley stepped between them. 'Now that's enough. The lady has told you she's never met you before. Be on your way.'

The man stepped aside as if to leave, but he continued. 'It was a few years ago. You had a small b-boy with you. Was he your son?'

'That's no business of yours,' Angelica said, but she realised she had indeed seen this man before. It had been close to dark, their encounter brief, but they had met.

'Damn your impertinence, man!' Stanley said. 'Be off with you before I call the police.'

'There's n-no need,' the man said, putting his hat on again. 'I'm g-going. I expect it will come to me sooner or later.'

With that, the man continued along the street, looking back over his shoulder now and then until he passed from sight.

'What a poor creature,' Effie said.

'Strangest fellow I've ever seen,' Stanley offered. 'As if anyone could forget meeting such a man.' He turned away from the street and offered his arm out towards the factory gate. 'Now, shall we continue?'

Once inside the building, they followed Hardy up a flight of ironwork stairs to the first floor, where they entered into a long room which housed a series of contraptions that Angelica had no understanding of. They were being operated almost exclusively by women, which she thought accounted for why the windowsills were laden with colourful, fragrant plants, turning Angelica's expectations of such a workplace on their head. This was unlike any manufactory she knew or had imagined. Because of the many tall windows, it was also a bright and airy space that was vaulted further down.

'These are the fly presses where the nibs are slit,' Hardy said, gesturing to one of the lime-green contraptions. 'Slitting the nib is the final part of the process before the nib is polished and set.' They continued walking between the lines of workers, who remained busy at their various roles. 'First the rolled steel or gold is marked and cut. Then it's pierced, creating the hole that allows air into the pen so the ink can flow. It's then embossed with one of our own unique patterns before it's raised, ground, and slit, as you've just seen.'

'And if you'd now care to follow me,' Stanley said, dashing ahead of Hardy towards another set of wide ironwork stairs by the far wall, 'I'd like you to see where we create the barrels and caps for our fountain pens. I'm sure you'd also like to see some of the finished products.'

At that moment a call went up from one of the workers behind them. 'Mr. Hardy, sir!' It came from one of the women they had passed.

'If you'll excuse me,' Hardy said. 'It's likely a bit of trouble with one of the presses.'

'Not at all, Mr. Hardy,' Stanley said. 'We must keep the cogs of business turning. I can take the tour from here.'

'Very good, sir,' Hardy said, and with a bow of his head he went to attend to the troublesome press.

Stanley continued towards the staircase, which ran up to a galleried iron balcony that turned back on itself on both sides, giving views of both this floor and the upper floor, where Angelica imagined the barrels and caps Stanley had just mentioned were being made. The height of the stairs and the openness of the supporting ironwork made Angelica feel a little dizzy by the time they reached the top. As they turned and surveyed the upper floor, she could see a number of other machines, where mostly men were at work.

'This is where our pens really take their form,' Stanley said as they made their way along the narrow gallery to their right. 'And a great deal of skill and craftsmanship is required to do so, I can tell you.'

Angelica clutched at the rail every step of the way, realising that height was not something she had much of a head for. At the end of the gallery they paused to watch the men work at their various roles.

'Here the barrels are turned on the lathes,' Stanley continued, indicating the machinery to their left. 'And here are the engravers who work in all materials from wood to solid gold,' he added, indicating the workers to their right.

Angelica watched one of the engravers for several seconds as he remained hunched over his work, gently working his burin over a silver pen cap, seemingly oblivious to her presence. 'Such focus and patience,' she said. 'It's quite remarkable.'

'Indeed it is,' Stanley said. 'Now, let me show you just what such attributes combine to create. If you'll step this way,' he added, heading back to the staircase, where there was also an office, 'I'd like you both to see some of our recent commissions before they're delivered—one of which is a most luxurious example for none other than Lord Calthorpe.'

As they reached the office, Stanley opened the glass-panelled door, inviting Angelica and Effie through. To Angelica he said, 'You know, there will still be a place here for Master William once his education is complete.'

Angelica stopped, allowing Effie to go inside ahead of her. She gazed warmly into Stanley's eyes and smiled. 'I really cannot fathom what either of us has done to deserve such kindness,' she said, 'but to my dying day I shall be most grateful. It is enough that you continue to pay for my son's education, but to offer him a place in your business when he's old enough is . . .' She trailed off, searching for the right words to convey her feelings. 'Well, it fills my heart with joy to know that even at his early age his future is secure.'

'It was Georgina's wish,' Stanley said. Then the light in his eyes seemed to intensify as he added, 'But more than that, it has over these past few years since Georgina died become my solemn desire to see that neither of you want for anything again.' He laughed to himself. 'And I'm afraid Alexander would be quite lost now without William by his side. You know how inseparable they've become.'

Angelica felt suddenly light on her feet. What had she done to deserve such kindness indeed? They continued slowly into the room, smiling at one another without further discourse. It was Effie who broke the silence. She was standing beside the desk where Stanley had set out a piece of black felt cloth, on which sat several of Hampton and Moore's finest-quality fountain pens.

'The workmanship really is quite exquisite,' she said. She went to pick one of the pens up, but she stopped herself. 'May I?'

'Of course,' Stanley said, 'but these pens are merely there to whet your appetites.' He went to the corner of the room and knelt before a black-and-gold-painted safe, which he unlocked with a key and opened. From it, he removed a felt roll case that he set down on the table. Then he unfurled it. 'There!' he said, withdrawing a gold pen that shone with such brilliance that no amount of shade could diminish it. He held it up. 'This tool of the mind, which has taken a great many hours of skilled labour to produce, shall very soon be in the hands of Lord Calthorpe—and who knows what important documents it may come to sign.'

His face was beaming as he spoke, and it was easy for Angelica to see the passion that burned in his eyes as he took in the pen's fine tracery. At the end of the barrel was set as large a diamond as it could accommodate, and both Angelica and Effie gasped at the sight of it.

'I must confess,' Stanley said as he removed the cap, which made a precise click as he did so, 'the diamond was Alfred's idea. I'm more for the metals, but he says there's good profit to be made through the inclusion of precious stones when the commission is rich enough to call for such things, even if the jewellery trade as a whole is in decline.'

Angelica watched Stanley slide the cap back on to the barrel with another click and set the pen carefully down on the felt again. 'It appears that you and Mr. Moore are creating quite a legacy for your children,' she said. 'I trust Mr. Moore's children will also follow in their father's footsteps?'

'Sadly that cannot be the case,' Stanley said, turning to her with a grave expression. 'Alfred's wife, Dorothy, died during the birth of their first child, and Alfred, the poor fellow, has never recovered. His love for Dorothy was so great that he refuses to remarry, despite all good intentions to encourage him to do so.'

'And did the child also perish?'

'No, the child somehow managed to survive

the ordeal. Alfred has a daughter, Louisa, a year younger than Alexander. But, of course, a pen factory is no business for a woman. The man needs a son and heir, but will he listen?'

Angelica wanted to question why the management of such a factory was no place for a woman. After all, was a woman's mind really so different from a man's that it should not be considered equal to the task? And yet here was a factory, like so many in Birmingham and elsewhere in the country, owned and managed by men, employing women to carry out all the unskilled tasks, such as pulling levers on press machines, while the men were given the skilled work—the engraving and delicate turning of the lathes—which were clearly deemed too complicated for a woman's mind to comprehend.

Stanley edged closer to her, and in a lower voice said, 'I do not share my business partner's sentimentality. A man must have a wife. As much as I loved Georgina, I hope to remarry.'

Their eyes met again, and there was such intent in his expression that Angelica could not fail to comprehend his meaning.

'It has always been my desire to father a house full of children,' he continued. 'Poor Georgina was unable to fulfil that desire, although I am blessed with Alexander, of course.'

'Of course,' Angelica agreed, still looking into

his eyes, trying to be sure of his intentions. 'He's a fine boy.'

Angelica was aware then that Effie was standing close beside her. She reached across and picked up Lord Calthorpe's pen, brushing Angelica's arm with hers as she did so. It broke the spell Stanley seemed to have over Angelica, as his eyes were instantly drawn to the pen.

'Be careful not to drop it,' Stanley said, with more alarm in his voice than seemed necessary.

Paying Stanley no attention, Effie studied the pen in closer detail. 'Isn't it beautiful, Angelica?' she said. 'You shall have a fine Hampton and Moore fountain pen for your next governess position. It will be my parting gift to you.'

'Thank you, Effie. You're too kind, as ever.'

'But what's this?' Stanley said, his face suddenly frowning. 'Do I take it that you mean to leave Priory House?'

Angelica glanced at Effie before answering, trying to gauge whether her interruption and mention of their earlier conversation had been deliberate. Effie was still looking at the pen, giving nothing away. Angelica supposed she had heard Stanley talk of marriage and of children. Was Effie jealous? If so, of whom? Surely Effie had no designs on Stanley Hampton. Or did she? It made no matter. The question was a timely one. Angelica's answer was sure to test her understanding of Stanley's meaning when he had spoken of remarrying. If his affections were now set on her, how could he let her leave Priory House, and just how far was he prepared to go in order to keep her there?

'I have no one else to govern at Priory House,' she said. 'I was waiting for the right moment to tell you, but I suppose this is as good a time as any.'

'You can't leave,' Stanley said, sounding quite perturbed.

'What else is there for me? I've enjoyed your hospitality long enough. I fear I shall now only become more and more of a burden to you.'

'A burden? My dear Angelica, you could never be that.'

'But I should have no purpose.'

'What about our card games? Stay, I implore you. If only for that.'

Angelica looked away. 'It's not enough, Stanley.'

Stanley drew a deep breath and held it, as if considering what to do about the matter. A moment later he took the pen from Effie and said, 'Effie, would you mind stepping outside the room for a moment?'

Effie's lips parted, but she didn't speak. She looked momentarily lost for words. A few seconds later she gave an awkward smile and said, 'Of course.' Then she left the room.

'Angelica,' Stanley said as soon as the door had

closed. His eyes were back on hers. The intensity that had been there previously now returned. 'What if there were a greater reason for you to remain at Priory House than trifling card games?'

'But I am a governess without a charge,' Angelica said. 'What possible reason could there be?'

Stanley sighed. 'Please don't tease me, Angelica. I think you know what's in my heart. It has been there this past year or more. Don't you see it?'

Angelica began to feel light-headed. She saw it clearly enough, but she needed to hear him say it. 'Do speak plainly, Stanley. What greater reason?'

Stanley turned away. He leaned on the desk as though in need of support. When he turned back to her, his face was lincd with anguish, as if the answer to his next question might destroy him.

'Will you marry me, Angelica? Will you continue to live at Priory House as my wife?'

Angelica and Effic did not remain long at the pen factory. The carriage met them outside the main gate where they had arrived, and after saying their goodbyes to Stanley, who for business reasons was unable to return with them, they were soon sitting opposite one another, heading back to Priory House. Effie had barely said a word since Angelica and Stanley had left his office to break the news of their engagement.

Stanley was beaming with joy as he rushed over to her, eager to tell someone, anyone, that he and Angelica were to be married, but it was clear at once that Effie did not share his joy. She smiled unconvincingly as Stanley told her, and her smile wavered to nothing as she turned to Angelica and gave her congratulations.

For reasons Angelica could by now gather, she was not surprised at Effie's reaction. Effie was indeed jealous of one of them, and the disappointment Angelica read in her eyes told her that it was in all probability Stanley she was jealous of. She thought it just as well that Stanley's business affairs would keep him in town for the remainder of the afternoon, because she felt there was a pressing conversation to be had with Effie, if only Effie would talk to her, and it was a conversation in much need of privacy.

Thankfully, as soon as the carriage pulled away and the busy sounds of the street veiled their words, Effie spoke out at last, releasing the questions she had kept bottled up since news of the engagement broke.

'Why?' Effie asked, her eyes imploring Angelica to give her an answer she could understand. 'Earlier today, you said you had a poor opinion of men, and yet here you are, this very same day, engaged to be married!'

'I'm sure today has been very confusing for

you,' Angelica said, trying to sound sympathetic. 'It's been equally confusing for me.'

'Do you love him?'

Angelica sat forward and took Effie's hands in hers. 'No,' she said with sincerity, 'but I do love my son, and how could I refuse the man who holds my son's future in the balance? Marrying Stanley will ensure William's future absolutely. I will no longer have to worry whether Stanley's charity will one day end at his whim. And what if he were to marry someone else? How would his new wife feel about William and me? How long would it be before her influence sent us back to the lives we had once known? And what of our friendship then?' She gave Effie's hands a gentle squeeze. 'Marrying Stanley also means that I shall remain at Priory House, where I'll forever be closer to you. Isn't that what you want?'

A tremulous sigh escaped Effie's lips. She nodded. 'Yes,' she said, sounding almost breathless. 'I want that very much.'

'Well then, isn't it for the best that I marry Stanley? For William's sake, and for ours?'

Angelica let go of Effie's hands. She reached up to brush her cheek, and as she did so, Effie held her hand there and leaned affectionately into it.

'I love you, Angelica,' she said. 'You must know it by now. I don't know why I feel the way I do about you. If I had been born a man, I would have asked you to marry me as soon as I met you.'

'Love?' Angelica said, surprised to hear that Effie's affections for her ran so deep. 'I'm afraid I'm not a woman anyone should fall in love with. We should both pity Stanley.' She shook her head and sat back again. 'I am not a good woman, Effie. In fact, I would go so far as to say that I'm a monster.'

Effie sat back with her, confusion creasing her brow. 'Why would you say such a thing?'

'Because it's true, Effie. I lied to Georgina about my reasons for leaving London, and I lied to you.'

'How do you mean?'

Angelica gazed out of the carriage window at the grey town buildings that sped past them, wondering whether it was wise to go on, but she was curious enough about Effie's proclamation of love for her to test it. 'The true reason I left London and brought William here is because I killed a man.'

Effie gasped and put a hand to her mouth.

'If I had not left I would otherwise have been found out and hanged for it long before now. I had fallen in with people I would have done well to steer clear of. There was a man called Reginald Price. One day he forced himself on me. He was quite brutal. William discovered us and the man began to beat him. I could take his brutality, but I could not stand by and watch him beat my son. I thought he was going to kill William and I panicked. I grabbed the first thing that came to hand. It was the knife Reggie carried, in a sheath on his belt. I pulled it out, and without thinking of the consequences I drove it deep into his back.'

Effie winced. She shook her head, as though unable to believe what she was hearing. Then her features softened again, turning to sympathy. 'What else could you have done?' she said. 'He might have killed you both.'

'Perhaps. But I'm afraid that's only the half of it. Price had a friend called Tom Blanchard. He must have seen what happened because he knew what I'd done. I expect he'd gone to meet with his friend that evening. When William and I left Price's house, Blanchard followed us home and waited for us to leave again. He had the most deplorable plans for us, too, threatening to turn me over to the authorities if I didn't obey him.'

'What plans?'

'Prostitution,' Angelica said. 'I'm sorry to say it wouldn't have been for the first time, either.'

'It wouldn't?'

'No. When little William was born I knew I wanted more for him than the life I'd brought him into. I couldn't rely on my husband to provide well enough for the two of us, let alone for our child as well. We needed more money. I gave William the best I had to offer.'

'Yourself?'

Angelica nodded. 'I knew a woman whose husband had encouraged her into prostitution to help make ends meet. She introduced me to Reggie Price, who found regular work for me and several other women. He saw to it that none of our clients got out of hand, and if they did, he dealt with them. Before I knew it, I'd become so caught up in that world that it was impossible to walk away from it. I tried, the evening before I left London, but Reggie wouldn't hear of it. Apparently I was his best girl, you see. That's why he turned on me, and then on William. I should have left William with his father, but as I've said, he was always so busy with his work.'

'You did what you had to do,' Effie said, 'for both your sakes.'

'Yes, I suppose so,' Angelica said. 'Imagine my horror when I learned that Tom Blanchard had similar ideas, only his were far worse. He wanted to keep me locked in a pretty room in a nice little house, sending client after client in to see me. He meant to put William to work when he was older, too, selling our flesh to be abused by whoever would pay him. It was not the new life I had imagined for us—who could want the kind of life Tom Blanchard had to offer?'

'What did you do?'

'Blanchard was also cruel to William. His type are rarely kind to children. He began to hit him,

108

and I knew it would only get worse. I would have run from him, but he had only to tell the authorities what I'd done in London.'

'Did you kill him, too?'

'Yes. Just moments before my first client was due to arrive I encouraged him to the upstairs room, where I was to allow this man who was coming to do with me whatever he wished. With William in the room below, I steeled my nerves and cut Tom Blanchard's throat with a piece of glass I'd taken from the washhouse in the yard.'

Effie gasped again.

'You see,' Angelica said, 'I'm a monster, and I'm sorry I lied to you before, but how could I have told you all this when we first met? You would not have wished to know me then.'

'Why are you telling me this now?'

'Because I care about you.'

'You do?'

'Yes,' Angelica said, sitting forward again.

'I don't think you're a monster,' Effie said. 'What choice did you have? You had to do something, if not for yourself then for William. I think you're a very brave woman.'

Angelica smiled. 'You're so sweet, Effie, but I doubt the magistrate would be so accommodating. Can I trust you not to tell anyone?'

'On my life.'

'Good,' Angelica said. She placed her hands

on Effie's knees. 'I've also told you this so you can better understand why my experience of men has not been a good one. I want you to believe me when I say that, while I have agreed to marry Stanley, men are of no physical interest to me— none at all. Do you understand?'

Effie nodded. Then, as Angelica held Effie's gaze, she leaned across the narrow divide between them and kissed her softly on the lips. Effie did not pull away. She returned the kiss as fully as it had been given, and in that moment Angelica knew that Effie understood her very well.

CHAPTER EIGHT

Two days after Stanley and Angelica were engaged to be married, Angelica was out in the grounds at Priory House, cutting flowers for her room. It was something she enjoyed doing for herself when the mood took her, even though it was usually the duty of one of the servants. It was another warm day, as fine as it had been all week, the air filled with birdsong and the gentle whisper of the wind. She wore an apron over her light summer dress so as not to spoil it, and a wide bonnet on her head to keep the sun from her eyes. Over her arm she carried a large wicker trug, which was already half full with roses of all colours.

She was walking alongside one of the flower borders that ran around the grounds by the perimeter wall, quietly humming a tune to herself as pleasant thoughts drifted in and out of her mind—of living at Priory House, not as governess, but as its mistress. She wondered what changes she would make, if any; Missus Redmond and Mr. Rutherford, the butler, ran a tight enough ship between them, but she liked the thought that Priory House and all its servants would ultimately soon be hers to control. Even Stanley for that matter.

She hovered her secateurs over the stem of another rose that took her fancy and clipped it into her trug. Then, as she moved on again, movement caught her eye. She was close to the main gates now, which stood open as they usually did during the day. She ventured closer, peering ahead, and after a while she saw the movement again. Someone was there. At first, she thought it must be the gardener, perhaps tidying the clematis, but it was not.

As she drew close to the gates, she came face to face with the man who had spoken to her previously outside the pen factory. She had hoped their paths would never cross again, but here he was, clearly having gone to some lengths to find her. Seeing his face again, despite the familiarity, was no less shocking.

'I didn't m-mean to startle you,' he said, politely removing his hat as he spoke. He had a grey suit jacket in one hand, his shirtsleeves rolled up as before, presumably on account of the warm weather, and perhaps because they were otherwise too long for his withered arm.

'What are you doing here?' Angelica demanded, keeping her distance. 'What do you want?'

'That's a very g-good question,' the man said. He stepped closer, but remained outside the gates. 'I remembered where we m-met.'

Angelica's breath caught in her chest as her hand tightened around her secateurs. Her eyes narrowed on him. 'Do you indeed? And where might that have been?'

The man swallowed a few times before he answered, as if having difficulty getting his reply out. 'H-Hockley,' he stammered. 'I saw y-you and your little boy outside a h-house on Kings Terrace. You d-dropped your purse and I went to pick it up for you, but you b-beat me to it. I-I was going to the same house y-you had just left. When I knocked, I received no answer. Y-you are the lady I was g-going there to see that night, aren't you?'

'I most certainly was not,' Angelica lied. 'As I said before. You are quite mistaken.'

'But I know I'm n-not,' the man insisted. 'Are you the lady of this fine house?'

'I soon will be, as if that's any business of yours.'

'A m-marriage,' the man said, smiling. 'How l-lovely.'

'Look, where is this leading?' Angelica asked, growing impatient to be rid of the man, but not before she was sure he was satisfied that it was not her he had seen that night. She had to understand what he intended to do about it if he would not believe her.

'I-I was just thinking that you've d-done very well for yourself, haven't you? You wouldn't want to r-risk it all now. I wonder who else m-might believe me if I told them that the lady of Priory House was a p-prostitute. Does your future husband know?'

Angelica wanted to slap his face for his impertinence, but she did not. He was right, after all, and clearly he was not about to let the matter go. She began to wonder what else he knew. More specifically whether he was aware that a man had been murdered at the house on Kings Terrace just moments before their paths had crossed in the street outside. She suspected he did not know, or she thought he might at least have hinted at it by now. She also thought that if he suspected her for a murderer and knew what she was capable of, he would be more wary of her. To the contrary, his lopsided eyes, which seemed to consume her, told her that he was well and truly besotted with her. She thought if he started blabbing about her in connection with Kings Terrace, however, someone might eventually make the connection.

She looked away and stared through the trees beyond the gates for several seconds while she thought what to do. It seemed that her past was not yet ready to let her go on with the happy life she was building for herself and William, and something had to be done about that.

But what?

She quickly decided that it was no use trying to appeal to the man's sensibilities by telling him she had been forced into prostitution, on that occasion at least. No, she had to deal with the matter head on, and here and now, rather than later with Stanley if this wretched man followed through with his threats. Whether Stanley chose to believe what he heard or not, it would do nothing for her reputation. It could even jeopardise their marriage, and she could not risk that.

'Very well, you're right,' she said. She saw no sense in prolonging the lie. 'It was me. I was the woman you were going to see that night.'

A childish grin slowly spread across the man's twisted face. He looked excited beyond measure to hear Angelica admit it.

'Do you need money?' Angelica asked. 'Is that it? How much will your silence cost me?'

The man shook his head, still smiling at her. 'I d-don't want your money.'

'Then what do you want?'

'I w-want,' he began, then paused to lick the spittle from his lips. 'I w-want what I was going to get that n-night at the house on Kings Terrace.'

Angelica laughed at the idea, but the man standing before her did not seem to share her humour, mocking as it was. His features twisted further as the light in his eyes darkened.

'You're n-not taking me seriously, are you?' he said. 'I don't l-like to be laughed at.'

'I'm sorry,' Angelica said, not wishing to anger him. She had no idea what he might do if she did. 'It was rude of me. I can see you're very serious.'

She paused, thinking again. 'If I agree to come to you, to a place of your choice, do I have your word that it will be just the once, and that will be the end of the matter?'

'You have my w-word,' the man said. 'Just the once.'

Angelica doubted that. There was no question in her mind that he would insist on seeing her again, and again and again for all she knew. That was, after all, the way of the blackmailer, but she went along with him.

'What's your name?' she asked, speaking more softly now.

'H-Hector,' the man stammered, turning the brim of his hat in his hands. 'Hector P-Perlman.'

'Well, Mr. Perlman, if I'm to go through with this, you'll understand that I'd like to get it over with as soon as possible.'

'Hector, p-please,' the man said. 'Call me Hector.'

'Very well, Hector. I have no other engagements this afternoon. How does three o'clock suit you?'

Perlman began to breathe heavily with antici-pation. 'It suits me v-very well,' he said. 'I have a h-house and a small w-workshop in the Jewellery Quarter, not far from where we m-met the other day. Y-you can come to me there.'

'What about your wife? Your family?' Angelica asked. 'Aren't you married?' She stopped herself. 'No, of course you're not,' she said, wondering who could love such an unfortunate, misshapen man. 'Very well. Let me have your address and I'll see you at three.'

'You'll w-wear a pretty dress, won't you?' Perlman said. 'I like pretty things.'

'Yes, of course,' Angelica replied, shuddering at the thought of him pawing at her in one of her beautiful gowns.

'Until three then,' Perlman said, handing her a torn slip of paper on which he had already written his address.

Angelica arrived promptly at the address Hector Perlman had given her. She had walked part of the way, and then taken a hansom cab into town, followed by an omnibus, getting off close to the Jewellery Quarter so that no one who saw her along the way could know where she was going. Having walked the last few hundred yards to Perlman's house, she felt so hot beneath the dark green satin gown she had chosen to wear, and so stifled by the heavy black lace veil she had attached to her hat so that no one would recognise her, that by the time Perlman answered her knock she thought she might faint.

Despite the appointment they had made between them, Perlman looked surprised to see her. 'Y-you came,' he said, his face beaming with joy.

'Of course,' Angelica said, eager to step inside

and get in off the street, as much for the shade as for not wishing to stand so openly at his door a moment longer than she had to.

She entered into a narrow hallway that was brightly coloured in shades of yellow above the dado rail, and blue beneath it. There were stained-glass wall hangings here and there that were obscure in their design; abstract, yet oddly appealing in their way.

'I m-make those in my workshop,' Perlman said. 'Do you l-like them?'

'Yes, they're very beautiful. You sell them, I suppose?'

Perlman nodded. 'In a m-manner of speaking. Someone s-sells them for me, you see. He's cheating me, I know, but who would wish to b-buy something so beautiful from someone who looks like m-me?'

Angelica did not answer. She thought anyone else but her might have felt sorry for him, but she felt nothing.

'This w-way,' he said, and then he led her up a straight flight of stairs to a landing area that was similarly decorated with more of the same type of colourful wall hangings. There were none of the mirrors typically found in such in-between spaces of a house, but that was understandable. She suspected poor Hector did not like to look at himself any more than she did.

They quickly came to more stairs and climbed

them to the next floor, but that was not the end of the journey. Another, narrower set of stairs took them higher still, on to a landing area that was bright with sunshine from the skylights above.

'Almost there n-now,' Perlman said, stepping across the bare floorboards towards one of the attic rooms. 'This w-way,' he added, inviting her into another bright room that had no windows other than a single skylight above them. The room contained very little. There was no furniture at all. Just a single iron-framed bed and a mattress, with no linen or pillows, and a washstand with no bowl.

'H-here we are,' Perlman said, studying Angelica, taking in the lines of her gown all the way down to her shoes. 'Splendid,' he added, smiling. 'N-now, remove your hat and veil, won't you? I should like to see your pretty face.'

Angelica took off her hat as instructed and set it down on the bed. Her hair was pinned up. She patted it to make sure everything was still in place.

'N-now I'd very much like to undress you,' Perlman said, stepping close to her.

'Don't you think my gown pretty?' Angelica said, hoping to keep it on for as long as she could.

'Oh, y-yes,' Perlman said, 'It's very p-pretty, but I'm sure what lies beneath is far p-prettier.'

Angelica drew a sharp breath and held it as Perlman moved behind her suddenly and began to unbutton her gown. She felt him clumsily tugging at it, impeded as he no doubt was by his withered arm. Several seconds later, she felt his hands on her shoulders, and then her gown was sliding to the floor. She heard his breathing then, coarse and excited as he began to unfasten her petticoats and crinolette. His actions became faster and faster as his excitement grew, moving on to the laces of her corset and then to the shoes on her feet, which he gently helped her out of, stroking each foot as he did so. Before long she was standing before him in nothing more than her chemise and drawers.

Angelica took a step back. 'I can manage the rest,' she said, feigning a weak smile. 'If you'd like to watch, I mean.'

Perlman gave a nod. He smiled back at her, and Angelica continued to undress herself, feeling more nervous than she would previously have thought possible. She had stood naked in front of many men before now, assumed all kinds of poses and positions for their pleasure and their shilling, but this was different. She was not doing this for a shilling as she once had, and this man, Hector Perlman, was not the kind of man she would have taken money from. When she had finished undressing, she stood naked before him, making no poses, yet doing nothing to hide her dignity either. She was there for a purpose, and she wanted it over with as quickly as possible.

She was surprised, however, when instead of launching himself at her, as she found most men in such situations usually did, he began collecting up her clothes.

'What are you doing?' she asked, confused.

'They m-make the room untidy,' Perlman said. 'I want a clean c-canvas for your beauty.'

It was a flattering notion, if rather bizarre, Angelica thought, although given his penchant for pretty things, she understood his reasons. She watched him collect everything up, and then he left the room briefly while she stood there naked, waiting for him to return. When he did, her clothes no longer with him, he reached into one of his pockets and produced a key, which he turned in the lock without explanation before putting it away again.

'There's no need to lock the door,' Angelica said. 'We're alone, aren't we?'

'Oh, yes, w-we're quite alone. I rarely have visitors—only the m-man who comes to collect my work to sell, and he isn't due for several days.'

'Then why do you need to lock the door?'

'Because I'm afraid y-you might not wish to continue once we've started.'

As unpleasant as this man was to look at, Angelica had been with men in London who looked little better and smelled far worse, and for much less than she stood to gain now. 'I assure you I have no intention of reneging on our agreement.'

'G-good,' Perlman said. 'But just in case.'

'I really don't like being locked in,' Angelica persisted, wondering just what this man intended to do with her once they had started.

'It doesn't m-matter what you like. This is about what I l-like, isn't it?'

'Yes, of course, but—'

'Then p-please,' Perlman cut in, 'lie down on the bed. I w-won't hurt you, I promise. Not unless you m-make me.'

As vulnerable as Angelica was, she stood her ground. 'Not until you unlock the door.'

Perlman slowly lowered his head. When he raised it again he screamed at her, 'Lie down!'

The outburst startled Angelica. She felt a shiver run through her as her hands began to tremble. She had never before seen such raw aggression in a man's eyes, not even from the likes of Tom Blanchard. She shuddered to think what this man was capable of, and she did not want to draw the beast within further out of its shell to find out. Still trembling, she sat on the edge of the bed, swung her bare legs up on to the mattress and lay down.

He was standing over her in seconds.

'That's b-better, isn't it?' he said, smiling at her. 'It's just a door. I'll unlock it again when we've f-finished, and perhaps one day, once you've become more used to me, I won't feel the n-need to lock it.'

'I knew it,' Angelica said. 'You lied to me when you said this was to be just the once.'

'But you're so b-beautiful, Angelica. How could it possibly be just the once?'

Angelica gave no answer. Neither of them spoke again. Unable to look directly at him now, out of the corner of her eye she saw him roll his sleeves further up. Then he unbuckled his belt and dropped his trousers. He stood watching her for several long seconds, admiring her beauty as he became more and more aroused by it. He touched her leg, gently with the back of his hand, and she flinched. She turned away, and suddenly he was over her, forcing her legs apart. She knew it was no use trying to struggle. She wanted to relax, to make it easier, but she couldn't. A second later, she felt his body jerk as he penetrated her, once, twice, and then without warning his hand was around her throat.

Perlman must have thought himself fully in control of the situation—his far weaker prey lying naked and defenceless beneath him—but he wasn't. Far from it. Angelica had to concede that things weren't going quite as she had anticipated, but no matter. She reached a hand up behind Perlman's ear and began to caress the back of his neck. She moved her hand higher and began to fondle the hair at the back of his head, which caused him to make little noises in his throat, like a cat purring on her lap. His grip around her neck lessened and she pulled him down into the soft cushion of her breasts as he continued to thrust and jerk, back and forth, his groans becoming more and more audible as he neared climax.

But, for his lies, Angelica would deny him.

When she sensed he was moments away from orgasm, she curled his hair around her hand and pulled his head back, at the same time reaching into her own hair for the dip pen she had used as a hair pin. She drew it out, took a firm grip, and before Perlman's eyes opened again, drove the steel nib hard into his left eye socket.

Perlman did not scream. He simply began to twitch and convulse on top of her as a line of blood ran like a tear from his eye. She rolled him off her, turning with him until she was on top, her hand still pressing on the pen, his body still twitching beneath her. When at last he was still, she tilted her head to one side and stared at his now-lifeless face with renewed fascination, thinking that she had given this man exactly what he would have received that night at the house on Kings Terrace had she been there.

CHAPTER NINE

Winson Green, Birmingham
1896

I shudder to think of the depraved things Hector Perlman would have had Angelica do for his silence, over and over again, had she not killed him. I knew nothing of his murder at the time, however. She told me about him much later. I was concerned only with my love for her then, and to hear that she was going to marry Stanley Hampton, as good a man as he was, upset me more than I could say, regardless of Angelica's assurances that she was not marrying him out of love. But Stanley's proposal had forced my hand, and it would prove to be a blessing, for a time at least.

Their wedding was a quiet affair with only a handful of friends and close family in attendance. I do not believe Stanley could have faced a larger gathering, despite it having been close to three years since Georgina's death. Even as the poor man stood there and said his vows before God, I am sure he felt racked with guilt and pain for the loss of his first wife, but what could he do? Stanley Hampton had fallen in love with

Angelica Chastain, and I can tell you from my own experience that that flame, once kindled, could never go out.

For myself, I would sooner have forgone the torment of attending their wedding. The intimate company of so few people made the proceedings all the more unbearable for me. There was nowhere to hide myself away, nothing to distract my attention from the happy couple when I was feeling anything but. If only I could have looked forward, and could have seen the life that was in store for Angelica and me. Then I might have rejoiced in their marriage for what it was. But it did take time. I am sure that, during those early years of their marriage, Angelica was too focused on making a good show of things, of keeping Stanley happy and safeguarding William's future, to risk it all on us. We shared our moments, but they were so few and far between that they became sweet torture to me, never knowing when we would be together again, having to watch Angelica and Stanley in all their post-marital bliss.

One such time was when our friend Violet invited us all down to Brighton. She had taken a large suite at the Grand Hotel for the entire summer, with rooms to spare. The boys, now turned eleven, were home on their school holidays, and Stanley had apparently been overdoing things at the pen factory and was in need of respite. How could I not go with them? In truth, I wanted to see Violet again, so when the boys pleaded with Stanley to accept her invitation, the matter was decided, although it was soon plain to see that Angelica would rather not have gone.

Brighton
1886

Angelica could not think of many worse places to be than in the lamentable company of the officious Violet Cosgrove. She could by now see the woman in no more favourable light. Their interactions since Georgina died had become more and more disagreeable, and never more so than since she had married Stanley. As close a friend of the family as Violet was, she hadn't even attended their wedding, citing her ongoing health issues as the cause, but Angelica knew the real reason: Violet couldn't bear to see Angelica in Georgina's place, and her snub was her way of letting Angelica know it.

They were partway through afternoon tea, all seated together in the suite parlour. It was a bright, spacious room between the various accommodations Violet had taken for herself and for her guests whenever she had company. It looked immediately out through a narrow iron balcony, over the promenade and below to the sea. Although warm and sunny outside, the parlour air was a little too cool for Angelica, on account of the sea breeze and the fact that Violet insisted on keeping all the windows open. It was, of course, for the benefit of her general health and well-being, so there was nothing to be done about it.

'I hope you don't mind taking tea up here,' Violet said. She lifted a small dog from her lap and it immediately began to bark with excitement—a shrill yap that made Angelica wince. 'The Captain can be somewhat expressive at times. Apparently some of the more sensitive hotel guests are upset by it, so we leave them to it.' She brought the dog closer to her face and let it lick her lips. 'Don't we, Sammy?' she added in a soft, playful tone that was unlike any Angelica had heard from her before.

'The Captain?' Alexander said, scrunching his brow. He was sitting beside Violet, his father to his right and then William, Angelica and Effie, all in a circle.

Violet settled the dog back on her lap. 'Yes, or Sammy,' she said over the dog's continued yapping. 'He answers to both. I named him after Captain Samuel Brown. I thought it fitting, as I seem to be spending so much time here in Brighton. Captain Brown was the man who designed Brighton's first pier.'

'Can we go and see it?' Alexander asked.

'Of course,' Stanley said. 'We shall have lots to see before we leave.'

'Can we go now?' William said.

'Tomorrow,' Angelica cut in. 'I'm sure we're all tired after so much travelling.'

'Yes, tomorrow,' Stanley agreed. 'That's a promise. I see they have an aquarium, too. Would you like to see that?'

Both boys began to nod with enthusiasm.

'You really are the best of fathers,' Violet said, 'but then I always knew it. The way you were with young Alexander as he was growing up, when poor Georgina was still with us, was always a joy to see.' She turned to Angelica. 'You married very well, didn't you, my dear?'

The look Violet gave as she finished speaking, the raised eyebrows and the rearward tilt of her head as if looking down her nose at Angelica, was as much to say that while she had married well, Stanley had not. Were they alone, Angelica might have said something about the remark, but she bit her tongue, glancing instead at Effie, who came to her rescue.

'What type of dog is The Captain?' Effie asked, changing the subject.

The interest put a smile on Violet's face, prompting her to put her teacup down and lift the dog up again to another round of excited yapping. 'He's a Japanese spaniel,' she said. 'Did you know that they were first introduced to England when a pair was presented to the Queen in 1853?'

'No, I didn't,' Effie said.

Violet nodded and began to laugh to herself. 'I thought if the breed was good enough for Queen Victoria then it was good enough for me.' She set the dog down on the floor beside her chair and it immediately began to shiver. A moment later it had disappeared beneath the table. 'How I would have liked to introduce him to Georgina,' she added. 'I'm sure she would have adored him just as much as I do.'

Angelica found it difficult to understand how anyone could like such a thing, let alone adore it. She could feel it near her ankles. She gave a small kick, and although she never made contact with it, it began yapping again.

'Do you like dogs, Angelica?' Violet asked.

Until meeting The Captain, Angelica had held no opinion either way. Now she could feel its tiny teeth on her shoe leather. 'I prefer them when they do not try to bite my ankles,' she said over the yapping, which had become constant, if thankfully muted beneath the tablecloth.

'He's overexcited from seeing all these new faces around him,' Violet said. 'That's all it is. I expect he'll grow tired soon.' She turned sideways to Effie, and speaking in a low voice that Angelica was clearly meant to hear, added with a chuckle, 'Between you and me, dear, I think The Captain is a good judge of character.'

The afternoon wore on at a painfully slow pace for Angelica. The dog's incessant yapping was giving her a headache, and the boys soon became restless, and no doubt as eager as she was to get up and go somewhere else—anywhere, in her case, that was not within earshot of Violet Cosgrove. She spoke of Georgina so much that it was as though she were there in the room with them. Angelica certainly felt her presence, but then how could she not when Violet so purposefully continued to remind them all that Angelica was sitting there in her place, with a 'Georgina this' and a 'Georgina that'. It took a while, but it eventually prompted Stanley to say something.

'Look, would you please stop talking about Georgina?' he said, his voice slightly raised.

'But of course,' Violet said, as if she had only just realised that Stanley might be upset at constantly hearing his late wife's name. 'I'm so sorry. You're still mourning, aren't you? I can see it on your face.'

Angelica could see it, too. Would he ever get over Georgina's death? Stanley didn't reply. Instead, he took a deep breath and buried his face in his teacup. A few long seconds passed in silence, then Violet brushed the matter off with a smile and turned her attention to the boys.

'I hear your schooling is going very well, Alexander,' she said. 'I'm told you're quite the sportsman, and top of your class in your academic studies.'

'Not in all of my studies,' Alexander said.

'Well, I'm sure it's just a matter of time. You're your father's son, after all.' To William, she added, 'You must be very glad of the opportunity to share such a fine education alongside Alexander, although I expect you're having a hard time trying to keep up with him.'

'I'm very glad,' William said, smiling at Alexander, too young and innocent to see the remark for the slight it was.

Angelica was about to speak out in William's defence, but Alexander beat her to it. 'William is very good at mathematics,' he said. 'He's much better than I am.'

'I like mathematics,' William said.

'Yes,' Angelica said, indignantly, 'and when it comes to numbers he's at the top of his class.'

'Is he indeed,' Violet said, studying William with a look of surprise as she spoke, as though someone with his low-class background could never be top of anything.

Angelica could feel her blood begin to boil. She could easily have turned the other cheek to all of Violet's remarks towards her for the sake of their happy sojourn to the seaside, but she wasn't going to sit there and let Violet shift her vitriol towards her son. Clearly, in Violet's eyes, William would never be Alexander's equal, just as Angelica would never be equal to the company in which she now sat. No amount of learning, or her marriage to Stanley, could change that. For herself she didn't much care, but in time it would be different for William. It had to be.

She decided enough was enough for one day. 'Would you boys like to see the hotel gardens?' she said, standing up. 'I hear they have some very interesting statuary.'

Both boys immediately shot to their feet, and their sudden movement caused The Captain to start yapping again.

'But we haven't quite finished our tea,' Violet protested, with enough innocence to suggest that she was at a loss to understand why Angelica wanted to leave.

Angelica moved around the table, collecting William's hand and then Alexander's. She leant in close to Stanley's ear. 'Coming here was a mistake,' she whispered, and then she and the boys left, but not before she heard Violet's parting jibe.

'You see, dear,' she said to Effie. 'No breeding, and evidently no manners either.'

CHAPTER TEN

The following afternoon, Angelica was out on the balcony, looking down at the people ambling along the promenade in their predominantly dark attire, despite the warm sunshine. From the suite's enviable position on the Grand Hotel's top floor, she was so high up that they put her in mind of a trail of ants. They had had an early lunch, which meant the afternoon still had plenty to offer, so she planned to take a stroll initially, then see where the remainder of the day led her. Stanley was in their room getting changed and the boys were running about the suite somewhere, playing hide and seek for all she knew, as tireless as eleven-year-old boys always seemed to be. She was about to go and round them up when Effie stepped out, wearing a light, white gown that was not dissimilar to her own.

'It's another lovely day,' Effie said, throwing her head back with the summer breeze.

'Yes, we've been very lucky,' Angelica agreed, taking in the wider view of the shimmering sea that stretched away from the beach and the West Pier for as far as her eyes could see. 'Need I ask how Violet is feeling?'

Effie pulled a face. 'Not good, I'm afraid. She's tired and wants to lie down.'

'You'll still come for a walk with us, won't you?' Angelica asked. 'I should enjoy your company.'

'And I yours, if only it were just the two of us,' Effie said. She looked back to be sure they were alone. 'You know this is torture for me. I should have stayed at home.'

'I wouldn't have come here if you had.'

Effie laughed to herself. 'I don't doubt it,' she said. 'I hadn't realised quite how bad things had become between you and Violet. I'm sorry.'

'Don't you apologise, Effie. It's not your fault she hates me.'

'I'm sure she doesn't hate you,' Effie said. 'She and Georgina were the very best of friends. She's just having a difficult time accepting you, that's all. But she will, eventually.' She turned away, as if she were about to go back inside. 'Anyway, I can't come with you. I've already told Violet I'll stay with her until she's feeling better. There's a shelf full of old books in my room. I'm sure I'll find something to keep me amused.'

They went back inside, just as Stanley came out from the walkway that led to their room. Angelica was surprised to see that he looked exactly the same as he had at lunch. She didn't mind, but she imagined he'd soon be feeling too hot in his three-piece suit, and his shirt had such a tall, stiff collar.

'Violet needs to lie down and Effie is going

to keep her company,' Angelica said as Stanley joined them. 'So it's just you, me and the boys for our stroll. I thought you were changing.'

'I've changed something,' Stanley said, smiling at Angelica as he raised his eyebrows. It was an odd yet endearing little smile that she usually only saw when it was time for bed and he was feeling amorous.

Angelica looked him over again. 'What have you changed? I can't see anything different about you.'

Still smiling, only more broadly now, Stanley said, 'I've changed my mind.' He leant close to Angelica and whispered in her ear. 'I could use a lie-down myself, if you know what I mean.'

Angelica had to smile. 'Whatever's got into you,' she said, suddenly feeling awkward in front of Effie, who could hardly have mistaken Stanley's meaning, whether she had heard him or not.

'It must be all this sea air,' he said as the two boys ran into the room, closely followed by The Captain, who was soon jumping up at them and yapping at their heels.

Much to Angelica's irritation, his bark quickly drew Violet from her room. 'Where is he?' she called as she entered the parlour. She sounded bright as a button, all trace of her former tiredness having evaporated at the sight of her dog. 'Where's my little Sammy?' she continued as she approached. She clapped her hands together and stooped to catch him as he ran at her and leapt into her arms. 'There he is,' she added, rubbing noses with the animal and pulling a cutesy face that Angelica found quite grotesque.

'Can we go outside now?' William said. 'I want to find some more washed-up glass for my collection.'

'Ah,' Stanley said, glancing at Angelica. 'Slight change of plans. I thought we could all follow Violet's lead and have a short rest before we go out. What do you say?'

'I say that's boring,' Alexander said with a frown.

William nodded. 'Can't we go out by ourselves?' he said. 'We must be old enough.'

'We could take The Captain for a walk,' Alexander said, looking at Violet for her answer even before they had been given permission to go.

'Yes, could we, please?' William added.

Violet looked very uncomfortable with the idea, but before she could answer, Angelica said, 'I'd much prefer it if you waited. You're not yet familiar with the area, and the sea can be very dangerous.'

The change in Violet's expression was sudden. Now she appeared to be all for it. 'I suppose The Captain will soon need his toilet,' she said as she began to smile at the boys. 'I'm far too weary to take him out myself at the moment.'

Both boys were soon smiling back at her.

'We'll keep to the boulevard,' William said to his mother, his eyes pleading for her agreement. 'I can collect glass from the beach later.'

'And we promise not to go far,' Alexander added.

Angelica turned to Stanley, but she already knew his answer.

'You can't always be with them,' he said. 'And they seem to manage perfectly well while they're away at school.'

'School is different,' Angelica said. 'There they have others to look after them.'

'That may be so, but they can't be little boys forever.' Stanley laughed. 'If little boys didn't someday grow up, who then would captain our industry and dictate the course of our evolution?'

Angelica knew he was right. She had to stop fussing over William and let him grow into the man he was bound to become, but she wasn't ready. A part of her would never be ready.

'I'll fetch his lead,' Violet said, giving Angelica a sideways smile as she spoke, evidently taking pleasure in her discomfort. It was as if she now wanted the boys to go out only because she knew Angelica did not.

'Very well,' Angelica said. 'But you're to stay on the boulevard and keep the hotel in sight.'

'We promise,' both boys said at once.

'And Alexander,' Violet said, making a point

of addressing him specifically. 'You must keep a tight hold of Sammy's lead at all times. Just you. At *all* times,' she reiterated, making it clear that she would only trust the dog's care to him and not to William.

Angelica swallowed her anger, even though it pained her deeply to see the look of disappointment that washed over William's face as he came to understand Violet's meaning.

An hour and a half later, Angelica and Stanley were sitting in the lavishly furnished hotel lobby, waiting for the boys to return. Stanley was in high spirits, his smiling cheeks still flushed from his earlier exertions in the bedroom, although their romantic interlude was long past in Angelica's mind. She was staring at the main entrance, squinting against the bright sunlight, worried about where the boys had got to.

'I didn't expect them to be more than half an hour,' she said, fussing without awareness at the lace trim on her dress. 'How long does it take to walk a dog anyway? It's only a small thing.'

Stanley stopped whistling to himself. 'You really do fuss over them far too much,' he said. 'I'm sure they'll be along shortly with a perfectly good explanation.'

Another ten minutes passed before they came running in, and Angelica was delighted to see that it was William, not Alexander, who held the dog's lead. She shot to her feet and went to meet them, kissing them both on the forehead as the dog began to yap and dance around her ankles.

'William, please take that thing away from me,' she said, and William pulled the dog away towards Stanley, who was sauntering over to them in no particular hurry. To Alexander she said, 'I distinctly heard Mrs Cosgrove tell you that you alone were to hold The Captain's lead.'

'It didn't seem fair, so we shared,' Alexander said. 'I'm sorry.'

'Please don't apologise to me,' Angelica said. 'It's as it should be.' She stroked the back of Alexander's hair. 'It was very kind of you to think of William like that.'

'He would have done the same for me.'

Stanley arrived beside them, bringing William and The Captain back with him. 'So where have you boys been?' he asked. 'I'm sure Mother is keen to know.'

'There was a Punch and Judy show on the promenade,' William said.

'Yes, and we lost track of time,' Alexander added. 'Shall we take Captain Sammy back up to Mrs Cosgrove?'

'Had you returned twenty minutes ago,' Angelica said, 'then my answer would have been yes. As it now stands, she and Effie have already gone out for a stroll, no doubt to look for the pair of you.'

'Can we go to the aquarium then?' Alexander asked. 'You said you'd take us.'

'So I did,' Stanley said. 'In that case, the aquarium it is, but surely not with The Captain here.'

'No,' Angelica said. 'His infernal barking would upset the fish and send them all into hiding. You'll have to leave him in Mrs Cosgrove's room. I shouldn't think she'll be out much longer.'

'I'll take him,' William said, his voice full of excitement.

He picked the dog up and began to run off, but Stanley caught hold of him. 'Not so fast,' he said. 'You'll need the key.' He handed it to him. 'Do you remember the way?'

'Yes,' William called back, quickly passing the hydraulic lift, or 'vertical omnibus' as it was known, as he made for the stairs.

'Did you mean to carry that cumbersome key ring around with you all afternoon?' Angelica asked.

'Of course not. I just thought I'd hang on to it until I knew what we were doing. I'll leave it at the desk before we go.'

'Do you mind if I don't go to the aquarium with you?' Angelica said. 'I don't really care for it, and it would be good for you to spend some time alone with the boys.'

'Yes, it would,' Stanley said. 'No, I don't mind

at all, but what will you do with yourself until we get back?'

'I think I'll go and look for Effie and Violet—see if I can't change Violet's opinion of me.'

'That's a splendid idea,' Stanley said. 'It would make the remainder of our stay more agreeable if you can.'

'Yes, well, don't hold your breath. You've seen how she is.'

William wasn't gone long. When he came running back down the stairs he handed the key back to Stanley, panting heavily, as if he'd sprinted all the way.

'Your mother could have saved you the trip,' Stanley told him.

'What do you mean?' William said.

'I mean, I'm taking you boys to the aquarium by myself. Your mother is going to see if she can catch up with Effie and Violet. She could have taken The Captain with her.'

'She most certainly could not!' Angelica said.

'No,' Stanley agreed with a grin. 'One step at a time, eh?'

Angelica was back in the hotel lobby when Stanley and the boys returned from the aquarium. Through the parlour palm she was sitting behind, she saw them enter, full of smiles, as if they had had the most wonderful time together. It warmed her heart to see William so happy. She watched them go to the reception desk for a key, unaware that she was sitting there watching them. As they made for the hydraulic lift, she stood up and followed along behind them. It was good timing because she hadn't long arrived back at the hotel herself and was about to go up to their suite. She caught up with them outside the lift.

'Room for one more?' she said, surprising everyone as they stepped inside.

'Mother!' William called. He leapt at her and held her tight, pressing his smiling face into the folds of her dress.

Angelica laughed. 'Did you miss me?' she said as the smartly uniformed attendant closed the lift cage and they began to rise.

William nodded. 'We saw a manatee!'

'Did you indeed?'

'And lots of sea lions,' Alexander added.

'Yes,' Stanley said. 'Apparently they're breeding very well.'

The lift arrived at the top floor and the attendant stepped aside to let everyone out.

'Thank you,' Stanley said, handing him a coin.

As they headed along the corridor to their suite, Stanley turned to Angelica and asked, 'But what about you? Did you manage to find Effie and Violet?'

Angelica shook her head. 'No,' she said. 'I suppose they had too much of a head start on me. I did find something interesting though—the waterfall grotto. We should take the boys to see it tomorrow.'

They arrived outside the door to the suite, and Angelica heard talking coming from inside. 'They must be back already.'

She opened the door, and before they were all across the threshold, Violet came rushing to greet them, although her enthusiasm was evidently not for them.

'Where's my Sammy?' she called in her cutesy voice. 'Have you missed me terribly? Oh, I'll bet you have.'

Her words caused immediate alarm. The dog had already been brought up to the suite as far as everyone but Violet was aware. Violet took one look at Alexander, her eyes drifting down to his empty hands, as if looking for the lead she had previously placed into his care, and then her jaw dropped.

'Where is he?' she demanded. 'What have you done with him?'

Effie approached. 'What's happened? Is everything all right?'

'No, everything is most certainly not all right!' Violet yelled. 'They've lost The Captain!'

'Lost him?' Effie said.

Stanley explained. 'When the boys came back from taking the dog for a walk, you'd both gone out, so I said to bring him up to the suite because we were going to the aquarium.'

'Oh dear,' Effie said. 'When we came back to the suite, the main door was ajar.'

'I thought we'd been burgled!' Violet said. 'Now I see that something far worse has happened. You've lost my Sammy!'

'Perhaps he's still here somewhere,' Angelica offered. 'Is he in the habit of hiding from you?' She thought it a reasonable question. If she was forced to spend her days in Violet's close company, she would have soon found places to hide.

'Hide from me?' Violet said with annoyance. 'My little Sammy? Don't be absurd!'

'It is a very large suite, Violet,' Effie said. 'It's worth a good look before we jump to any conclusions.'

Violet's face brightened a little. 'Perhaps he's shut himself in one of the wardrobes and fallen asleep,' she said. 'Oh, the poor thing. Sammy! Where are you?' she called as she headed off to look for him.

'I think someone would have heard him by now,' Stanley said. 'Still, you never know.'

Every wardrobe, every cupboard and every drawer was opened and closed in the search for Sammy. They checked under the beds and out on the balcony, and all the while William looked as worried as Angelica had ever seen him. It didn't take long to realise that the dog wasn't there. William was close to tears by the time the search was over.

'You see?' Violet said. 'You've lost him, haven't you?' Her eyes were on Alexander. 'I'm very disappointed in you,' she told him. 'I trusted my Sammy to you. I suppose it was you who brought him up to the suite and forgot to close the door when you left?'

Angelica waited to hear Alexander's answer with great interest. What would he say? Were the two boys as close as she believed them to be? Would he stand up for William and take the blame for him, knowing that Violet's wrath would fall more lightly on his shoulders than on William's? On the other hand, if he did, would William let him?

Very slowly, Alexander began to nod his head. 'Yes, and I'm really very sorry,' he said, looking down at his shoes. 'But I'm sure we'll find him. He must be in the hotel somewhere.'

Violet drew a deep breath, as though contemplating what to say next, but before she was able to, William burst into tears.

'It wasn't Alex's fault,' he said. 'It was mine!'

'Yours!' Violet snapped.

'Yes, and I think I closed the door, honestly I do.'

'I don't care what you think,' Violet said, growing more and more red-faced by the second. 'Clearly you didn't close it, did you? I should have known better than to let my Sammy anywhere near the likes of you!'

'Now, just a minute,' Angelica said, stepping between them, but Violet wouldn't let her speak.

'And you!' she said, her eyes narrowing on Angelica. 'You're supposed to be his mother, aren't you? How could you let this happen?' She scoffed. 'Your type are rarely dependable.'

Stanley was suddenly at Angelica's elbow. 'How dare you!' he said. 'I won't have you speak to my wife like that.'

'Your wife is dead, Stanley,' Violet retorted. 'And this . . .' She trailed off, waving a hand at Angelica. 'This woman is no fitting substitute.'

Angelica had never seen Stanley look as angry as he did at that moment. His jaw was clenched and his head began to quiver as he fought against his rage. She wondered what he would say or do next, and she was proud to see that he didn't grace Violet's arrogance with a reply.

Instead, Stanley drew a sharp breath, turned on his heel, and firmly said, 'Come along, Angelica, boys. We're packing our bags and leaving on the next train home.'

CHAPTER ELEVEN

Winson Green, Birmingham
1896

I suppose our sojourn to Brighton was never destined to be a happy one. Violet's dog was soon found, washed up on the beach, and she may never have known what had become of him had she not made the entire hotel staff and half the guests look for him. By the time the poor little thing's body was discovered, news of her loss had reached far and wide. It didn't take long to work out who it belonged to. I had never seen Violet so distressed, or young William for that matter when he heard the news. Naturally, I stayed on with Violet to help console her, but I'm afraid I was an unsatisfactory substitute for her Captain Sammy.

I was glad to stay, though, for a while at least. I was so very jealous of Stanley during those early years of their marriage that it somehow made me feel better to know they were far away. If only I could have remained in Brighton indefinitely, but with all my heart I wanted to return. I yearned for what Stanley had: Angelica, and a place for us both, where we could shut out the rest of the world—just as Stanley had when he took

Angelica into their bedroom that afternoon. With that in mind, as soon as I returned to Birmingham I took a little room for us in town, away from the ever-inquisitive eyes of the servants and everyone else who knew us.

Over the years our friendship continued to grow, and so did our love for one another. I remember it all now, of course, as one recalls a dream. Those days came and went so fast, as beautiful and vivid as the rising of the sun, and yet they are somehow too distant now, too perfect, to have been mine. Before I knew it a new decade was upon us. It was 1890 and Birmingham was no longer a town, but a thriving city. They were the happiest of days, while they lasted. I felt so alive, so full of joy. I think of those good years often now, when I am in need of comfort, although they fill my heart with great pain, for I know they shall never return.

But they were good times.

William and Alexander finished their schooling that year, and how fast they had grown. I swear I never saw Angelica looking more happy than when William was with her. It's silly, I know, but I was even a little jealous of him at times. Whenever William was around he seemed to demand her attention and her affections, without ever trying to, although his own affections were soon to be drawn in another direction, in the form of Alfred Moore's daughter, Louisa.

Angelica was keen to tell me all about the day William met Louisa as a young woman for the first time, and about what happened afterwards. I knew Angelica had a troubled past, but I was soon to learn just how troubled it truly was.

Birmingham
1890

Watching herself in the mirror as Effie continued to dress her, Angelica considered that she had come to enjoy being with her far more than she had imagined. She glanced over at the brass bed, the white sheets unmade and still warm, the soft pillows still carrying the impressions of their heads from having stared up at the ceiling in silent satisfaction for several heavenly minutes afterwards. They would of course have to make the bed up again before they left. It was, after all, the middle of the afternoon, and such careless-ness could easily give their little secret away. But there was no rush. As far as anyone they knew was concerned, they were out enjoying a stroll in the park, which they did often, and Angelica had no place to be until it was time for dinner, when Stanley would expect her opposite him at the dining table as usual.

She felt another tug on her corset laces and gasped. 'Not so tight, Effie! I can barely breathe as it is.'

Effie's face appeared beside hers in the mirror, the afterglow still apparent in her cheeks. 'You can get your own back when you dress me,' she said with a giggle. 'Now, hold still while I tie the bow, or I shall have to tighten it all over again.'

Angelica held her breath and tried to remain still as Effie continued to pull and tug at her corset strings. They were both far less adept at dressing one another in their many layers of clothing than their own maids were, but they took their time and managed well enough. The intimate undressing and redressing was all part of the titillation.

'I meant to tell you,' Effie said a moment later. 'I received a letter from Violet yesterday.'

'How is she?' Angelica asked, more out of politeness than genuine concern.

'She's much improved, although I don't suppose we shall see her any time soon. She's still in Brighton and plans to remain there. It appears her physician was correct to suppose that the sea air would be more agreeable to her.'

'I'm glad to hear it,' Angelica said, although what she really meant was that she was glad Violet was not coming back to Birmingham, not that her health had improved. She would never forgive her for the way she had treated her and William on their last visit.

There was another tug on her corset strings as Effie fixed the bow. 'There,' she said, stepping aside, dressed only as far as her black knee-length stockings and flesh-pink fine wool combinations, which were a new trend in recent years to replace the individual cotton drawers and chemise. She took up her corset from the chair beside them and held it up to Angelica. 'Now it's your turn, and you can make it as tight as you like.'

They swapped places, and Angelica studied her friend's reflection in the mirror for several seconds, watching the rapid rise and fall of her breasts. She could not resist her. She reached beneath her arms to hold her corset in place while Effie fastened it, but as she did so, instead of holding the corset, Angelica reached higher and ran her palms gently down over Effie's breasts until she could feel her erect nipples, hard and prominent beneath her undergarment. She heard Effie sigh as she continued to tease her. Then she stopped suddenly.

'More,' Effie gasped.

'Next time,' Angelica promised, returning her attention to the corset.

'Tomorrow then?'

'It's Saturday tomorrow, Effie. You know I can't see you. William and Alexander are home from school now, remember? They formally begin their apprenticeships on Monday, and tomorrow we have Alfred Moore and his daughter Louisa with us for dinner. I shall need all day to pre-pare.'

'Yes, of course. I forget everything when I'm with you.'

Angelica smiled to herself, thinking that Effie hadn't changed a bit over the years since they'd met. Although now thirty years old to her thirty-two, she still seemed so young and innocent. 'I could only see you today,' she continued, 'because my husband's foreman, Mr. Hardy, kindly offered to show the boys how everything at the pen factory works.'

Effie finished fastening the front of her corset and Angelica began to adjust the ties at the back.

'Speaking of children,' Effie said a moment later, 'you married Stanley almost seven years ago. I'd expected you would have had at least two children together by now, and judging from the frustration I sense in Stanley almost every time I see him, I'm sure he expected it too. Can you no longer bear children?'

Angelica laughed. 'Stanley's wondering the same thing. He's convinced there's something wrong with me. He's even asked me to see a specialist. If only he knew.'

'Knew what?'

Angelica paused before answering. 'I suppose I can tell you,' she said. 'I don't want any more children. I've been taking precautions against it.'

'You have? How?'

'I procured a solution of sulphate of iron, which I soak into a small piece of fine sponge tied with a string made from several strands of sewing silk. Each time Stanley comes to me, I insert the sponge high up into my person with a length of candle. When the act is over I simply withdraw the sponge.'

'Doesn't he notice the string?'

Angelica shook her head. 'I have always made clear my preference for coital proceedings in the dark.'

Effie laughed. 'Poor Stanley. It really is quite mean of you. You knew how much he wanted more children when you agreed to marry him.'

Angelica pulled hard at the corset strings and heard Effie wince. 'I have already provided Stanley with another son to raise as his own. I think two strong, intelligent heirs to any man's fortune is quite enough, don't you?'

'Yes, I suppose so. I'm sorry. I didn't mean to upset you.'

'I'm not upset,' Angelica said, and then in silence she finished tying Effie's corset.

'I expect you've missed William terribly,' Effie said after a while, as if deliberately changing the subject. 'He must be all of fourteen years old now?'

'He's fifteen, and yes, I miss him every day. Further education for William and Alexander was Stanley's idea, of course, or I would have had William home with me much sooner.'

'I'm sure everything they learned during those

extra years will soon be put to good use at the pen factory,' Effie said, laying out Angelica's crinolette. 'I know Stanley has high hopes that they'll someday take over the running of the business.'

That much remained Angelica's hope, too. As she stepped into her crinolette and pulled it up around her waist to fasten it, she wondered how well William would take to working at the pen factory. Had she done all she could to secure him a prosperous future? She thought she had, for now at least. The rest was surely up to him, although he was still very young, and as far as her son's future was concerned, she knew she would continue to do all she could to ensure it was a happy one.

CHAPTER TWELVE

The following evening saw Angelica waiting with great anticipation for the arrival of their guests at Priory House. After so many years, she knew Alfred Moore and his daughter Louisa very well. She had watched Louisa transform from a small girl into the young lady she was today, but this was the first time William would see her since they were children, and Angelica had high hopes for them. She had spent most of the day with the housekeeper, Missus Redmond, ensuring that the entire household was as prim and proper as it could possibly be. She had also gone over the particulars of the meal more times than she knew was necessary, but she was determined that everything should be just right.

She sipped her Madeira wine and glanced over at the clock on the mantelpiece above the drawing room fireplace. It would soon be seven, at precisely which time Alfred and his daughter would arrive—punctuality being ever close to Mr. Moore's heart. Angelica had put on one of her finest pale blue evening gowns for the occasion. It had an awkwardly large bustle, but she thought it made the gown look all the more elegant. The men would of course be in their dinner suits and bow-ties, so as the only mature female in attendance, she had to make every effort.

She heard voices and laughter in the hall outside, and turned to the door as it opened. It was William and Alexander, still laughing at whatever it was they had been talking about as they entered. Alexander, who was trying to tie his bow-tie, had a broad smile on his face. She thought they both looked such handsome young men in their tails and white waistcoats, and she had to concede that if there was a love match here for Louisa, it would be hard to call.

'Mother!' William said as soon as he saw her. He kissed her cheek and turned back to Alexander, who was dawdling towards them, at the same time looking down at his bow-tie as his fingers became knotted with the silk. 'Help him, will you, Mother? He's been at it now for at least twenty minutes.'

'I'm sorry,' Alexander said. 'Every time I think I've got the hang of these wretched things, it all falls apart on me.'

Angelica smiled as she went to him. The tying of bow-ties was something she had become quite adept at since marrying Stanley. 'Couldn't you have helped him, William?' she asked as she untied the knot Alexander had made so she could start over again. 'Heaven knows Alexander has always helped you when you've needed him.'

'And I have always helped him, Mother, as well

you know,' William said, sounding exasperated. 'I've shown him a hundred times at least, but it's simply not fitting for one gentleman to help tie another's bow-tie. He's usually very practical. I really can't understand it.'

'Knots aren't my thing,' Alexander said as he tried to watch what Angelica was doing.

'You can say that again,' William said. 'You'd be of no use to the navy!'

'It's just as well I have no interest in the navy then, isn't it?'

William scoffed. 'They wouldn't have you!'

They both began to laugh together as Angelica snapped Alexander's bow-tie into place. 'There,' she said. 'Now, calm down, the pair of you. Our guests will be here shortly.'

The door opened again and Stanley popped his head in. He was dressed almost identically to the two boys, except that his waistcoat was of ivory silk jacquard. Angelica thought his attire looked a little tighter than usual and she made a mental note to call on his tailor.

'My shirt is missing a stud!' he said, brushing a hand over his chest where the small black stud should have been. 'Do you think anyone will notice?'

Angelica went to him, thinking that father and son were both very much alike when it came to dressing themselves. She wished Stanley would allow her to hire a valet, but he wouldn't hear of it. She checked the buttonhole, and then looked down into his waistcoat. She gave the hem a tug and the errant stud fell into her hand.

'Bless my soul!' Stanley said, laughing to himself as Angelica fixed the stud into place. 'It was there all the time.'

The sound of the front door opening drew everyone's attention.

'They're here,' Stanley said. 'I'll take them off Missus Redmond's hands and bring them in for a drink before dinner.'

The clock on the mantelpiece chimed seven as Stanley left. He was gone no more than a minute, and when he returned he had their guests with him. Seeing Louisa enter, wearing a beautiful yellow calf-length gown, Angelica's first thought was that she would do very well for William indeed. She was without question the prettiest fourteen-year-old girl Angelica had ever seen, with her doe eyes and long blonde ringlets. But what would William make of her?

Angelica stole a glance at him out of the corner of her eye, and she was delighted to see the colour rise in his cheeks as his eyes widened to better take Louisa in. Even before they had been announced, William had taken a step towards her, clearly keen to reacquaint himself with her now that he was old enough to appreciate her beauty.

'Our guests have arrived,' Stanley said, closing the door behind him. 'Alfred, Louisa, you remember young William here, don't you?' He laughed. 'And Alexander, for that matter. They were both much smaller when you last met.'

'I'm pleased to see you again, sir,' William said to Alfred as they shook hands, and Angelica couldn't help but notice his eyes stray towards Louisa as he bowed his head.

Unlike Stanley, Alfred Moore was a short, stout man, with a full, brown beard that was grey at the edges. His suit was also grey, his waistcoat ruby red to match his bow-tie, and he had the most strikingly unusual hair, which, although thinning, was a foot long and fell in waves of grey and brown streaks on to his shoulders.

'The pleasure is most certainly mine, young man,' Alfred said, his voice always sounding a little coarse to Angelica, hinting at his working-class roots. 'I've already heard good things about you from Stanley, and from Mr. Hardy, with whom I'm sure you and Alexander spent an agreeable day at our pen factory yesterday.'

'Yes, sir. It was most agreeable.'

'Good. Good,' Alfred said, adjusting his round, wire-framed glasses. 'I'm sure you won't remember my daughter, Louisa,' he added, turning to her. 'Perhaps unsurprisingly, given her father's prowess with numbers, she has a keen interest in mathematics, which is something I'm told you have in common.'

William raised his eyebrows. 'Really?' he said,

looking at Louisa, who seemed to shy away from his gaze. 'Perhaps we can discuss our shared interest in the Queen of the Sciences someday. The work of Gauss is of particular interest to me.'

Louisa gave a small curtsey. 'I'm sure your learning would quickly put mine to shame.'

'Then I would be very glad to teach you.'

Alfred took his pocket watch out from his waistcoat and checked the time, eyeing the clock on the mantelpiece as he did so. 'You're a full two minutes out, Stanley,' he said as they all made their way further into the room.

'Have a glass of sherry, won't you?' Stanley said. 'What do a couple of minutes matter between old friends?'

They both laughed, gravitating towards the drinks table as they did so, leaving Louisa and William alone together. Angelica hoped he was about to say something light and encouraging to her. She watched for Louisa's smile in response, but it did not come. Instead, with nothing further spoken between them, Louisa left William and came over to her and Alexander, whom she had known on and off since very early childhood. As bright as William was, Angelica began to question his ability to woo Louisa unassisted.

'Louisa!' Angelica said as she arrived. 'It's lovely to see you again. I swear you become prettier each time I see you.'

'Do you really think so?' Louisa said, smiling coyly as she looked at Alexander as if to ask whether he thought the same.

If Alexander understood her meaning he gave nothing away. His polite smile remained fixed. It was, however, immediately apparent that Louisa had eyes for him. Perhaps she always had. And yet Alexander seemed completely oblivious to her affections, for the time being at least.

'Yes, I do,' Angelica replied, glancing at William, hoping he would join them, but as she did so she saw him heading for the drinks table to talk with Stanley and Alfred. 'When I last saw your father,' she continued, 'he told me you have your mother's eyes. They're a beautiful shade of blue. Your mother must have been a very striking woman.'

'I believe so,' Louisa said. 'I never knew her, of course. I've only ever seen a few photographs of her.' Without pausing she turned to Alexander and said, 'How have you been, Alex? You look very smart. Quite grown-up.'

'Well, I am fifteen, Lou,' he said with a small laugh. Then he pulled a serious face and added, 'Schooling ages you, you know?'

'Yes, I suppose it must,' Louisa said. 'Do you like my dress?' She held the frame of her crinolette and gave a twirl.

'It's very nice,' Alexander said without conviction. He looked over at the drinks table. 'Will you both excuse me? There's something I'd like to discuss with your father.'

Clearly not marriage, Angelica thought as Alexander left them. 'Boys are easily distracted,' she said to Louisa, brushing her shoulder gently with the palm of her hand. 'I think your dress is exquisite.'

Louisa's smile returned. 'Thank you. You're very kind.'

'According to Aesop,' Angelica said, 'no act of kindness, no matter how small, is ever wasted. Do you believe that to be true?'

'Yes, of course. Kindness is among the greatest of virtues.'

Angelica laughed to herself, wondering how many times Louisa had been told that. She thought her very naive to unequivocally believe something she had no real experience of. Kindness was not always well meant. She had to agree with Aesop, however, that kindness, well meant or otherwise, was indeed never wasted.

She took Louisa by the hand. 'Come along,' she said. 'Let's go and find out what the men are talking about.'

As they arrived, Alexander was in full flow, speaking with great passion.

'Surely, the question of leakage has much to do with controlling the flow of ink?' he said, animatedly gesturing with his hands. 'If no air is permitted into the barrel—if the ink reservoir could be fully sealed when the pen is not in use—then the capillary action that allows the ink to flow from the nib would be prevented, and it would not be possible for the pen to leak.'

'Ladies!' Stanley said as Angelica and Louisa arrived. 'Alexander was just telling us about his visit to the factory yesterday.'

'Mr. Hardy was very instructive,' Alexander said.

'Yes,' William agreed, 'and now my unfortunate stepbrother finds himself tormented by the desire to invent a pen that doesn't leak!'

Everyone except Alexander and Louisa began to laugh.

'You really shouldn't trouble yourself,' Alfred said. 'It is an accepted understanding that fountain pens leak, and will likely ever do so.'

Alexander sighed. 'That is not Mr. Hardy's view, and having spoken with him at length over the matter, neither is it mine.'

William scoffed. He turned to Alfred. 'Surely it's the profit margin that matters,' he replied. 'And if everyone else's pens leak, then the pens created by Hampton and Moore are at no disadvantage.'

'Perhaps for now,' Alexander said. 'But imagine being able to offer our customers a pen they can carry in their breast pocket all day without fear of the ink ruining their suits?'

Louisa stepped closer to Alexander, drawing his

eye. 'I'm sure if anyone can solve the problem, you can.'

'Hear, hear!' Stanley said. 'You keep dreaming, my boy. There's plenty of room for invention and progress at Hampton and Moore. Why, I've half a mind to create a department solely to tackle the problem.'

'Think of the cost!' Alfred said, wide-eyed.

'That, my friend, is your job,' Stanley said with a laugh. 'Now, I think it's time we put our business to one side and enjoyed some dinner. I'm positively famished.'

As they went through into the dining room, they were met by the butler, Mr. Rutherford, standing tall inside the doorway, his chin proud, his hair slicked tidily back off his brow. He offered up a bottle of wine to Stanley, the dark glass contrasting against the white of his glove.

'The 1870 Haut-Brion, sir,' he said. 'I've decanted three bottles as requested.'

'Thank you, Rutherford,' Stanley said, turning to Alfred with a smile. 'Your favourite, I believe.'

'Good man!' Alfred said, patting Stanley's back. 'I thought you said it was all gone?'

'After your last visit, it nearly was, but Rutherford managed to find a few more bottles.'

Alfred laughed to himself. 'Then you're a good man, too, Rutherford.'

'Thank you, sir,' Rutherford said, and everyone went to their seats.

As she sat down, Angelica's mind was far from the wine and the meal. That William, who shared Alfred's love of financial matters, could someday gain his approval to marry his daughter, she was in little doubt. But what of Louisa? She shared William's interest in mathematics, but Angelica feared it would not be enough—at least not while Louisa harboured such apparent affection for Alexander.

Thankfully, Alexander seemed too blind, or too distracted by his leaking-pen problem, to see it for now, so she supposed there was time. This was, however, the best match she could hope to achieve for William and she did not want to see it slip away. If her son married Louisa, William would effectively own at least half the business when her father died. It promised her son too great a future for her to leave the matter to chance for long.

After dinner, Angelica found herself sitting alone in the dining room, the men having gone back to the drawing room for their port and cigars, taking William and Alexander with them, and Louisa . . . Where was Louisa? Angelica wasn't sure. Perhaps she'd had too much wine and hadn't been paying attention when Louisa said where she was going. Much to Angelica's chagrin, the girl had been moon-eyed over Alexander all through the meal, so she half expected that, if she cared to look, she'd find her peeping through the drawing room keyhole, unable to take her eyes off him.

She heard footsteps out in the corridor and rose from her chair. 'Louisa!' she called, going to the door. 'Missus Redmond, is that you?'

On opening the door she felt a cold blast of air on her face and she wondered where it had come from. Perhaps an open window somewhere, or had one of the servants left the main door open? It had been a warm day, though, and the air she felt was distinctly cold. She looked both ways along the corridor, first to her right, which led to the drawing room and the entrance hall further along, then left, towards the orangery at the back of the house where she had first sat down to afternoon tea with Georgina and her friends.

She heard the footsteps again, the sound coming from that direction. This time they were followed by the distinct creaking of a floorboard, which Angelica thought could only mean that whoever was there had taken the small flight of servants' stairs partway along the corridor.

'Hello!' she called. Why didn't whoever was there answer her?

The floorboards continued to creak, so she paced after the sound, keen to confront whoever was there. She suspected it was Louisa, playing a childish game with her. She began to laugh to herself as she ran up the stairs, wondering what it would have been like to have a daughter of her own. How they would have played chase, and hide and seek, in a big house like this. She reached the top of the stairs and stopped, looking and listening.

'Louisa!' she called again. 'I'm going to find you!'

There were mostly bedrooms on this floor, and too many doors to try at random in the hope that she had the right one, so she continued to wait and listen. A moment later she heard a hollow thump from inside one of the bedrooms not many doors down to her right. It was by now far too late in the evening for it to be one of the maids. It had to be Louisa.

She smiled to herself as she opened the door and peered inside. What she saw made her gasp and put her hand to her mouth. There were two people on the bed: a rough-looking man with his shirt off, trousers around his ankles; and a woman in a white lace dress that was piled up over her back. Both were on their knees, the woman facing away. The man pulled at the woman's hair and the thumping sound intensified as he continued to thrust his pelvis back and forth, banging the headboard into the wall with such violence that it began to chip the plaster.

Angelica tried to back away before she could be seen, but she found herself rooted to the spot. The woman on the bed began to turn her head slowly towards her, and still Angelica could not move. When she saw the woman's face fully, she gasped again. It was badly scarred and disfigured, but she knew who she was. Before another thought entered her head, the man stopped. Now he also turned to her, and she knew him, too. There was blood in his hair and on his face. He reached down beside him and lifted a gnarled cane towards her.

'Where's that boy of yours?' he demanded. 'I still owe the little runt a good beating!'

Angelica's heart was pounding hard. She felt suddenly dizzy and confused. There on the bed was Reginald Price, the man she had killed to save her son before fleeing London. He appeared just as he had on that fateful day, only it was not her on her knees before him, it was Georgina Hampton, just as she had looked on the day she was trampled to death. Angelica managed to turn away at last, but as she did so she cried out in terror. There was another man behind her—a man in a squat bowler hat and a tatty grey suit. It was Tom Blanchard.

But Blanchard was dead. They were all dead.

She caught the fresh-looking cut across Blanchard's throat and the lascivious smile on his face as she ran past him, down the stairway and along the corridor towards the main entrance. She called for help, over and over again, but she heard no sound. At seeing moonlight beyond the open door ahead, she ran faster, but before she reached it another man stepped on to the threshold, appearing in silhouette against the silver-blue light. She stopped the instant she saw him, and he came closer. He wore fine clothes and a top hat, but she could not see his face. Neither, it seemed, could he see her. He crouched suddenly, lowering an ear towards the ground, as if listening for her presence. He raised up again and drew the air in deep through his nostrils, trying to draw her scent.

'Angelica!' he chanted. 'Where are you?'

Angelica swallowed hard, trying not to make a sound as the faceless figure began to step delicately around her. She watched him intently, her entire body shaking with fear as he went. She thought she knew who he was. He was the one she feared the most. Now he had come for her, to undo all she had accomplished for herself and for William.

If she would let him.

As he passed her, ever listening for her, she ran for the open doorway, determined that he of all people would not find her. Once outside, she fled into the grounds, following the moonlit pathway around the house and past the lake, looking for somewhere to hide. When she saw the dome of the ice house, she bolted towards it and quickly took the stone steps down to the gate. It creaked as she opened it, and she cursed the rusting hinges. Beyond was a short tunnel that led to an oak door, which was invitingly open. Without a moment's hesitation, she went inside and closed it quietly behind her.

And in the darkness, she waited.

She waited a long time, sitting huddled on the cold stone floor, staring in the direction of the door in the hope that the figure had gone. When she felt certain he had, she stood up and went back to the door. Then she began to open it and her breath caught in her chest when she heard the gate outside creak and groan.

He was there.

She backed away, though she could not go far. The oak door slowly opened and she screamed as the faceless figure appeared before her again. This time he rushed at her, drawn by her scream.

And in that instant, Angelica awoke, a cold sweat on her brow, her heart still racing. She was alone at the dining table, the meal long finished. As soon as she realised she had been having a nightmare, she drew a slow breath to help calm herself, but it did no good. What if he really did find her? What then for this good life she now had, and above all, for William's future? She could not see it come undone at this man's hand. She would have to safeguard against it, but how?

'Effie . . .' she said under her breath.

She would ask her to procure a small pistol for her from her father's collection. If the man in her dream came for her, she would be ready for him.

CHAPTER THIRTEEN

Winson Green, Birmingham
1896

A pistol?

I was shocked at first to hear Angelica ask me to obtain one for her from my father's vast collection, but when she explained her nightmare to me, how could I refuse? I would have done anything within my power to lessen the day-to-day anxiety that so frequently forced these nightmares upon her. Perhaps having a small pistol close by would be enough to end them, or at least bring some comfort to her until time played its inevitable part in allaying her fears.

It was a small American-made Remington Derringer with mother-of-pearl grips, an early model I was afraid my father would miss, but with so many large and impressive pieces in his collection I took the chance that he would overlook such a tiny thing. Growing up with a father so obsessed with firearms, I was quickly able to show Angelica how it worked. It had an over-under barrel design that meant two bullets could be loaded and fired independently, which she thought was a good idea in the event that a second bullet might be called for. I shuddered to think of Angelica ever having to pull the trigger, but she couldn't have been happier with it. It seemed to put her at ease the moment she slipped it into her reticule.

I forgot all about the Derringer for a time, although I'm sure it helped Angelica because her nightmares seemed to pass. There were soon other things on her mind, however. During the three years that followed she became more and more preoccupied with the challenge of making a love match between William and Louisa, and more and more frustrated by the fact that Louisa only seemed to have eyes for Alexander. The boys were now settled into their roles at the pen factory. They were both ripe for marriage, but who would win Louisa's heart? I found it all very amusing to begin with, but I had no idea at the time just how serious Angelica was.

We were all soon greatly distracted, however, by far more serious matters—terrible events that would change the course of all of our lives forever.

Birmingham
1893

It was early autumn, though still warm and dry, the leaves on the trees here and there already beginning to fall as Angelica strolled through Cannon Hill Park, past the bandstand where Mr.

Featherstone had chanced upon her and William and had helped to change their fortunes. It hadn't rained for weeks. The groundskeepers had done well to keep the flowers blooming, but the dry summer had taken its toll on the grassy areas, which had all but lost their colour and were patchy in places, revealing the dusty, baked ground beneath. Effie was there, as were the two boys, now turned eighteen and men in all but legal right, and of course there was Louisa.

Louisa, Louisa . . .

How that name had become a source of frustration for Angelica. She had thus far been unable to turn the girl's affections towards William, and William remained hopelessly inept at doing so for himself. Thankfully, Alexander's apparent indifference to any romantic attachment to Louisa remained as strong as ever. They were all just good friends, although Louisa's every word, every gesture and glance at Alexander told Angelica that she wished it were otherwise.

They approached the lake where William and Alexander had first met, the two boys ahead, each carrying a picnic basket, and Louisa in the middle with the blankets for them to sit on. Angelica hadn't wanted any of the servants with them on this occasion. There wasn't much to carry, after all, and since Stanley had recently fallen ill and had now taken to his bed, there was far greater need of their help at Priory House.

'How is Stanley?' Effie asked from beneath her sun parasol.

'Still very weak, I'm afraid,' Angelica said with a sigh. 'Doctor Grosvenor was with him this morning. That was his third visit in as many weeks, and I don't believe he's any the wiser as to what's the matter with him.'

'I hope he soon recovers.'

Angelica smiled kindly. 'Thank you, Effie. I'm sure he'll be back on his feet again in no time. I wanted to stay with him today, of course, but he wouldn't hear of it. He said he'd already missed too many of our little Saturday afternoon outings, and he didn't want me to miss them too.'

'He's very sweet. Do you think he suspects what's going on between us?'

The question surprised Angelica. 'Why should he? Why should anyone for that matter? We're discreet, aren't we?'

'Yes, of course.'

'Well then,' Angelica said. She snapped open her fan and began to wave it in front of her face. 'I shouldn't think this heat would suit Stanley anyway.'

'I'm not sure it suits me, either,' Effie said. 'It really is quite stifling. Perhaps we'll find a breeze by the lake.'

When they caught up with the boys and Louisa, she had laid out their blankets, and William was already munching on an apple. Alexander was on his knees, bent over one of the baskets, handing out the crockery.

'Mutton pie, anyone?' he said as Angelica and Effie sat down.

'We might have to share it with the geese,' William said with a laugh, pointing to the waterline, where several assorted fowl had begun to look interested.

'I'd like some,' Louisa said. 'Just a small piece.'

'Don't want to get fat, eh?' Alexander said, showing little tact over the fact that Louisa had put on some weight in recent months. It put a small smile at the corner of Angelica's mouth.

'Do you think me fat now?' Louisa said, looking self-consciously at herself.

'No, of course not. I was just being silly as always.'

William tossed his apple core towards the geese. 'I think you look very well indeed,' he said, and Louisa's smile returned.

She glanced at Alexander and then, making sure she had his attention, moved closer to William until she was sitting right beside him.

'Thank you, William,' she said, putting her arm through his.

Angelica was initially pleased to see some progress at last, but it was quickly apparent that Louisa was only trying to make Alexander jealous.

'Would you like to have afternoon tea with me tomorrow, Willy?' she said, rather more loudly than she had to, making sure everyone, especially Alexander, heard her. She was even looking at Alexander as she spoke, as if keen to see his reaction.

'I'd like that very much,' William said, suddenly beaming at her. 'You've never asked me before.' He paused, his brow creasing. 'You do mean just the two of us, don't you?'

'Yes, of course. Just you and me. Alex isn't interested in such trivial pastimes as afternoon tea, are you, Alex?'

Alex looked up at Louisa from his mutton pie, and as he did so she snuggled closer to William, feigning indifference to his answer. It seemed to get Alexander's attention at last.

'Oh, I don't know,' he said as he put his pie down and sat up. 'I like a cup of tea as much as anyone. I'll come, too, if you like.'

Louisa couldn't have dropped William's arm any quicker. 'Would you?' she said, sounding all too eager as she edged closer to him again.

'Hang on a minute!' William said, finally latching on. 'I thought you just said—'

'It'll be even more fun with the three of us,' Louisa cut in. 'Could you please pass me a sandwich, Alex,' she added, taking the opportunity to move back beside Alexander so that he didn't have so far to pass it.

Angelica couldn't understand for the life of her how William had not seen Louisa's ruse to get Alexander to join her for afternoon tea coming. She supposed he was too flattered by her attention at last to mind, or too blinded by it. She saw that Louisa was all moon-eyed for Alexander again, so before Louisa could further capitalise on the little streak of jealousy she had instilled in Alexander, Angelica asked, 'Are you any closer to solving your leaking-pen problem, Alexander?'

Alexander put his plate down and turned to her, and Angelica could see the eagerness in his eyes as he answered. 'I heard only recently that the Americans have filed patents which solve the problem with a retractable nib design,' he said, suddenly seeming to forget Louisa was beside him. 'It seems a rather convoluted solution, if you ask me.'

'And no doubt far more expensive to produce,' William said, sounding very much like Alfred Moore in his desire to look after the pennies.

'Indeed. I'm sure there's a much simpler answer waiting to be found. We're already looking at a screw-on cap with a seal that would contain any leakage from the nib. I still feel, however, that the answer lies with the ink bladder itself.'

Louisa frowned and fidgeted. 'Must you always be so wrapped up in your work, Alex?'

'But it's very important work, Lou. At least, it is to me.'

'I didn't mean to suggest it wasn't, I—'

'Would you excuse me,' Angelica cut in, satisfied that Louisa now had little chance of turning Alexander's mind off the subject of leaking pens for the remainder of the afternoon. 'I'd like to take a stroll beside the lake.'

'That's a lovely idea,' Effie said. 'I'll join you.'

As they walked, Angelica began to shake her head, still thinking about Louisa and the match she wanted for William, and how she was going to help bring it about.

'They're not right for one another,' she told Effie as soon as they were out of earshot. 'Louisa and Alexander, I mean.'

'Louisa doesn't seem to think so,' Effie said, taking Angelica's arm.

'No, the poor thing. She's quite besotted, or so she thinks.'

'I like that word. I'm besotted with you, you know that, don't you?'

Angelica laughed. 'How could I not when you tell me so often.'

'Do I? I'm sorry.'

'Don't apologise. I like it. Stanley hasn't shown much affection towards me in a long time. He's still very kind, but I think his heart has cooled because I've not given him another child in all these years. I really can't remember the last time he kissed me.'

'I wish I could kiss you.'

'Heavens, not here,' Angelica said, alarmed at the idea.

'Stanley could kiss you here if he wished to. It's not fair.'

'Stanley would never kiss me in public, even when he was in the habit of kissing me more often.'

They continued walking beside the lake, taking in the few small rowing boats on the water and the general activity going on around them: the people strolling along the path further back, others sitting on the grass here and there, with and without picnics of their own.

Angelica still could not stop thinking about Louisa so, turning the subject back to her, she said, 'I think Louisa is merely clinging on to the one boy she's known all through her life as they were growing up. Alexander is a comfortable match for her, but I'm sure that's all it is.'

'Or she could genuinely have grown to love him,' Effie countered.

They turned around and headed back, not wanting to stray too far from the picnic. 'Yes, she could,' Angelica conceded, thinking if that were the case then the only chance William had of gaining Louisa's affections was if her love for Alexander somehow turned against him.

CHAPTER FOURTEEN

On her return from their picnic in the park, Angelica was surprised to learn that Doctor Grosvenor had been called back to Priory House. As soon as she, William and Alexander stepped down from their carriage—Effie and Louisa having returned to their own homes—Missus Redmond was quick to inform them that Stanley had become quite delirious while they had been out.

'One of the maids found him lying on the lawn,' Missus Redmond said, her voice, along with her expression, full of concern. 'The good Lord only knows how he got there. He was too weak to stand up again and had to be carried back to his bed.'

'Is the doctor still with him?' Angelica asked as they all paced inside the house.

'Yes, madam. He's been with him for the past half hour.'

'No news then?'

'Not yet, madam.'

Angelica marched up the stairs, leaving Missus Redmond clutching the lower newel post, her hand clasped to her mouth with worry. William and Alexander began to follow, but Angelica stopped them.

'Take Missus Redmond into the drawing room and sit her down with a glass of sherry,' she said. 'Wait with her until I come back. I don't think it's advisable for us all to go bundling into Stanley's room at once.'

With that, Angelica continued up the stairs, wondering what this new turn of events regarding Stanley's condition meant, and whether Doctor Grosvenor was yet any the wiser as to what was wrong with him. She did not knock when she arrived at her husband's bedroom door. She entered briskly and was met with a scene that made her jaw drop.

'What in heaven's name are you doing to my husband?' she said, anger rising in her tone as she took in the scene before her.

The bedcovers were pulled all the way down to the foot of the bed. Stanley was lying on his back, partially naked, while Doctor Grosvenor—a thin, white-haired man who appeared old enough to be Angelica's grandfather—bent over him with a metal tray in one hand and a large pair of tweezers in the other. His shirtsleeves were rolled up, and over one forearm was a bloodstained fold of cloth.

'Leeches?' Angelica said, as though unable to believe her eyes.

She went closer and screwed her face up in disgust. There had to be at least forty of the slimy black creatures clamped to Stanley's skin, and yet the doctor's metal tray still held more, which he would no doubt have administered had Angelica not walked in when she did.

Doctor Grosvenor looked at her with an expression that was as much to say, 'Yes, leeches. Of course leeches. What else?' Angelica, however, had long since heard that, although still practised, this cure-all treatment of bleeding patients for just about every ailment had fallen out of favour, having come to be considered of no benefit whatsoever for all but a few specific conditions, and in the overwhelming majority of cases to do more harm than good.

'Remove them at once!' she demanded. 'Then get out. Can't you see that my poor husband is close to unconscious already?'

'But it is only then that we know the patient has been bled enough,' Grosvenor replied with insistence.

Angelica gave a frustrated sigh. 'Your methods are both archaic and barbaric, and they are not welcome here!' she said, placing the palm of her hand on Stanley's brow. His skin was decidedly blue in places, and as a result Angelica thought his brow would feel icy cold, but it was surprisingly hot.

'He has a fever, madam,' Grosvenor said. 'It must be bled from him. I've been this family's physician since Stanley was born.' He paused and gave a derisive laugh. 'I think I'm best placed to know what's right for him, don't you?'

Angelica turned to the doctor, her face now glowing with anger. 'No, sir, I do not,' she said with a shake of her head. 'And your opinion, for what it's worth, is no longer welcome here either.' She went back to the door. 'You have five minutes to remove those wretched things and leave this house. If you are one minute longer, I'll have you thrown out!'

Angelica closed the door behind her and waited outside the room. When the door opened again, Doctor Grosvenor looked red-faced and flummoxed. He took one glance at Angelica, gave a huff, and proceeded towards the main stairway without saying another word, which was for the best as far as Angelica was concerned. She saw the doctor off the property herself and was glad to see the back of him. When she entered the drawing room afterwards, to explain to everyone what had happened, all eyes were immediately on her, each troubled expression asking how Stanley was.

Angelica went straight to the drinks table and poured herself a glass of brandy; she needed something stronger than Madeira wine. 'I've asked Doctor Grosvenor to leave,' she said, taking her drink to the settee beside Missus Redmond, who immediately began to stand up. 'Stay where you are, Missus Redmond,' Angelica told her.

'You asked the doctor to leave?' Alexander repeated. 'Why?'

William sat forward, his eyes suddenly full of hope. 'Is Stanley feeling better?'

Angelica sipped her brandy and slowly began to shake her head. 'I'm afraid poor Stanley is the worst I've seen him, no thanks to Doctor Grosvenor and his damned leeches. In a moment, I'd like both of you boys to go and sit with him. Missus Redmond, I shall need the carriage prepared.'

'Of course, madam,' Missus Redmond said, making to get up again.

Angelica put a hand on her arm to stop her. 'In a moment. First, I must tell you all what I plan to do.'

'What can you do that Doctor Grosvenor can't?' Alexander asked.

'I can summon a real doctor to Priory House— one of the best in the country,' Angelica said. 'The only difficulty I have is that he lives in London.'

'London?' Alexander said, his tone still challenging her. 'Why waste time bringing a doctor all the way from London when there are many far closer?'

'Doctors such as Grosvenor?' Angelica said. 'Isn't he supposed to be the best in the area? If so, what then for the rest?'

'That was his reputation,' Alexander said.

'Was,' Angelica repeated, emphasising the word. She shook her head. 'I'm afraid his practices are now woefully antiquated. Perhaps dangerously so. London is at the pinnacle of modern medical science, and as I've said, I aim to have Stanley seen by the best. Did Doctor Grosvenor ever once tell us what was wrong with Stanley? Has Stanley ever shown any signs of improvement under his care?'

Everyone shook their heads.

'No,' Angelica said, 'and I must do something about it. It may take longer to employ the services of a doctor from London, but what use are a hundred quick opinions and procedures if they're all wrong?'

She stood up, and everyone stood with her. 'You each have your duties,' she said. 'Go about them, and as soon as the carriage is ready I shall go into the city to send a telegram to London, asking the doctor I've spoken of to come at once.'

Later that evening, following a sombre dinner that no one at Priory House was really in the mood for, Angelica was on her way upstairs to look in on Stanley again when she heard a sound that was akin to a door being slammed. It came from inside the drawing room. She entered to find Alexander by himself, sitting on the stool at the piano, collapsed over the fallboard. She supposed the sound she had heard was that of the fallboard being slammed shut. Alexander sat up as soon as he heard Angelica approach. He was in his shirtsleeves, buttons undone at the neck, his hair tousled and his eyes drawn with worry and alcohol—if the bottle of port and empty wine glass sitting on top of the piano were anything to judge by.

'Angelica,' he said, slurring slightly. 'I thought you'd be upstairs in my father's room with William.'

'I was just on my way,' Angelica said, studying the port bottle, trying to gauge how much Alexander had consumed after the already generous amount of wine he'd taken at dinner. 'I also expected you would be there at your father's side with William.'

Alexander drew a deep breath and let it go again, shaking his bowed head as he did so. 'I can't,' he said. 'I can't bear to see him looking like that. He's so ashen. It's as if he's already . . .'

Alexander trailed off and turned away. He picked up the port bottle and filled his glass again. Angelica knew what he was going to say. She had thought it herself as soon as she'd walked in on Doctor Grosvenor and his leeches. Until she saw Stanley move his head in a fitful spasm for the first time, she had thought him already dead. But there was hope. One of the older maids, Sarah, who had been with the family since before Alexander was born, had been with

189

Stanley ever since the doctor left. She had sat there with a bowl of cool water, gently dabbing his brow, and she was still there now.

'When I last spoke to Sarah, she told me she thought your father's fever had begun to lift,' Angelica said, resting a hand on Alexander's shoulder. 'She always looked after you while you were growing up, didn't she? Now she's looking after your father.'

Alexander put his glass of port down again untouched. 'Is it terrible of me to not wish to see my father like this?'

Angelica offered him a kindly smile. 'No, it's not terrible,' she said. 'You must deal with such matters as you see fit. We're not always as strong as we'd like to be, are we?'

'I'm ashamed of myself. Why can't I be as strong as William? Apart from dinner, he's been at my father's bedside since you left to send that telegram. When do you suppose we'll hear from this London doctor of yours anyway?'

'It's my hope that he has already read my telegram and is making preparations to call on your father tomorrow. Perhaps he'll send a reply before he leaves to let us know he's coming. For now we have to wait. We can't know anything more until morning.'

'What if he can't come?'

'Then we'll call on as many local doctors as are available and have them all attend on Stanley until they reach a decision as to what's wrong with him.'

Angelica picked up the bottle of port and the full glass. 'It's getting late,' she said. 'Why don't you try to get some sleep?'

'William isn't getting any sleep.'

'He will. I'm going up to Stanley's room now to insist he rests, too. You'll both need your strength in the morning. I expect poor Sarah must also be quite exhausted by now.'

'Are you going to stay with Father?'

Angelica nodded. 'All night if I have to.'

'Won't you need your strength, too?'

'I'll try to sleep for a few hours once I'm sure your father is settled. My bedroom is next to his, after all. I'll leave the door between our rooms open so that I'll wake if he cries out. Sleep is no doubt the best medicine for your father until the doctor arrives.'

When Angelica arrived in Stanley's room it was almost eleven o'clock. She sent William to his bed, and Sarah to hers, and she continued to cool Stanley's brow as he turned this way and that, fitful and uncommunicative. The colour had already begun to return to his cheeks, and Sarah was right; Stanley's fever did appear to be lifting. Perhaps by morning he would be well enough to sit up in bed again and take some food. She waited with him until it was close to two o'clock in the morning, when the house was silent as snowfall, and Stanley was still at last. Then she, too, went to her bed.

At four o'clock that morning, Angelica awoke with a start from the heavy, dreamless sleep she had fallen into. Someone was shouting.

Stanley . . .

Had he awoken, feverish and delirious again? No, the voice was not Stanley's. It was too light—too young. Angelica listened for the sound again, but it did not come. As she sat up in her bed, meaning to investigate further, she saw the silhouette of someone standing in the open doorway between the two bedrooms.

'William?' she said, squinting into the moonlight that flooded into the room after him. 'Is that you?'

'Yes, Mother,' William said, sounding half dazed. 'I had a terrible dream, and then I couldn't sleep. I had to be sure it wasn't real.'

'You had to be sure *what* wasn't real?' Angelica said, getting out of bed.

William put his hands to his face. 'I had to make sure my dream wasn't real, but it was, Mother. He's dead. Stanley's dead.'

CHAPTER FIFTEEN

Three mournful weeks passed slowly at Priory House. Stanley's funeral service at St Bartholomew's church came and went, along with the many people who called at the house each day to pay their respects. Effie had been particularly supportive, although she and Angelica had shared no intimate companionship in that time. The pen factory had closed on the day Stanley died, and its doors did not open again until the man who had made Hampton and Moore such a success was laid to rest. In settling Stanley's affairs, all that remained was for the executor of his last will and testament to notify the beneficiaries.

Angelica was on her way to the pen factory on Legge Lane now to do just that. It was mid-morning on a Tuesday, the October clouds rendering the streets grey and dull as the carriage clicked along the cobblestones towards the Jewellery Quarter. She was wearing black, and just as Queen Victoria continued to wear black after the death of Prince Albert, so would she continue to do so for Stanley. She had even had the carriage repainted, the horses replaced, all in black so that everyone would know her grief.

Her eyes were closed beneath her veil, her thoughts drifting back over the days since Stanley had died. She recalled Alexander's tearful regret at not having had the courage to spend more time with his father in his last hours—how inconsolable he had been. She recalled how his attitude towards William had changed, growing cold where it had previously been as warm a relationship as any two brothers might have hoped to enjoy. The reason, although never voiced, was clear to Angelica. Alexander was jealous. William had been at his stepfather's side during his dying days, while Alexander, born of Stanley's own flesh and blood, had not.

As the carriage turned on to Legge Lane, so did Angelica's thoughts turn to the morning of Stanley's funeral. They had travelled to St Bartholomew's in this very carriage, she and the two boys together. How kindly William's words fell on her ears when she spoke of her own regret.

'I should not have waited,' she had said, dabbing the tears from the corners of her eyes. 'It was folly to waste so much time sending that telegram to London. I feel so responsible.'

William had reached across the carriage and held her hands in his. 'Do not trouble yourself, Mother,' he said to comfort her. 'The best doctor in the world could not have saved Stanley in so short a time. If anyone is to be held responsible, then it is Doctor Grosvenor and his damned leeches.'

Angelica felt the carriage jolt as it came to a

stop, shaking her from her thoughts. She had arrived outside the factory gate, and her thoughts swiftly caught up to the business at hand.

'Wait for me here,' she called up to the driver as she stepped down from the carriage, giving the man no time to step down himself to assist her.

'Very good, madam,' the driver said, touching the brim of his black silk hat.

Angelica made eye contact with no one as she paced across the factory floor on her way up to the main office, not even Mr. Hardy, whom she passed with a short 'Good morning' before making her way up the ironwork stairs.

Alexander and William were both waiting for her inside the office, each with his sleeves rolled up, as though they had been helping to catch up on the delays caused by Hampton and Moore's recent closure.

'Sleeves,' she said with a flick of her hand, indicating that they should both roll them down at once. 'You must set an example. Do you find Mr. Hardy with his sleeves rolled up, his collar unfastened?'

'Sorry, Mother,' William said, blushing.

Alexander merely sighed as he grudgingly did as he was told.

'Now then,' Angelica said, removing her hat and veil. 'You both know what I've come to talk to you about, so I'll be as brief as possible. I've just left the offices of our solicitors, Watkins,

Watkins and Brown. They have this morning received a grant of probate for Stanley's will, meaning that the document has been legally registered as his true last testament and that his estate can now be administered. As executor, I wish to afford no delay in carrying out his wishes, so I've come straight here.'

'Would you care to sit down?' William said, offering her one of the chairs.

'Thank you, but no. As I've said, I don't expect to keep you long from your work.'

Alexander had a bemused expression on his face. 'I thought Watkins, Watkins and Brown were the executors of my father's will. At least, that's what my father told me.'

'And how long ago was that?'

'It was not long after William and I returned from school.'

Angelica gave a small, humourless laugh. 'My dear Alexander, that was four years ago. Your father and I since decided that it was a waste of money to appoint solicitors as executors when we were both perfectly capable of administering the estate ourselves. They were to handle matters only in the event of both your father and I dying simultaneously.'

'I see,' Alexander said, although his bemused expression remained. 'Please, go on.'

'In his will, your father, God rest his soul, has bequeathed to you each the sum of two hundred

196

pounds, payable to you by twenty shillings a month. He leaves to you specifically, Alexander, his collection of pens, which he knew you were very fond of, and to you, William, his pocket watch, so that you may never be one second late for your financial meetings with the fastidious Mr. Moore.'

William chuckled to himself.

Alexander looked less amused. 'And what of the house?' he said. 'What of my father's share in the business? He told me it would be mine to continue in the event of his death.'

'Which, I imagine,' Angelica said, 'he also told you some time ago. But things change. Your father had a new will drawn up no more than two years ago. The house, he has left to me, so that I may never again find myself without a roof above my head. When I die, it will pass to you and William. The business is rather more complicated.'

'How so?' Alexander asked, his eyes narrowing.

'You must understand that your father's life had changed quite dramatically in recent years. He had remarried and gained another son in William. His previous will, the will perhaps to which you refer, was outdated. The problem we faced when deciding what was best for the business in the event of your father's untimely death was that you and William were still, at the time of writing the will, so very young. It was decided, therefore, that your father's share of the business would pass to me if you had not yet reached the age of twenty-one.'

'So the business is now legally yours?' Alexander said.

'Yes, but you will both continue to run it alongside Mr. Moore, as you have so competently done since Stanley became ill, and one day, when you are both past twenty-one and deemed worthy of the responsibility, you shall inherit an equal share.'

'Deemed worthy?' Alexander said. 'By you, I suppose.'

'Yes, of course, by me. Who else knows you better? But you have no cause for concern, surely? You and William are becoming fine gentlemen. You have both more than adequately demonstrated your ability to run the business together. As soon as you reach the age of majority, this pen factory will belong in part to both of you.'

Before any more could be said on the matter, Angelica took up her hat again and set it in place on her head. 'Now, I must go and speak to Mr. Hardy,' she said. 'Stanley has bequeathed to him the very generous sum of fifty pounds.'

With that, Angelica pulled her veil down over her face and left the office, wondering how Mr. Hardy was going to take the news that he was to be dismissed. With both Alexander and William now in management positions at the factory, and Mr. Hardy having taught them so well in the three years since they had begun their apprenticeships, there was no further need for him as far as Angelica was concerned. She saw him now as little more than a drain on the purse strings at a time of uncertainty and change at Hampton and Moore, and she had no doubt that her partner would see things the same way.

She supposed the fifty pounds Stanley had left to Mr. Hardy would help him on his way, but what news to give him first? It was difficult to know which Mr. Hardy would prefer, not that it mattered to her. As she headed down the steps to the lower shop floor, she decided to tell him about the money first, imagining that the good news would help to sweeten the bad.

CHAPTER SIXTEEN

Before dinner on the day Angelica sacked Mr. Hardy, she was leaving William's room when she saw one of the maids in her black-and-white livery approaching along the corridor.

'Sarah!' Angelica called to her. 'I need you to do something for me.' She turned back into William's room. 'I'll see you at dinner, William.'

She closed the bedroom door as Sarah arrived.

'Yes, madam?' Sarah said, her coarse tones never pleasing to Angelica's ears.

Angelica had one of Stanley's pens in one hand, and a small bundle of off-white fabric in the other, which she held out to Sarah. 'This pillowcase needs to be laundered,' she said, handing it to her. She glanced back at William's door and Sarah's eyes followed hers. 'It has a bloodstain on it.'

'So it does,' Sarah said, holding the pillowcase up to better study it. 'I don't know if it'll come out, mind. It's dried right into the cloth.'

'Well, ask the laundry maid to do her best, will you? One can ask no more.'

Angelica made to leave.

'It's one of the late Mr. Hampton's pillowcases,' Sarah said, drawing attention to the embroidered monogram.

'Yes, what of it?'

Sarah glanced at the bloodstain again, and then looked back at William's door. If there was something on her mind, she didn't speak it. 'Nothing, madam,' she said with a curtsey before she continued about her business.

Angelica continued about hers, taking the opposite direction, towards Alexander's room. The pen she was carrying was from Stanley's collection. According to his will, it now belonged to Alexander, whose room was several doors along, at the top of the main staircase. She stopped outside and knocked.

'Come in!'

Angelica pushed the door open to find Alexander getting dressed for dinner. He was buttoning up the neck of his shirt as she entered the room, which was dimly lit by the bedside lamp and the pale moonlight from the tall mullioned window. One of the panes was open, drawing in the night air, making the room decidedly chilly.

Alexander did not look pleased to see her. 'What is it?' he said, dour-faced. 'I'm rather busy, as you can see.'

It had not escaped Angelica's attention that Alexander's attitude towards her had cooled considerably since his father died, but he had never been quite so curt with her before. 'This is yours,' she said, holding out the pen she was carrying. It was an old and unremarkable black dip pen. 'It belongs in Stanley's collection.' She corrected herself. 'In your collection.'

Alexander took it from her. 'Where was it?'

'William had it. Stanley was in the habit of letting him borrow it. He's just finished using it to write a letter.'

'Thank you for bringing it to me. It's one of the earlier pens my father collected.'

'I think that must be why William liked to use it,' Angelica said. She went to the window and closed it. 'If you're not careful you'll catch a chill.'

'I feel quite warm, thank you.'

'Then perhaps you have a fever. Here, let me feel your forehead.'

Angelica went to him, but he backed away. 'Whatever's the matter?' she asked. 'Have you been at the brandy already?'

'A little,' Alexander said. 'Look, was there anything else? I'm trying to get dressed.'

'No, that was all. Unless you'd like me to help with your tie.'

'I can manage, thank you,' Alexander said, his tone now brusque to the point of sounding rude.

Angelica shook her head. 'Young man, I'll not leave your room until you tell me what's the matter.'

Alexander gave a loud sigh. 'Very well, if you

insist, I'll tell you. I don't like it. I don't like it one bit.'

'What don't you like? Whatever are you talking about?'

Alexander began to pace the room, if only to distance himself from Angelica. 'My father's will,' he said, raising his voice. 'And your treatment of Mr. Hardy. Yes, I've heard all about that. Will you be paring down the servants as well? Who's next? Perhaps we no longer need a butler, or what about the housekeeper? Is Missus Redmond to go as well?'

'I let Mr. Hardy go because, as far as the pen factory is concerned, you and William are perfectly capable of filling both his and Stanley's shoes, and because all the while Mr. Hardy remains, so will Hampton and Moore remain the same. You and William are young. You have fresh ideas. I don't want them quashed by Mr. Hardy's old values. You both respect him too much not to be guided by his opinion. As for the servants, I was considering taking on more. I always told Stanley he should have a valet. You can hire one for you and William if you like, subject to my approval, of course.'

'Oh, of course,' Alexander said, with more than a hint of sarcasm.

'And what is that supposed to mean?'

Alexander sighed again. He paused before replying, as if biting his tongue while he decided whether or not to hold back what he wanted to say. He chose to speak his mind. 'Well, it's your house now, isn't it, and your factory, too?' he said, his eyes narrowing on Angelica as he spoke. 'They were both to be mine when my father died. You knew that and you made him change his will. You want it all for yourself, don't you?'

Angelica drew a deep breath and slowly let it go again. She stepped closer to meet Alexander's accusing stare. 'My dear Alexander,' she began, 'you are not to believe that your father did not have your best interests at heart when he changed his will.' She gave an exasperated sigh. 'But I've explained all this to you already. The new will was written because at the time we thought you too young for such responsibilities, and—'

'There it is,' Alexander cut in. 'You say, *we* thought, when what you really mean is that it's what *you* thought, not my father. I know what my father wanted.'

'Do not presume to know what was in your father's mind after our marriage, Alexander. He loved me and he trusted me, as you now must. The house, the business . . . you'll have your share of them in time.' She went to place a hand on his shoulder in an attempt to reassure him, but he pulled away. 'If only you could see how irrational you're being,' she added. 'I understand why, of course I do, and I can forgive you for it.

Your father is dead. It's a very difficult time for you, as it is for all of us.'

Alexander went to the door and opened it, inviting Angelica to leave. 'I don't want your forgiveness,' he said. 'I want back what you've stolen from my father—and from me!'

There it was, Angelica thought, as blunt as any accusation could be. But however cold Alexander's words sounded, they did not come as a shock to Angelica. 'I think you must have had more brandy than you let on,' she said as she swept out of the room.

Fifteen minutes later, Angelica was sitting in the drawing room with a glass of Madeira, as was her custom before dinner, when she heard what she thought sounded like someone shouting. It was a distant, unclear sound, easily dismissed to imagination, so she gave a shrug and continued to sip her drink as she ruminated over her recent conversation with Alexander. A few seconds later, however, she heard a thud from one of the rooms above that was enough to shake the chandelier. This she had most definitely not imagined. It jarred her nerves and made her jump in her seat. She stood up and called for the butler.

'Mr. Rutherford!'

She went to the door and heard the shouting again, more distinctly this time. It was definitely coming from the floor above. She went to the main staircase, still calling for the butler.

'Mr. Rutherford! Where in God's name are you?'

At the top of the staircase it became clear to Angelica that the sound was coming from one of the bedrooms. She hurried along the corridor to find out for herself what was going on, and as she reached the source of the sound, she realised it was coming from William's room. She abandoned the courtesy of knocking first and instead thrust the door open to see both William and Alexander on the floor in the middle of the room. William was lying on his back with Alexander sitting on top of him, beating him senseless. Beside them was the pillowcase she had not long since given to the maid, Sarah, to have laundered.

'Alexander! Stop it at once!' Angelica yelled, moving towards them, but Alexander did not stop. He continued to beat William, who did nothing to stop him.

'Mr. Rutherford!' Angelica called again. She grabbed Alexander's shoulders in an attempt to stop him, but he was too strong for her. He would not stop. 'Alexander! You're going to kill him! Please!' she pleaded, just as Mr. Rutherford arrived.

Rutherford's face as he entered the room was filled with alarm at the sight that greeted him. Wasting no time, he rushed in behind Alexander and thrust his arms beneath his, bringing his hands up behind Alexander's head in a full nelson hold. Then he stood up from the squat he'd lowered himself into, pulling Alexander up with him.

'Now then, Mister Alexander,' Rutherford said as Alexander continued to struggle. 'Calm down, won't you?'

Angelica went to her son. 'William,' she said, gently stroking his brow, trying not to look at the blood on his face.

William did not stir.

'William!' she said again, louder this time and with a degree of panic in her voice as she realised he could not hear her.

She looked up at Alexander, who by now had stopped struggling. 'Look what you've done,' she said, her words cold and detached. 'You've killed him.'

CHAPTER SEVENTEEN

There would be no dinner served at Priory House that evening. When the police arrived, everyone who had anything to say about the incident in William's bedroom was gathered, solemn-faced, in the drawing room. Angelica was seated in one of the armchairs, while Mr. Rutherford was on the settee beside Alexander in case he tried to do anything foolish, and there was the maid, Sarah, who was sitting in another of the armchairs. Alexander hadn't said a word; his indifferent expression having remained fixed the entire time since his attack on William had been discovered. On the table before everyone was the bloodstained pillowcase, which had been deemed important in helping to ascertain what had driven Alexander to act as he had.

'Come along now, sir,' the policeman said, standing before everyone. 'Your silence won't help anyone, not least yourself.'

The plain-spoken policeman had introduced himself as Sergeant Beauford. He was a tall man with a tidy head of salt-and-pepper hair, and he had a thick moustache that sat like an inverted chevron on his upper lip. He stooped over the low table and picked up the pillowcase.

'Now what about this?' he said, looking at

Angelica. 'You said you gave it to the maid, madam.' He turned to the maid. 'Sarah, is it?'

'That's right, sir. Sarah Smith.' Her voice sounded tremulous. A moment later she began to cry. 'I'm afraid it's all my fault. I saw it was the late Mr. Hampton's pillowcase. Well, it was in Mister William's room with blood on it and all, and I thought Mister Alexander should know about it, so I took it to him.'

Alexander spoke at last. 'You have no blame in this, Sarah,' he said. 'My actions were entirely my own, and I do not regret them.'

Angelica shot to her feet, furious. 'You monster!' she said, her tone seething. 'How can you sit there before me and say such a thing? Explain yourself!'

'Now, now, Mrs Hampton,' Beauford said, waving Angelica back into her seat.

Alexander sat forward. 'I gave your son every opportunity to explain to me why my father's bloodstained pillowcase was in his room,' he said, his face reddening as he spoke. 'He denied all knowledge of it. I asked him whose blood it was and how it got there, and he just stared at me, but the answer was clear enough.'

'And just what answer was that, sir?' Beauford said.

Alexander looked bemused. 'Isn't it obvious? It was my father's blood, coughed into his pillowcase when William went into his room in the middle of the night and smothered him with it, immediately before he raised the alarm and reported him dead. At seeing the blood, he removed the pillowcase and replaced it with a fresh one so no one would know what he'd done. Then he hid the evidence in his room until the dust had settled.'

Beauford began to shake his head. 'Now why would young Mister William want to kill your father, whom I might add was already a very sick man by all accounts? Where's the motive?'

'My father's business, of course,' Alexander said. 'William was to inherit a sizeable chunk of it.' He scoffed. 'He could hardly do that while my father was alive, could he?'

'But as I understand it,' Beauford said, 'your father left the business to Mrs Hampton, not to her son.'

A cold expression washed over Alexander as he turned back to Angelica. 'Of course. It was you who brought the pillowcase out from William's room to have it laundered. You knew it was my father's pillowcase and that there was blood on it, and yet you've raised no question over it. Did you think you were protecting William? Or perhaps you were both in on it together.'

'This is preposterous!' Angelica said.

'Is it?' Alexander snapped back before Angelica could continue. 'You had everything to gain, and through you, so did William.'

Angelica gave a humourless laugh. 'If your accusations bore any truth, and they do not, do you really suppose that I would hand such a damning piece of evidence to a maid for laundering?'

Alexander did not answer.

'No one in their right mind would do such a thing,' Angelica continued. 'They would burn the pillowcase, or at least bury it deep in the ground where it would never be found.'

'Then what were you doing with it when you left William's room earlier?' Alexander asked.

'Yes, Mrs Hampton,' Beauford said. 'I should like to hear the answer to that question myself.'

'And hear it you shall,' Angelica said. 'Mr. Rutherford, would you go and fetch Missus Redmond.'

Rutherford shot to his feet. 'Of course, madam,' he said, a look of puzzlement on his face.

'Missus Redmond?' Beauford said, looking equally puzzled.

'She will bear witness to what I'm about to tell you,' Angelica said.

Rutherford wasn't gone long, presumably because, like all good attentive housekeepers, Missus Redmond wasn't far from the keyhole. They both stood together beside Sergeant Beauford.

Angelica glanced at Alexander before speaking. She thought he looked less confident now that Missus Redmond had been called in. Here was someone he had clearly not accounted for during his damning accusations. But then how could he? Angelica picked up the pillowcase. She did so very slowly, drawing everyone's attention to it. Then she stood up and let the material unfold to reveal the bloodstain.

'This is my blood,' she said, looking at Alexander. 'I was in my late husband's room this afternoon, where I accidentally knocked over a glass vase. It smashed and I cut myself. I grabbed the first thing that came to hand to stop the bleeding, which happened to be this pillowcase. I called for Missus Redmond to have someone clear up the mess, but by the time she arrived, I'd dealt with most of it myself. Missus Redmond insisted on tidying up the rest in case I cut myself again.'

Beauford turned to Missus Redmond, who was already nodding.

'It wasn't worth calling one of the maids to do it,' she said. 'If I hadn't cleared up the rest of the glass, Mrs Hampton would have done it before the maid arrived.'

'I didn't want the entire household to know I'd broken the vase,' Angelica said.

'Of course not, madam,' Redmond said. 'So we managed it between ourselves. The cut on madam's arm wasn't so bad, but it wouldn't stop bleeding, so I suggested she continue to hold the pillowcase there until it did.'

'Where exactly did you cut yourself?' Beauford asked. 'Can I see it?'

'Certainly,' Angelica said, putting the pillow-case down and unbuttoning her cuff. She pulled up her sleeve to show the cut, which, now fully dried and healing, was no more than an inch long.

Beauford leaned in for a closer look, his moustache twitching as he did so. 'I see,' he said. 'Well, that explains it then.'

Angelica buttoned her cuff again. 'I was in my husband's room collecting his pocket watch for William, which Stanley had left to him in his will. It was in the dressing table drawer, which was stiff when I opened it. The table rocked, and the vase went crashing to the floor. I then took the watch to my son in his room, which is why I was leaving his room with the bloodstained pillowcase when Sarah passed. The bleeding had stopped, so I gave her the pillowcase for laundering.' She turned to Alexander again, now with a cold stare. 'You see, it was all perfectly explainable. Why didn't you come to me about it? I could have cleared the matter up in seconds. My poor William . . .' She put a hand to her mouth as her words trailed off. A moment later, she added, 'I'm afraid your irrational behaviour has led you astray. You and William both stood to inherit your father's half of the business between you when you were old enough and responsible enough, which I'm afraid is now something you have very much brought into doubt.'

'Brought into doubt?' Alexander repeated.

Angelica shook her head, smiling sardonically. 'Do you really suppose that you have not forfeited all that you stood to inherit? When you almost killed my son, your stepbrother, you lost your place in my heart forever. Even now he is fighting for his life, and you had better pray that he survives your insanity, or it will be your life as well as his.'

Beauford cleared his throat. 'I think I've heard all I need to hear,' he said with a sigh as he looked down at Alexander. 'Unless you've anything further to add, sir, I'll have to ask you to come along with me.'

Alexander did not have anything further to say. If he was sorry for what he had done then his featureless expression did not show it, although Angelica suspected he was feeling very sorry indeed, as much for himself as for poor William now that his actions had proven to be without foundation. As Alexander was led to the door, Angelica couldn't help but consider the deeper ramifications of his actions. He had been very foolish. There was no doubt that he would go to prison for what he had done, bringing shame upon himself. As a result he would lose everything. All that his father had built would fall entirely to William, and what of Louisa's affections now? With Alexander out of the way, surely William's chances of winning her hand were greatly improved, and in doing so William would have it all.

Angelica began to think ahead, and she tried not to smile in front of Sergeant Beauford and the servants as she pictured her son one day in the future with everything she had ever desired for him. Yes, Alexander had been very foolish indeed, just as Angelica knew he would be.

CHAPTER EIGHTEEN

Winson Green, Birmingham
1896

1893 was a black year for the Hamptons. Stanley was dead and, as a result, Alexander was now facing trial for his savage attack on poor William. When I heard the news I was naturally mortified. We were all still deeply mourning Stanley's death, and suddenly William's life, too, was hanging in the balance. Angelica told me everything that had happened that evening, leaving no detail out. Looking back now, I can see that she was perhaps unnecessarily thorough in her explanation, as if trying too hard to ensure that I could see matters no other way than as Sergeant Beauford had. But she had been thorough for a reason, and it was only later that I came to understand just how far she was prepared to go for William's happiness.

Angelica and I saw much less of each other after that. She was mourning Stanley's death, and had William to console, and there was little place for anyone else in her life at the time. I understood, of course. I tried to be patient, each day willing the cloud that had descended over her to lift and allow our lives to resume their former happy rhythm, but as much as I was led to believe it, they never truly did. Angelica had me wrapped around her finger, and I took it all in, blinded as I was by my love for her.

It was easy then to convince myself that Angelica's bereavement, and her other family matters, were the only reasons we were suddenly seeing so much less of one another, but they were not. I saw her at Alexander's trial and she seemed momentarily brighter. It lifted my hope that we would again soon be as we once were, but before long Angelica was to be deeply troubled by other matters that overshadowed all else that had happened that year.

Birmingham
1893

A month had passed since Alexander almost beat William to death. His trial was held at the recently built Victoria assize courts on Corporation Street. Designed by Aston Webb and Ingress Bell, the richly ornamented building was an eclectic blend of French Renaissance and Gothic architecture, constructed in red brick and faced with intricate, deep-red terracotta mouldings. With its picturesque towers and projecting pillars, Angelica thought it more like a fairy-tale castle than a court of law, although she expected Alexander had had no such fancy when he was first brought there.

The trial did not take long to conclude, and by the time the jury had reached their decision and the judge was ready to give his sentencing speech, the courtroom was heaving under the weight of all the people who had come to see judgement passed on this young man from the prominent and well-respected Hampton family. The case had made all the local newspapers and some further afield. Now, irrespective of the judge's verdict, it seemed that public opinion would ensure the young man in the dock would face a life of shame for what he had done. Angelica only hoped it would not have too detrimental an effect on the Hampton and Moore penmaking business, although in time she intended to disassociate the business from the Hampton name, thus limiting any damage it might cause.

Alfred Moore was seated beside Angelica, close to the dock and the judge's ornate canopied chair, and although Alfred had said very little since the proceedings began, it was clear to Angelica that he was deeply troubled by everything he had heard. His sunken features bore a solemnity that was matched only by the accused, and every now and then as the proceedings progressed, he would shake his head and pull at his beard as if unable to believe his ears.

'Who would have thought it?' he said, speaking in a whisper as if to himself as the jury's verdict was announced. He turned to Angelica. 'Stanley

Hampton, God rest his soul, would turn in his grave if he knew what a remorseless monster his son had become.'

'At least the jury reached the right verdict,' Angelica said through her veil.

'How could they not?' Alfred said. 'I'm afraid Alexander was poorly advised by his council when he entered a plea of not guilty. I suppose they were hoping for a lesser charge and subsequent sentence.' He gave a low harrumph. 'We'll soon see how that little gambit turns out.'

Angelica hoped the judge would show no leniency towards Alexander for what he had done to her son. She thought it a pity that transportation was no longer an option.

'Jealously was at the root of it, I suppose,' Alfred continued in a contemplative tone. 'He was angry at William for sharing his father's affections, and no doubt his wealth. That's what it was.'

'Perhaps,' Angelica said, unsurprised by Alfred's shift in sentiment towards Alexander. He had crossed a line no gentleman should cross. He had betrayed his class, proving himself to be of no higher moral standing than a common thug.

She turned to William, sitting to her left beside Louisa, who had insisted on being next to him so that she could help him through the ordeal of reliving the terrible incident all over again. William had spoken very little all day, and then largely only to protest at having to attend the hearing at all. Angelica glanced at him, trying not to draw his attention to the fact that she was again studying the stitches and contusions on his face, and the swelling around his right eye, which even now made it difficult for him to see properly. It chilled her to her core to think that he might have lost the use of his eye altogether had Alexander not been pulled off him when he was—or worse, that Alexander might have killed him, as she had at first supposed.

The ordeal had, however, served to bring William and Louisa closer together, and for that Angelica was thankful. Now it seemed as though Louisa could no longer bear to look at the young man in the dock, even though she had previously been so besotted with him. There was no doubt in Angelica's mind that Louisa fully shared her father's disappointment in Alexander, and it gave Angelica great comfort to know that their opinions in that regard were never likely to change.

Ahead of them, the elderly judge in his bright red gown and his wig stirred into life and someone called, 'Please be upstanding for His Lordship, Judge Phineas Whyte.'

Many of the crowd began to cough and clear their throats as they rose, as if they had been holding back until the general noise in the room was sufficient to mask the sound.

When the room settled again, the judge stood before them. He looked over the assembly briefly from the top of his glasses, and then with a gravelly voice, his eyes squarely on Alexander, he said, 'Mr. Alexander Hampton, as we have heard, it is the verdict of this jury that against the charges of inflicting bodily injury, with or without a weapon, upon the victim, Mr. William Chastain, you are found guilty. In weighing up the mitigating circumstances of the case, I have taken into account your fractious state of mind following the recent and untimely death of your father. However, your attack on Mr. Chastain was one of a most savage and brutal nature, and in light of the evidence and statements presented to the court here today, I find your paltry excuses for the attack to be entirely without foundation or provocation by the victim. Under the Offences Against the Person Act 1861, I therefore offer no leniency and sentence you to ten years' imprisonment.'

The room suddenly erupted with a tremendous din as the people began to cry out, some against the judgement, but the great majority all for it. Angelica sat down again and flung her head back, her eyes lifting all the way to the coffered, Tudor-style ceiling as she began to smile and replay the judge's words in her mind: *Ten years' imprisonment*. She thought that would do very well.

She felt a hand on her shoulder and she twisted around in her seat. Effie and her parents were in the row behind her, and here was Effie returning her smile to show her shared satisfaction at the justice William had received. Angelica raised her veil and smiled more fully now as their eyes met, and she wanted nothing more than to embrace Effie. Perhaps it was because they had not shared a moment's intimacy since Stanley died, or because of the euphoria she felt at hearing the judge's sentencing statement, but she was surprised by the level of emotion she had begun to feel towards Effie. How Angelica had missed her—she who had never once let anyone close to her heart before. She raised a hand to her shoulder and risked a touch, and then a gentle squeeze of Effie's hand before letting it go again lest anyone should notice the affection in her eyes and realise there was more to it than simple friendship.

'It's an outrage!' someone further back in the crowd shouted.

Angelica knew the voice. She immediately stood up and spun around to see Jack Hardy pumping his fist in the air in protest. A few other voices quickly joined him in support.

'Order in the court!' the bailiff shouted. 'Order!'

Angelica turned back to the dock, where Alexander was now being led out in handcuffs to begin his long sentence, deprived of all the finery and advantage he had been born into. As the room fell silent again and the prisoner was led away, he lifted his bowed head and she caught his eye. She raised an eyebrow and a wry smile creased her lips, letting him know how satisfied she was. In return, Alexander could do no more than grit his teeth and pull a sour face. The promising life that was once before him was now no more, and there was nothing he could do about it.

With the trial concluded, Angelica simply wanted to return to Priory House and once again start her life afresh, putting everything that had happened, first with Stanley and now with Alexander, behind her, but as soon as she stepped outside, she knew that was not to be. Jack Hardy was there in his sagging black suit and bowler hat, standing beside a lamp post opposite the building's main arched entrance, tapping out his pipe. As soon as he saw Angelica, he put it back into his jacket pocket, and with his eyes squarely fixed on her, he came striding across the road.

'You go on with Louisa,' Angelica said to William. Louisa and her father, and Effie and her parents, were already walking ahead to their carriages. 'I believe Mr. Hardy wishes to speak with me. I shan't be long.'

William didn't seem to mind in the least. He was no doubt keen to return as quickly as possible to the privacy of the carriage, where people could no longer stare at the cuts and bruises on his face.

He simply gave a nod, and arm in arm he and Louisa continued on their way.

Angelica met Mr. Hardy in the street, which was empty of traffic due to there being no thoroughfare as yet because the area outside the assize courts was still under construction.

'Good day to you, Mr. Hardy,' she said in an assertive tone. 'If you have something to say to me, then say it quickly.'

'In a hurry to be somewhere, are you?' Hardy said with a mocking smile. 'I, on the other hand, have precisely nowhere to be. You saw to that well enough, didn't you?'

'Your services at Hampton and Moore were no longer required.'

'Right. So you said. But we both know that's not the real reason now, don't we?'

Angelica huffed. 'I don't know what you mean.'

Hardy stepped closer until Angelica could smell the tobacco on his breath. 'I mean I know what you're up to. I've had Alexander's trust for a while now, and even before his father died, he told me he had his doubts about you.'

'Oh yes,' Angelica said. 'Alexander's doubts . . . He voiced them to me before he tried to kill my son.'

'And that's really why you sacked me after his father died, isn't it? Working as closely together as we did, you thought sooner or later he might confide in me and tell me about his concerns, and maybe I'd believe him, eh? Well, you were too late. He'd already confided in me, and he told me plenty about you, too.'

'What could Alexander possibly have told you about me?'

'Enough to be going on with,' Hardy said, sounding confident. 'Let's just say that whatever Alexander knows about you, I know about you. While I grant you that may not be much just now, if there is something you've not been on the level about, I'll find out what it is.'

Angelica gave a dry, humourless laugh. 'And just what do you suppose that could be, Mr. Hardy?'

'Oh, I don't know, but I think a little digging into your background could be a good place to start looking. As I said, it's not like I've got anything else to do with my time at the minute, is it?'

'Time is a precious thing, Mr. Hardy. You would do well to use yours to find yourself a new position in another factory before you find yourself without a roof above your head.'

'I've enough money to keep me going for a while. Stanley saw to that in his will, didn't he? It's like he knew I'd be needing something to help his son out when the time came, and now it has. As soon as I heard the poor young man had been arrested, I knew all of Alexander's suspicions were right. Now, you said if I had something to

226

say, then I should say it quickly. I just wanted you to know that I'm on to you, and I mean to do something about it.'

Angelica laughed again, but there was a nervousness to it this time. 'Then you, sir, are as delusional as Alexander Hampton! Good day to you!'

'Good day, madam,' Hardy said, touching the brim of his hat as Angelica turned on her heel and left for her carriage.

The return to Priory House was an uneasy one for Angelica. All the way home, first through the grey city streets, and then the leaf-strewn late-autumn countryside, she silently cursed Hardy for so quickly denying her the pleasure she had felt at seeing justice done for her son in the courtroom. She would have liked to savour the moment, and converse with her travelling companions in celebratory tones at the outcome, but she had other things on her mind now, and in truth William appeared to draw no satisfaction from it. He had forever lost a brother, after all, however hard Alexander had beaten him, and for reasons William would never truly understand.

She tried to recall what she had told the Hampton family about herself. Surely it had not been much, and then mostly before Alexander was old enough to take any interest in such matters. But he had clearly become inquisitive as his years matured. What had Stanley told him?

Again, she thought hard on what she had said about her past, of France and of marriage to an Englishman, of his trade and of his death. Surely that was all.

But perhaps it was enough.

There were certainly things in her past that she would rather no one know about, least of all Jack Hardy, who was now clearly on a crusade to clear Alexander's name, or at the very least enact revenge for him by upsetting everything she had achieved since coming to Birmingham.

She could not allow that.

By the time the carriage arrived back at Priory House in the grey of the late afternoon, Angelica understood that for now at least she had to keep a close eye on Hardy. She needed to know what he was doing and where he was digging for information. To do that, she first had to learn his address, and she knew just where to find it.

CHAPTER NINETEEN

The pen factory on Legge Lane was in darkness when Angelica arrived. She had decided to go there after the workers had been dismissed for the day because, although by her late husband's benefaction she now owned half the business and had every right to go there whenever she chose, she wanted to be discreet. She held her oil lamp before her, and in its pale amber glow she thought the various contraptions that combined to manufacture Hampton and Moore pens sinister-looking things as she made her way between them, like apparatuses from a torture chamber. The fly presses cast long, contorted shadows, which moved around her as she went, reaching in towards her one minute, and then receding again the next as she passed them. It was so quiet she could hear her lamp hissing in front of her like a snake.

She stooped and lifted the hem of her dress as she reached the ironwork stairs and began to climb them, wondering why she felt so nervous. It was not because she was afraid to be there at the factory alone after dark. If she were, she would have asked her driver to come inside with her instead of waiting with the carriage in the street outside. No, she was nervous because of Jack Hardy. She had felt that way since they exchanged words outside the assize courts earlier—that creeping, almost suffocating feeling that calamity was close at hand if she could not prevent it.

At the top of the stairs, she entered the main office and set her lamp down on the desk. It was not a large room; the lamp's glow lit the space sufficiently to see what she was doing. The filing cabinets were to her left: tall oak chests four drawers deep with brass handles. She slid one of the drawers open and welcomed the noise it made as she peered down over its contents. This was where she would find Hardy's address. Here were all of Hampton and Moore's employee records, past and present. She withdrew the section in the folder marked 'H' and took it to the desk. Hardy's details were easy to locate.

Angelica slid the lamp closer. 'Navigation Street,' she said under her breath.

She knew where Navigation Street was—it was not far from the town hall to the south—but what to do about it? To know what Hardy was doing she would have to follow him, but she couldn't very well do that herself. He would all too easily recognise her, and it would be a laborious task that she was ill-equipped for. She had to hire someone—someone capable, whose discretion could be guaranteed, no questions asked. She closed the folder again and returned it to the filing cabinet, thinking she would have no trouble remembering the address. She was just about to close the drawer, anticipating the grating sound it had made on opening it, when another sound made her catch her breath. It was distant. It sounded like a door opening or closing, she couldn't be sure which.

Angelica caught up her lamp as she made for the door to see who was out there. She went to the railing that ran alongside the walkway above the lower shop floor and held the lamp out over the edge. She couldn't see anyone, but the light from her lamp only reached so far, and more than half the floor below was hidden from view by the level above it. She squinted into the darkness, her breath now short and rapid. Then she gasped as she saw the glow of another lamp.

'Who's there?' she called, supposing it had to be her driver for some reason, although she could not fathom why.

When no answer came and the lamplight drew closer, its bearer still out of sight for now, she knew it could not be her driver or he would have answered her call. She lowered her own lamp and watched the other grow brighter, until very soon whoever was carrying it came into view, although Angelica still had no idea who it was. The figure wore a cape with the hood drawn up.

He or she was heading straight for the staircase.

'Who is it?' Angelica called again, growing impatient. 'Why don't you answer?'

This time she thought she heard laughter. It was no more than a faint giggle.

'Effie, is that you?'

Angelica went to the top of the staircase. The figure at the foot of the stairs was now bathed in lamplight, and even before she pulled her hood back, Angelica knew she was right.

'Surprise!' Effie called, laughing again, more loudly this time. 'Did I scare you?'

Angelica took a deep breath, thankful at least that it was not some robber come to break into the factory safe. 'Not at all,' she said, straightening her back and pushing her chin out to give the impression that she was completely unfazed by the matter. 'But whatever are you doing here at this late hour?'

'I should ask you the same thing,' Effie said as she began to climb the stairs. 'But I already know why you're here.'

Angelica caught her breath again. 'You do?'

Effie nodded. 'I was desperate to see you after the trial, so I called at Priory House. Missus Redmond told me you said you were coming here to collect a ledger for William.'

Angelica relaxed again. Effie did not know the true reason for her visit to the factory, only the lie she had told Missus Redmond in case she or anyone else should wonder why Angelica had gone there so late in the day.

'Yes, William's starting back on Monday,' she said. 'With everything that's happened, he's a little out of touch with the accounts.'

'He's taken over the books from Mr. Moore?'

'Yes, I'm afraid poor Alfred isn't getting any younger,' Angelica said. 'I had reason to check his work recently, and I'm sorry to say that I found a number of errors in his calculations. I suggested it was time for William to look after the finances, and Alfred, although reluctant to begin with, soon saw the sense in it. He knows how good William is with numbers.'

Effie reached the top of the stairs and threw herself at Angelica, clearly not at all interested in talking about business and finance. She kissed Angelica full on the lips before she could raise any objection, not that she wanted to. Now, as Effie drew away again, her cheeks flushed in the lamplight, it was Angelica who was laughing.

'Steady, Effie!' she said. 'You almost knocked me down.'

'I'm sorry,' Effie said, panting a little. 'I've been wanting to do that for so long now, I couldn't help myself. You can't imagine how wretched I feel when I'm not with you. Do tell me when we can be together again, please. I know it's been difficult for you lately, but I—'

'Effie,' Angelica cut in, still laughing, although it was now at Effie's giddy desperation. 'You must slow down and catch your breath or you'll faint.' She took Effie's hand and led her into the office. 'Come in here where we can be more comfortable.'

Effie's eyes lit up. 'What, in the factory office? I didn't necessarily mean I had to be with you right here and now, but I'm game if you are.'

'Heavens, no! Not in here,' Angelica said, aghast at the thought. 'Look, sit down and let's talk. I know I've been aloof lately, but you know how it's been. How can I focus on us while all this is going on?'

'But it's over now,' Effie said as she sat down, both their lamps now on the desk, lighting up the room.

'Almost,' Angelica said. 'I still have a few things to attend to, and then we can spend as much time together as you like.'

Effie sighed. 'Do you promise?'

'Yes, of course. I promise.'

'And would you really like to spend more time with me? You're not just saying that?'

Angelica leaned in and kissed Effie's lips, a far softer, more gentle kiss than the one Effie had greeted her with. 'Did that feel genuine enough to you?' she asked, smiling at her.

Effie did not answer straight away. She teased her tongue over her lips, savouring the moment

234

for as long as she could. 'Yes,' she said, smiling back.

'Good. Then give me a few days. That's all I need. We'll meet for lunch on Thursday afternoon. How about that?'

'And after lunch?'

'A bit of shopping, and . . .' She trailed off, teasing, knowing full well what Effie meant. 'Do we still have our room in town?'

Effie gave Angelica an eager nod as her face lit up with anticipation.

'Thursday it is then,' Angelica said. 'Now come along. Let's get out of here.'

Angelica went to the door, but before she had crossed the threshold, Effie called to her, 'What about the ledger for William?'

Angelica turned back. 'The ledger, of course,' she said, smiling awkwardly. She hadn't really intended to take anything away with her, but she supposed it wise to in case William heard why she had gone there and asked after it. 'How silly of me. You see the effect you have on me? You've made me forget why I came here.' She went to another of the filing cabinets, and from one of the drawers removed one of several thick, well-thumbed ledger books. 'Here it is,' she added, turning back to Effie.

'I can't wait for Thursday,' Effie said, with such sincerity that it caused Angelica to reflect on just how much she was looking forward to it, too. Her time with Effie, just her and Effie, was always so relaxing and carefree. She wanted to feel that way again, but first she had other matters to attend to, matters which, if left unresolved, would make it impossible for her to ever feel relaxed or carefree again.

Outside, she saw Effie into her carriage and bade her goodnight, and then, before Effie's carriage had pulled away, she dismissed her own driver under the pretence of returning home to Priory House later that evening with her friend. Moments later, both carriages left in opposite directions, leaving Angelica standing in the street, her black gown and cape blending into the shadows between the lamplight.

A few people passed her by, carriages came and went. When she saw an available hansom cab approaching, she stepped out to hail it, meaning to hire the driver's services for the evening. She had several places to visit, none of which she wanted any of her acquaintances to know about.

The first place Angelica had the cab driver take her was Navigation Street. Before she went about trying to employ someone to follow Jack Hardy and observe his activity, she wanted to see for herself where the man lived. When the cab was almost upon his address, she thumped on the roof to let the driver know she wanted to stop. She had imagined that Hardy lived in a tidy little terraced house, but instead she found herself looking out at the unmistakeable facade of a taxidermy shop.

The shop was on the corner of the street at a crossroads. Above the display windows and the entrance, mounted beneath the guttering, she counted a dozen deer heads, complete with antlers. They were all in a line, one beside the other, each staring back at her with their dead eyes. She thought it quite macabre. On the step outside the entrance, completely blocking the door, she saw a young dromedary, which presumably was there to indicate that the shop was closed. Her eyes drifted up to the glow she could see at one of the windows above. She supposed it had to be Hardy's lamplight, his accommodation rented from the taxidermist.

Angelica immediately wondered what Hardy was up to, and she had little doubt that his activity concerned her. She would have liked to remain there, just to see if he went out that night, and to follow him if he did, but it was not worth the risk of discovery. She had to keep to her plan and find someone to do that for her. Her eyes remained fixed on the lighted window as she continued to consider how best to do that. There was only one kind of place where she could hope to hire someone for a job like this, no questions asked, and that was in one of the city's many public houses.

She banged on the cab roof again. 'Deritend,'

she called to the driver, thinking it was best to start her search for such a man further afield, so there was less chance of anyone recognising her. She had known plenty of men in London who would have jumped at the chance to assist her for the right price, and she imagined Birmingham was no different.

Deritend, however, quickly became a dead end. An hour soon passed, during which time Angelica visited several public houses, raising nothing more than curious eyebrows and unwelcoming frowns, but she had expected nothing less. Respectable women did not frequent such places, least of all by themselves. They were built by men for men, largely for the purposes of drinking and the company of prostitutes. Nevertheless, Angelica was determined to see her plan through, even though few of the landlords she spoke to had anything more to say to her than to ask her to leave.

'We don't want any trouble, miss,' was the typical reply. 'On your way with you.'

Leaving Deritend behind, Angelica instructed the cab driver to take her back towards the city centre, where she hoped for better luck. As the journey continued, she wondered what he must think of her, travelling to so many pubs by herself at night, but she had paid him well and he minded his business.

'We're in Digbeth now, miss,' the driver called

to her from his seat high up behind the carriage. 'That's the Anchor Inn on the corner there. Do you want me to stop?'

'Yes, thank you,' Angelica called back, thinking that the Anchor Inn offered much the same odds of her finding the kind of man she was looking for as any other.

The cab pulled over by a lamp post outside the pub, where two men were smoking pipes and laughing together. The laughter stopped as soon as Angelica stepped down from the carriage, and she sensed both men were staring at her as she passed them. She paid them no attention, pausing briefly to take the place in before entering. It was a small, homely-looking pub on Bradford Street, with lodgings on the two floors above. The sounds coming from inside told her it was busy, which was good. The busier it was, the more people there were, and the more people there were, the better her chances of finding someone to follow Jack Hardy for her.

The din grew louder still as she opened the door, and this time it did not quieten down when she entered, as it had in the other pubs she'd visited that night. Here, only a handful of the quietest, ruddy-faced drinkers seemed to notice her. She stared back at them until they looked away, and she continued to take the place in. Because the pub occupied a corner location on the street, it was arranged in a narrow L-shape, with bench seating beneath the windows, before which were set a few tables and chairs. She made for the bar, which although only a few paces away, was a jostle to get to.

'Be with you in a minute, dear,' the woman behind the bar called when she saw Angelica.

She was pulling a pint, the sleeves of her green dress rolled up to her elbows, her once-white lace bonnet and shawl stained with beer slops and tobacco smoke. At length she came over.

'Staying here, are you?' she said, as if there could be no other reason why Angelica was there.

'No,' Angelica said. 'I should like to speak with the landlord, if you please.'

The woman laughed. 'I'm afraid that's not possible.'

Angelica frowned. 'It's not?'

'No dear, he died five years go. I took over from my husband, you see. If a landlady will do, then I'm all ears.'

They had something in common, Angelica thought. 'I have also taken over my late husband's business,' she said above the general hubbub. 'One of my employees was recently dismissed, and I have reason to believe he may do something foolish in retaliation. As nothing has yet happened, I cannot very well go to the authorities, so I wonder if you know of anyone who may be trusted, for an agreeable price, of course, to follow the man and keep an eye on him for me.'

The landlady had what Angelica considered to be a hard face, even when she was laughing, with a strong jawline and sunken cheeks, which she now sucked in, accentuating them further as she seemed to think on her answer. A moment later she rose up on her toes and began to look to her left and to her right, past Angelica into the bar, as if trying to pick someone out.

'I'm sure he's in tonight,' she said, further screwing up her face as she tried to squint past all the other patrons.

Her words raised Angelica's hopes.

'There!' the landlady said a moment later. 'See the bald fella in the corner?'

She pointed behind Angelica, to her right. Angelica turned and tried to see who she was pointing to, but her view was blocked.

'That's Ben Lynch,' the landlady continued. 'He's always looking to make a shilling. I'd pop over and have a word with him if I were you. He don't bite.'

'Anyone serving!' came a gruff call from the other end of the bar.

The landlady gave a tut and turned to see who it was. Then she turned back to Angelica and winked. 'I'll spit in his beer for his cheek,' she said. 'Do excuse me.'

With that, the landlady left, mumbling words Angelica couldn't hear over the raised voices around her. *Ben Lynch,* she mused as she turned around and made her way in the direction the landlady had indicated. She had only taken two steps when she felt someone's hand on her forearm. She pulled away, and turned to see a middle-aged man with a top hat beneath his arm and a smile on his clean-shaven face, which seemed to Angelica uncommonly pale.

'My humble apologies,' the man said, bowing as he spoke, 'but I couldn't help overhearing your little dilemma and felt it my duty to make your acquaintance. You see, Ben Lynch isn't the person you're looking for.'

'And I suppose you are?' Angelica said, not yet sure what to make of the man.

He was well dressed, in grey pinstripe trousers, a black frock coat over his emerald waistcoat, and a matching green silk at his neck. On closer inspection, however, Angelica thought his clothes had seen far better days, and the leather on his shoes, which held little shine, was crumpled and cracked in the way only age and poor maintenance could account for. He was well spoken, although Angelica suspected it was a case of imitation over breeding. It didn't fool her. His elocution was clearly all part of the act, designed to belie his criminal-class status.

He thrust a hand towards Angelica and smiled again. 'I'm known as Gentleman John,' he said, 'and unlike that oaf, Ben Lynch, I'm very good at following people.' He nudged her arm and raised his eyebrows at her. 'Just don't ask me for any references, if you know what I mean.'

Angelica did not shake the man's hand, gloved as her own hands were. The fewer things, or people, she touched in such places that night the better, as far as she was concerned. 'You expect me to trust you?'

Gentleman John gave a small laugh. 'Only so far as you expect *me* to trust *you*. You stated why you want this ex-employee of yours followed, but we both know that's not the real reason. If it were, you would surely conduct your business by daylight, and in a more respectable manner than this.' He paused with a finger raised to his top lip. 'If it were,' he repeated, 'then you would likely not be conducting such business at all, but would have someone else do it for you. This is therefore personal to you.' He smiled again. 'Things are not all as they seem between us, are they? But surely we can use that to our mutual advantage. Now, I see that Mr. Lynch is just leaving.' He waved his hand in the direction of the corner seat where a bald-headed man was getting up. 'Shall we discuss the matter?'

His wits were sharp. Angelica liked that about him. His persona was also well suited to the job, even if it failed to stand up to close scrutiny. He would blend in on the city streets by daylight. With the appearance of a gentleman, he would also be above suspicion of such shady activity as

243

she would have him perform. At least, far more so than the likes of Ben Lynch, whom Angelica now saw fully for the first time as she made her way to the corner table. His clothes were stained and threadbare, and he carried a fetid odour about him which she could not fail to notice as she passed him and sat down, ignoring his lascivious leer. Yes, she thought, Gentleman John, or whatever his real name was, would do very well.

Gentleman John set his top hat down on the table and lowered himself into the chair opposite Angelica, facing the window. 'Now then,' he said, 'it doesn't matter who you are or why you're here —your reasons are your own. My interest lies solely with the job at hand, and how much it pays. You say you want someone followed?'

Angelica glanced around to be sure no one could overhear her conversation this time. The room was still noisy with the sound of raised voices trying to be heard. No one was paying them any attention. Just the same, she lowered her voice as she replied, so that Gentleman John had to lean over the table to hear her.

'His name is Jack Hardy. He lives above the taxidermist's shop on Navigation Street. Do you know it?'

'Madam, I know Birmingham like the back of my hand.'

'Good, then starting early tomorrow morning

you must wait for him to leave his accommodation and follow him, unnoticed.'

'That much goes without saying.'

'I want to know where he goes,' Angelica continued, 'who he speaks to, and why.'

'A catalogue of his day-to-day activity,' Gentleman John said. 'I understand.' His eyes narrowed. 'Now, to the price.'

'I believe the price to be a generous one,' Angelica said. 'I'll give you four pounds for your time and trouble. Half now and half on completion of the work.'

Gentleman John sat back in his chair and drew a thoughtful breath. 'That could be a tidy sum indeed, depending on the duration of the work, of course. How should I know when my work is done?'

'It will be done once I'm satisfied.'

Gentleman John nodded. 'Which is as it should be, of course. But if the work were to run into weeks, even months, four pounds might seem—'

'If you're as good as you suggest,' Angelica cut in, 'I anticipate that the work will last no more than a week or two.' She fully expected that Hardy would act fast. 'Forty shillings a week is more or less twice what any London labourer might expect to earn. Should the job finish sooner then it will be all the more to your advantage. That much, however, is to be your gamble.'

'Yes, I see that,' Gentleman John said, tapping a finger against his top lip again. 'Four pounds, all in,' he added, reiterating the deal. He studied Angelica in silence for several seconds, weighing things up before he smiled and said, 'Very well. I'll do it, however long it takes.'

Angelica had brought no reticule with her that evening, no coin purse in which to carry her money, in case she should draw the wrong kind of attention and be robbed of it. Instead, she carried her money inside her left glove, safely in the palm of her hand. She removed it, slipping the elbow-length cuff from her forearm, and shook the coins free into her lap. Then she slid two gold sovereigns across the table to Gentleman John, whose eyes were on them from the moment he saw them. He was quick to pick them up, and he made no inspection of them—not now, at least. He was still smiling as he slipped them into his waistcoat pocket.

'I shall begin my work tomorrow then,' Gentleman John said. 'But how shall I report my findings to you? I very much doubt you wish me to call on you at home.'

Angelica raised her eyebrows, letting him know that she most certainly did not. 'I'll come here to see you each evening at nine o'clock,' she said, putting her glove back on. 'If you're not here, I'll assume you have nothing to report.' She stood up and moved around the table to leave. 'I hope my money is well spent,' she added, her eyes suddenly narrowing on him.

Gentleman John's smile began to waver. 'Very well spent indeed, I assure you.'

'Good, because I don't want the bother of having to hire someone to come and look for you.'

CHAPTER TWENTY

The November rain continued to spatter and streak at the window as Angelica gazed absently out from the comfort of the bed, listening to the chaotic yet peaceful harmony. She was sitting up against the headboard, lost in her thoughts, while Effie lay beside her with her head on her lap, having drifted off to sleep for all Angelica knew, because she hadn't spoken or stirred in several minutes.

But Angelica was no longer thinking about Effie.

Her thoughts had turned to the unwelcome situation that had arisen with Jack Hardy, as they often did when she had nothing else to occupy her mind. In particular, she was thinking about her arrangement with Gentleman John. Two nights had passed since she first met him at the Anchor Inn, and despite having returned there on both nights since, she had not seen him again.

She hoped he would be there that evening with news for her, but she had begun to wonder whether the man was following Hardy at all, or if he had simply taken her money with no intention of working for it. Was that Gentleman John's game? Was he a confidence trickster who had preyed on her needs to his own financial advantage? He certainly bore all the traits, pretending to be the gentleman he clearly was not. If that was the case then he had not taken her parting threat seriously, and it would be to his ruin.

Angelica drew her fingers slowly back through Effie's hair and she stirred. 'Were you sleeping?'

'No,' Effie said, craning her neck around to look up at her. 'I was just daydreaming. You?'

'I was daydreaming, too.'

'What about?'

As much as Angelica would have liked to confide in Effie and tell her everything, she knew she could not. She did not doubt that Effie loved her, but she knew the truth would tear that love apart in a heartbeat and she could not risk it. She did not want to. Theirs was a love Angelica had never felt before, not with either of the men she had married, and certainly not with any of the other men she had been with.

'I was thinking about you,' Angelica lied, knowing it was just what Effie wanted to hear.

Effie giggled. 'That's funny because I was thinking about you. Tell me what you were thinking.'

Angelica drew a long breath and sighed as she thought on her answer. Then, from within the lie came a simple truth and she voiced it. 'I was thinking about how much I enjoy our time together, just the two of us, and how much I'd like to spend every day with you if I could, without fear of what others might think of us.'

'I often think the same thing,' Effie said. 'Can't we go away together, somewhere quiet and peaceful where no one knows us?'

Angelica began to picture such a future, far from any great town or city, a simple house on a hill above a lake, or perhaps overlooking the sea, where so few people lived that they would rarely see another soul if it was not by their own choosing. She thought she would like that very much, and she was growing tired of pretending, but while she quickly began to desire that future now that she had imagined it, she knew it was not possible.

'I can't leave William,' she said. 'He's still young, and he has so much responsibility ahead of him. I'm sure he'll need me by his side.'

'What about Louisa? If things continue the way they are, I won't be at all surprised if they're soon married.'

'I do hope so,' Angelica said, 'but there's the business to run, and if he and Louisa do marry, their children will need their grandmother.'

'I see,' Effie said, sounding dejected. 'So we're to go on pretending?'

Angelica stroked Effie's hair again, letting the loose chestnut strands fall through her fingers on to the bed sheets. 'We must,' she said. 'At least for the time being.'

'Someday then?' Effie said, tilting her head back as she looked up at Angelica again.

Angelica bent down and kissed her forehead. 'Someday,' she said with a smile. 'Someday, I promise. Now, come along. We can't lie here all afternoon.'

'Can't we?' Effie sighed. 'I like listening to the rain.'

'So do I, but you know we can't. William knows I've been out shopping with you today, remember? I told him I'd travel home with him when he's finished at the factory.'

'Oh yes, I remember.'

Angelica slipped out from beneath the bed-covers, letting Effie's head fall back on to the sheet.

'Of course,' Effie said, 'if we did move away somewhere quiet together, you'd need have no fear of that man you told me about from your nightmares ever finding you. Do you still fear him?'

Angelica feared him now more than ever, and while her dreams were not real, Jack Hardy was, as was the threat he posed by digging into her affairs. 'Yes, I do,' she said, even before she had turned back to face Effie.

'So my father's pistol still gives you comfort? I only ask because you've had it a while now and he's sure to miss it someday.'

Angelica returned to the bedside and sat down.

She took Effie's hands in hers, thinking that she might soon have even greater need of it.

'It gives me such comfort,' she said. 'Do not ask me to return it now. Besides, your father hasn't missed it yet and it's been three years. If he was ever going to notice it gone, wouldn't he have done so by now?'

Effie sat up, letting the bedcovers fall down over her breasts as she looked intently into Angelica's eyes. She seemed suddenly distressed to know that, after all this time, Angelica was still afraid of the man in her nightmares.

'I don't care if my father does miss it,' she said, clearly having changed her mind at seeing how desperate Angelica was to hold on to it. 'If it still gives you comfort then of course you must keep it.'

'Thank you, Effie,' Angelica said. Then she grabbed a pillow and playfully swung it into Effie's back. 'Now get up and help me dress. I don't have long.'

Promptly at nine o'clock that evening, Angelica arrived at the Anchor Inn in Digbeth wondering whether her journey was once more to be in vain. Perhaps there really was nothing to report. Maybe Jack Hardy was all wind and no sail, and wasn't really a threat to her. No news was, after all, good news in this case. It had rained on and off all day, and it was still raining as the hansom cab she had hired pulled up outside. She wiped the condensation from the window with the back of her glove and peered out through the rain that fell in golden droplets around the lamp post the driver had stopped beside. The pub seemed quiet this evening. She could hear no revelry spilling on to the street, nor could she see the shadows at the windows that she had seen on every other night. The rain had kept people home, but what of Gentleman John?

Angelica leaned forward and began to push open one of the low half-doors in front of her, but as she did so she paused. A figure had dashed out from the pub doorway, heading straight for her. She squinted through the rain to better see who it was, then she recognised the man's clothing and a wave of excitement caught her. It was Gentleman John, dressed exactly the same as he had been the night she first met him.

He had no over-frock coat to ward off the rain or the evening's chill. He had one hand on his top hat to prevent it from falling off his head as he ran, and the other on his pocket watch, which he was just slipping back into his waistcoat. Angelica sat back again as he arrived, but before addressing her, he stopped and looked up at the cab driver, as if wary of him, or of what he might overhear of their conversation. A moment later he stepped closer.

'It's too quiet in there tonight,' he said in a

whisper, although over the now hissing rain even Angelica struggled to hear him. 'I thought you might appreciate talking out here in the privacy of your cab. I find that the seasoned drinker is very adept at listening to other people's conversations.'

Angelica moved across the seat and waved him in. 'What news do you have?' she asked, eager to hear what the man had to say, and glad to see that he had not simply taken off with his payment after all.

Gentleman John stepped up via the footboard, removing his hat as he did so. He pulled the low half-door open and sat beside Angelica, closing it again to keep the rain out.

'As you have the use of this cab,' he said, 'perhaps you'll permit me to show you?'

'Show me?'

'Why, yes,' Gentleman John said. 'Show you where your Mr. H went this afternoon. It may be nothing, but it piqued my interest enough to come here this evening. It's not far.'

'Then by all means,' Angelica said, raising her hand in the general direction of the cab driver, whom she imagined was by now soaked through and miserable, despite his waxed canvas cape.

'Driver!' Gentleman John called over the rain. 'Hurst Street, if you please!'

A second later, the cabby flicked his reins and they were moving, the horse's hooves clacking at a moderate trot over the wet cobbles, leaving Angelica wondering precisely where in Hurst Street Hardy had gone, and why the man sitting next to her thought it important. She did not know the street well, only that it was, or had once been, at the centre of the Jewish community, so she had little clue as to why Hardy had gone there. As it wasn't far, however, she supposed she would soon find out.

As they continued on their way, Angelica began to wonder what other activities Hardy had been engaged in since she had hired Gentleman John. She found it difficult to believe that Hardy had done nothing noteworthy in all that time until now.

'What else has Mr. H been up to?' she asked, adopting the use of Hardy's initial only, as Gentleman John had. 'Surely he left his accommodation before today?'

'Oh, yes, he went out,' Gentleman John said. 'But not often. On Tuesday morning he visited a tea room in New Street and sat reading his newspaper for a little over an hour. If it interests you, it was a copy of the *Birmingham Daily Post*.'

'Did he meet with anyone?'

Gentleman John turned to Angelica and raised an eyebrow. 'If he had, you might have seen me sooner than this. He spoke to no one other than the serving girl. When he left, he called at a greengrocer and bought a bag of apples. Then he went home.'

'And on Wednesday?' Angelica asked, keen to hear more about Hardy's day-to-day life.

'Wednesday was without a doubt the most interminably dull day of my life,' Gentleman John said with a sigh. 'On Wednesday, Mr. H never left his home at all.' His features suddenly brightened. 'This morning, however, Mr. H was up and out early. I watched him buy a copy of the *Birmingham Daily Gazette* this time, from a loud young newspaper-seller at the Bull Ring. Then I continued to follow him to the same tea room he'd visited two days before, where he sat down with his pot of tea to read said newspaper. Now, a lot of people buy the *Gazette* for the advertisements, so I thought to myself, perhaps he's after buying something, or maybe a service of some kind, just as you have bought mine. It wasn't until this afternoon, however, that I discovered I was right.'

'Hurst Street!' the cabby called, cutting through their conversation.

'Ah, here we are,' Gentleman John said, looking along the quiet lamplit street for whatever it was that had so interested him.

'Already?' Angelica said, surprised at how quickly they had arrived.

'I said it wasn't far.' Gentleman John sat forward, squinting through the rain. 'A little further!' he called to the cab driver, and they were off again, now at a slower pace as Gentleman John continued to look for the location Jack Hardy had visited that afternoon. Several seconds passed. 'It doesn't quite look the same in the dark,' he told Angelica. Then, after several seconds more, having passed a number of back-to-back houses and a chapel, which she noted was called the Unitarian Domestic Mission, he shouted, 'Here! Stop the cab!'

They pulled up outside what at first appeared to be more of the same working-class housing, but then Angelica noticed a brick archway and realised this was what Gentleman John had been looking for.

'Mr. H went through there,' he said, pointing directly at the arch, confirming Angelica's thoughts. 'I could only follow him so far in such a confined space for fear of being seen, but through that arch lives the man Mr. H went to see. Now, I don't know if you can make them out from here, but on the wall there, just to the left of the arch, there are three plaques stating the service provided at each of the three addresses. Can you see them?'

Angelica could, but she could make nothing out. 'So, on which door did Mr. H knock?'

'That's just the thing,' Gentleman John said. 'I don't know. By the time I reached the arch, Mr. H had already entered through one of them.

I listened at each door for some small clue, but could hear nothing, so I waited, and I waited, until my presence began to feel decidedly suspicious. I took a stroll, not far, and when I returned, it was just in time to see Mr. H walking out from beneath the arch, leaving me none the wiser as to precisely whom he'd gone to see, which is why I thought it best to bring you here. Perhaps if you were to look at the plaques, it may become obvious to you whose services Mr. H sought to employ.'

Angelica was keen to see them. She pushed open the low door in front of her and stepped down from the carriage, not caring for the rain. Gentleman John followed in her shadow, and when they reached the arch and the plaques beside it, he struck a match, sheltering it with his hand, and held it up to the first name.

'Daniel Beckman, tailor,' Angelica said under her breath as she read it. 'The man is certainly in need of a new suit, and by your account he was here long enough to undergo a fitting.'

If Beckman was the man Hardy had come to see then it gave her no cause for concern. But there were tailors all over Birmingham. There was no need to search through the advertisements in the *Birmingham Daily Gazette* to find one.

Gentleman John cursed and shook his hand as the match burnt down too close to his fingertips.

He quickly lit another and held it before the second plaque. 'Into books at all, is he?'

'Not to my knowledge,' Angelica answered absently as she read the details on the plaque. 'Jonathan Teller, book gilder,' she said. 'Did Mr. H have any books with him? Did he leave with any?'

Gentleman John took a moment to answer. 'No, I don't believe he did,' he said with some hesitation.

'You seem uncertain. Did he or did he not arrive or leave with a book or books?'

Gentleman John shook his head with equal uncertainty. 'Well, it's like this. While I never saw him with any books, he still had his newspaper with him, you see, so I can't discount the possibility that he had one or more books concealed within its sheets.'

Angelica moved on. 'Light another match, and quickly, will you? I'm getting soaked.'

Gentleman John struck another match and held it to the last of the plaques. This time as Angelica read it, she took a step back.

'Are you all right?' Gentleman John asked, clearly noticing her reaction and the distress that was suddenly evident on her face.

Angelica was not all right—far from it. She was convinced that this was the man Hardy had discovered among the advertisements in his newspaper that morning. Who better to talk to when digging into someone's life—or their past, in this case? 'Mathias Pool,' she read out. 'Heraldic and genealogical studies.' Hardy had employed Pool to reveal her ancestry. She was certain of it.

She turned on her heel and marched back towards the waiting hansom. 'Keep following him,' she said, her tone now curt. 'I want to know if he returns, and this time be sure of whom he visits, whether you're discovered or not.'

Gentleman John walked after her, but Angelica had already climbed back into the cab. A second later it was moving. 'Do you mean to leave me here in this accursed rain?' he called after her, but he received no reply.

CHAPTER TWENTY-ONE

Winson Green, Birmingham
1896

If only I had insisted on Angelica giving back my father's Derringer on that rainy afternoon. But how could I have known then what I know now? Back then, my heart was suddenly so full of joy again. It was just like old times. All I wanted to do was make Angelica happy.

But Angelica was not happy.

She did well to hide her fears from me, as intimate as we were. Although I could not see it at the time, even then she was manipulating me, using me as she used everyone around her. Was her love for me nothing more than an act? I am bound to question it now. There was acting on her part, of that I am in no doubt, just as there were lies, but there was love, too. I am equally sure of it. I never felt it more strongly than I did on that day when she spoke about the two of us someday moving away and living out our lives together in peace and privacy. Yes, I was happy then, blinded by love and ignorant to the scheming that was unfolding around me, and I had good reason to be.

A little over a week had passed since that wonderful, rainy afternoon in town. We were having dinner together at Priory House with William and Louisa, who had become inseparable since Alexander's trial. I was so excited because Angelica had told me she had a surprise for me, and what a surprise it was, although it hurts me to think about it now.

Birmingham
1893

It was early on Friday evening, eight days after Angelica had visited Hurst Street with Gentleman John. With every passing day the knot in her stomach had twisted tighter and tighter. Even so, she was determined not to let Jack Hardy upset the pleasant dinner she was currently enjoying with William and their guests, Effie and Louisa. Angelica did not consider that their company alone warranted the usual fifteen or so courses that would have been more appropriate if Louisa's father had been dining with them. Instead, she had planned a less formal family dinner of only six courses, which had been taxing enough given her fractious state of mind. Had Louisa and Effie not been there, she would likely have skipped dinner altogether, taking only a light supper, but they were there for good reason.

As the fish course ended and the servants cleared away the plates, William sat back and drew a long breath. He had a quizzical expression on his face as he looked first at Effie, and then at Angelica. 'You two seem very conspiratorial this evening,' he said, his eyes narrowing further. 'What's going on? What's all the excitement about?'

Effie giggled for the umpteenth time that evening and just stared at Angelica, as if waiting for her to explain why she was in such high spirits, and why they had been whispering to one another since their soup bowls had been set in front of them.

Angelica raised a glass of wine to her lips and took a sip, taking her time to answer. 'I was going to tell you after dinner,' she said, 'but I suppose the cat is now out of the bag.' She took another sip of wine, this time lingering over the finish longer than William seemed to care for.

'Well?' he said. 'Are you going to tell me, or aren't you?'

Louisa, who was sitting beside William, placed a hand on his arm. 'Patience, William. All things come to those who wait.'

On hearing that, Angelica had to smile to herself. Here was another of Louisa's pithy moral expressions, plucked from the mouths of others or from the books and poems she had read, and through them she had once again revealed her naivety. To Angelica's mind, all things came to those who waited, but only when they were prepared to apply their own influence on the situation. She had come to see Louisa as a young lady of little substance, but what did that matter when she would someday inherit her father's half of what was already a very lucrative business?

'We're taking a little trip together,' Angelica said, smiling at Effie, who was already smiling back at her, the excitement in her eyes almost palpable.

'When?' William demanded. 'And where to, for that matter?'

'We're going to Brighton to visit Violet. You remember Violet, don't you?'

William raised his eyebrows. 'How could I forget her? I killed her dog, remember?'

'Nonsense, William. I've told you a hundred times that you mustn't blame yourself for that. You made a mistake, that's all. I thought you were over it.'

'I am,' William said with a sigh. 'But why are you going to see her? I thought you hated her.'

'I don't hate her, William—it was years ago. We're going by train in the morning. That's why Effie's staying with us tonight.'

'As soon as that!'

'You'll be fine, William. I'm sorry I've not given you much notice, but I need to get away.

Things have been very stressful since poor Stanley took ill.' She paused and smiled at Louisa. 'If you'd like to, Louisa, you can stay here with William while I'm away.'

Louisa blushed at the thought. 'I'm sure my father would disapprove.'

'Your father need know only what you tell him,' Angelica said with a wink that caused Louisa's blush to rise further in her cheeks until she became quite red-faced. She looked down at her lap to hide her embarrassment. Then she glanced sheepishly at William.

'Mother!' William said. 'You know full well how inappropriate it would be to have Louisa stay here in your absence, whether her father knows about it or not.'

'It was just a thought, William,' Angelica said. 'Someone to keep you company in the evenings, that's all.' She considered, somewhat wildly, that it would certainly help to speed their marriage along if Louisa were to fall pregnant. 'I'm just saying that I don't mind. Stay or don't stay, Louisa. It's entirely up to you.'

The meat course arrived, breaking the tension as the *filet de bœuf à la Pompadour* was served, and Angelica did not need the ensuing silence to tell her that she had perhaps gone too far with her marital machinations. It was an unnecessary suggestion anyway. It was plain to see that Louisa was now as smitten with William as she had once been with Alexander, and there was no doubt in Angelica's mind that William returned her affections. He had but to ask for her hand in marriage and she would surely give it, but there was no immediate rush. It could wait until her business with Jack Hardy was resolved.

Jack Hardy . . .

Would the wretched man not give up his quest to uncover her secrets and ruin her? According to the latest information she had received from Gentleman John two nights ago at the Anchor Inn, he most certainly would not. Their conversation was still playing on her mind.

'Well, what news do you have?' she had asked as they sat in their usual corner of the pub, which was busy enough that night to drown out their discourse. After several fruitless visits and as many sleepless nights, wondering when Gentleman John would show up again, she had become impatient to see him and hear his report.

Gentleman John had barely had time to sit down. He removed his top hat with one hand as he did so, and with the other he flicked his coat tails out in a flamboyant manner, as if to suggest that his answer would not be rushed.

'As I'm sure you have by now gathered,' he said, loosening his collar as he made himself more comfortable, 'I observed little of note from Mr. H for several days.'

'Yes, yes,' Angelica said, her impatience frustrating her. 'Get to the point of the matter.'

'Very well. This afternoon, I followed Mr. H back to Hurst Street. This time I remained close to him as he strolled beneath the arch, as silent as his own shadow.'

'And did you see which door he knocked on this time?'

'I did, and when he left again, he had a smile on his face as wide as the moon. The door he knocked on was that of Mathias Pool, whom you will surely recall provides services in the fields of heraldic and genealogical studies.'

'I knew it,' Angelica said, her pulse quickening. She recalled Mathias Pool's profession very well. It was that which had so troubled her sleep since first seeing his plaque on the wall.

'I stayed with him,' Gentleman John said. 'From Hurst Street I followed him along Hill Street, all the way to the train station at New Street, where I watched him buy a ticket.'

'Where to?' Angelica asked, her concern growing with every word Gentleman John spoke. Clearly Hardy had received information from Pool, information that had taken him over a week to obtain. Now Hardy was making travel arrangements. She feared she already knew where Hardy was going, but she wanted to hear Gentleman John say it, if only in the hope that he might prove her fears wrong.

'London,' Gentleman John said, and the word caused Angelica such pain it was as if he had thrust a dagger into her chest. 'He has a ticket for Saturday morning.'

London . . .

Of course Jack Hardy was going to London. Where else would he find the answers he was looking for? Where else would he find the tools with which to bury her?

Gentleman John began tapping his fingernails on the table, as if something were vexing him. 'Mr. H looked at me rather suspiciously as I listened in on his conversation with the ticket seller,' he said. 'I think he must have recognised me from the arch at Hurst Street earlier. I managed to follow him home again unseen, and I waited until it was dark, to be sure he didn't go out again, but I'm not sure how much use I can be to you now.'

Angelica drew a deep breath and sighed. 'You've been very useful,' she said, removing her glove as she had the night she first met Gentleman John. From within it, she produced the remainder of his payment. 'An extra half sovereign for your shoe leather,' she said as she slid the coins across the table. 'Buy yourself a new pair.' And with that, Angelica had left, knowing all she needed to know, leaving only the matter of what to do about it.

What to do about it indeed?

She was still pondering the question now, but the silence in the dining room was becoming tedious. She turned to Effie and grinned. 'I have another little surprise this evening,' she said. 'This one's for you, if you can withstand any more excitement.'

'I really don't know that I can,' Effie said. 'Taking the train to the seaside with you, and visiting Violet, of course, was surprise enough when you first told me.'

'Perhaps I'd better not say then.'

'Don't be mean, Mother,' William said. 'Now we all want to hear what it is.'

'Very well,' Angelica said, 'we're breaking our sojourn to the seaside and staying in London for a night or two. While we're there I thought we could see some of the sights, and on top of that I have the best surprise of all.' She paused. 'Perhaps I should tell you after dinner so your excitement doesn't overflow and ruin your appetite.'

Effie jiggled in her seat. 'It's already ruined. Now do stop teasing and tell me, please!'

Angelica's eyes widened as she looked into Effie's. 'When we first met, you said how much you loved the opera, so that's what we're going to do.'

Beyond the rented room Effie kept for them in town, Angelica had not heard her squeal with such delight. 'We're going to see an opera together?' she said, as if unable to believe it. 'Where? The summer season at the Royal Opera House has finished and the winter season has not yet begun.'

'In London there is always opera,' Angelica said. 'The D'Oyly Carte Opera Company at the Savoy Theatre are performing Gilbert and Sullivan's new comic opera, *Utopia, Limited*, also known as *The Flowers of Progress*.'

Effie gasped and held her breath. Angelica thought she was about to cry; her eyes were so full of emotion. She let her breath go again and put her knife and fork down. 'There,' she said. 'I positively can't eat another mouthful.'

'Didn't I tell you?' Angelica said. 'I should have held back the surprise until after dinner.'

Effie shook her head. 'I don't know what to say. I know it's early yet, but I think I just want to go to bed so the morning will arrive all the sooner.'

Everyone laughed.

'Have some dessert, at least,' William said.

'Yes, you must, Effie,' Angelica agreed. 'It's one of your favourites—vanilla soufflé. Besides, I want to talk to you about the other sights we're going to see while we're in London.'

'They could never eclipse the opera,' Effie said.

'I'm sure it's going to be a wonderfully entertaining performance,' Angelica replied, thinking it a pity she would have to miss it. Her thoughts drifted back to Jack Hardy again, as they so often did, and she imagined that her time in London was going to be far less agreeable than Effie's.

CHAPTER TWENTY-TWO

Angelica hadn't gone back to the train station at New Street since she had first arrived in Birmingham. Seeing it again now after so many years immediately rekindled unpleasant memories for her: the feigning of hers and William's deaths, their flight from London. That was thirteen years ago, and yet it suddenly felt as if it were yesterday. As she and Effie followed their porter along the station platform, she pictured herself as she was back then, climbing down from one of the carriages with little William, while Tom Blanchard grappled for her arm, seizing it violently even before she had fully alighted from the train. She did not wish to go back to London, but unless she wanted to risk the return of those dark days—risk losing the life she had made for herself, and above all, for William—she knew she must.

Jack Hardy could not succeed.

A puff of steam sounded sharply from one of the locomotives on the other side of the platform, drawing Angelica's attention back from her memories. She turned her head towards the sound and watched the white steam billow up into the arched iron framework, where it began to dissipate beneath the glass roof. She wondered whether Hardy was yet aboard their train to London, and the thought led her eyes back to the carriages beside her. She imagined he would be travelling in second, or perhaps even third class, but they had already passed the third-class carriages and she had seen nothing of him. He would surely not be in first class—at least she hoped not, or there would be a greater chance of him seeing her.

They were halfway along the second-class carriages when Effie slowed down and began to hobble. 'There's something in my shoe,' she said as she stopped altogether.

'Porter! Please wait,' Angelica called, and the porter, whom they had previously had difficulty keeping up with, stopped and frowned as he pulled out his pocket watch. 'The train leaves in five minutes, madam.'

'Effie, can you make it to our carriage?' Angelica asked. 'It's not far, and we can better deal with it there. We don't want to miss the train, do we?'

'I don't think I can,' Effie said, her eyes filled with apology. 'It's really quite painful to walk on.'

'I'll help you take the weight off it. Hurry now, put your arm around my shoulders. That's it.'

They hobbled towards the first-class carriages, Angelica thinking that the last thing she wanted to do at that moment was to draw so much attention to herself. She began looking into the second-class carriage windows before quickly turning away again in case Hardy should see her. Then she looked back over her shoulder. There were plenty of people about, and no one stood out. Not at first. But then she saw him and caught her breath. There was Jack Hardy, a small case in one hand and a newspaper in the other. His step was brisk—too brisk for the slow progress she and Effie were making. In a matter of seconds he would reach them. Perhaps he would offer to help, thinking them strangers at first. He had only to pass them and look their way once to know it was her.

'Faster, Effie, please,' Angelica said, and Effie made greater effort, although it caused her to wince and yelp with every step, drawing more and more attention.

Angelica chanced another quick look back, and this time Hardy was so close she could almost read the headlines on his newspaper. She turned her face towards Effie and bowed her head as she braced for the inevitable confrontation. As they reached the beginning of the first-class carriages, however, and nothing happened, she carefully glanced back again, just in time to see Hardy stepping up into one of the compartments in the second-class carriage they had just passed.

'We're nearly there, Effie,' she said, seeing that the porter had stopped a little ahead of them and was taking their travel bags into one of the first-class carriages. 'It's probably just a small stone. That's all it is. I really don't know why you chose those dainty lace-up shoes over an honest pair of travelling boots.'

'I'm wearing a new gown,' Effie said, pulling her long coat aside to show the shimmering, heavy reddish-brown fabric. 'I didn't want to wear black boots with it, and the shoes match so well. It's easy for you these days. You only ever seem to wear black.'

They arrived beside the porter and Angelica tipped him. 'Thank you,' she said as they were both helped up into their compartment.

The porter closed the door behind them with a thud that jarred Angelica's already fragile nerves. 'I see it's one of the older trains,' she said with a frown as she helped Effie with her shoe, at the same time taking in the dull mahogany woodwork and the faded blue upholstery. 'I was hoping it might be one of the newer ones with a corridor and a toilet.'

'At least we have the compartment to ourselves,' Effie said.

'Yes, for now, although I expect that will change when we make our first stop.'

A shrill whistle sounded from somewhere out on the platform and the carriage shuddered as the locomotive let off its steam. Then, with a jolt, they were moving.

'You'd better sit down with me before you fall down,' Effie said.

'I've almost got it,' Angelica replied. 'There it is,' she added a moment later, holding up a sharp little stone no larger than a match head. 'I'm afraid it's made a hole in your stocking.'

Effie smiled. 'I have others with me, and we're going to London, aren't we? I'll buy a very fine pair if we can find the time to go shopping.'

'I'm sure we will,' Angelica said. She sat down opposite Effie. 'That's if there's time after visiting all the sights you've listed, not forgetting the opera this afternoon. Do you want your railway rug yet?' She gestured at the rugs they had each rented from the station before they boarded.

'No, I don't think so,' Effie said. 'It's cold out, but it's a lovely day. My gown is warm and the sunlight through the window should help to take the chill off.' She smiled playfully at Angelica and stretched her stockinged foot across the space between them. She began to rub her toes against Angelica's knees. 'You do realise that when we're speeding through the countryside, no one will be able to see us?'

'It had crossed my mind,' Angelica said, raising an eyebrow. 'But we'll have plenty of time for that once we're in London.'

'You're no fun, Angelica,' Effie said, pouting as she withdrew her foot. 'At least help me on with my shoe, will you. I can't even reach halfway in this corset.'

Angelica slipped Effie's shoe back on to her foot and tied the lace, and as she settled down for the journey her thoughts drifted to Jack Hardy again, and the reason she was really going to London. It was certainly not for fun. She had to find out exactly where Hardy was going, and to do that she supposed she would have to follow him, as Gentleman John had. But how could she hope to be successful with Effie at her side? Hardy would surely check in to a hotel, as they would, but how could she discover which hotel if she could not follow him?

To her delight, the answer to her questions came to her more quickly than she expected. She did not have to follow Hardy, and neither did she have to know where he was staying. If she was right about his reason for visiting London then she knew exactly where he would go. All she had to do was go there and wait for him to come to her, and in doing so confirm her deepest, darkest fears.

They were staying at the Savoy hotel on the Strand, which had only opened its doors a few years earlier, in 1889. It made perfect sense to Angelica, as that was where the opera performance was being held, and she knew Effie would appreciate the en-suite bathrooms and the endless supply of hot water, not to mention the novelty of having electric lights and lifts, the Savoy being the first hotel in the city to boast such modern conveniences. Their adjoining rooms had windows facing the Thames, which Angelica had mixed feelings about. On one hand, it was a lovely aspect to look out from— the course of the river and the bridges below them, winding away to the east for as far as her eyes could see. On the other hand, like seeing the train station again after so many years, the river brought back memories she would sooner forget, however much she knew she now had to face them. All the while she was in London, they would not allow her a moment's peace if she did not.

'Angelica?' Effie called to her from the doorway between their rooms. 'Is everything all right?'

Angelica turned away from the window, putting her memories aside for now. 'I was just admiring the view,' she said. 'They really are lovely rooms, don't you think?'

'Yes, it's all rather lavish. The yellow and white decor, and the gilt details here and there make me forget it's November. Shall we unpack, or would you like to eat something first?'

'If you'd allowed me to bring a maid with us, we could have done both,' Angelica said.

Effie frowned. 'But that would really have

spoiled our fun, wouldn't it? Perhaps the concierge can send someone up?'

'No, I'm sure we can manage perfectly well,' Angelica said, putting a hand to her head.

'Are you sure you're quite well?' Effie asked, coming to her side. 'You look a little pale. Did you catch a chill on the train?'

Angelica's complexion was indeed paler than usual, but it was not from a chill. It was on account of the creeping nausea she had felt since arriving back in the city she had fled. It was the last place in England she wanted to be, but she could not turn her back to it now. Still, if it caused her to pale, then it served her purpose. It would make it easier to do what she now had to do.

'Perhaps I should sit down,' she said, moving slowly towards the chaise at the foot of her bed. 'I don't know what's come over me. I have a pain in my head and the most unpleasant feeling in my stomach.'

Effie took on a serious expression. 'Shall I call for a doctor?'

'No, no. I expect I just need to sit down for a moment.' She lowered herself on to the chaise. 'It's probably all the excitement.'

'Yes, and you've certainly been through a lot lately,' Effie said. 'Perhaps now we're away, it's all catching up with you.'

Angelica nodded. 'That's probably all it is. Could you please pass me a damp flannel?'

Effie went to the washbasin and began to soak a flannel in cold water. She wrung it out, and by the time she returned with it, Angelica was lying down with her eyes closed. She felt the cool flannel against her forehead and began to question whether she could really be so cruel to Effie, who had always been so kind and so loving towards her. She had known no other love or friendship like it. But if there was to be any hope of their friendship continuing, what choice did she have? Effie would surely not wish to know her one day longer if Jack Hardy succeeded in exposing her lies.

'Would you be more comfortable on the bed?' Effie asked, lifting the flannel away.

Angelica slowly opened her eyes, and as she looked into Effie's she told herself that she would go through with this for Effie's sake—for the love they shared—knowing it was better to be parted for one afternoon than for the rest of their lives if she did not. She nodded and sat up, and Effie helped her around to the side of the bed. Angelica practically fell on to it, as if all her strength had suddenly drained from her.

'Angelica!'

'I'm all right,' Angelica replied, though her voice sounded weak.

'You're not, Angelica. Look at you. You can barely hold your head up. I'm fetching a doctor.'

Angelica quickly found the strength to grab Effie's arm as she made to leave her side. 'No, really. I'll be fine by this evening, I'm sure. I just need to rest. Please don't call for a doctor.'

It was then that the reality of the situation seemed to dawn on Effie. 'I don't suppose you're well enough to go to the opera, are you?'

'I'm sorry, Effie,' Angelica said, closing her eyes again so she didn't have to see the disappointment on her friend's face. 'I really don't think I am.'

'Then I shan't go either,' Effie said. 'I'll stay here and look after you.'

Angelica had anticipated this. 'That would only make me feel worse. You love the opera. You must go, or I shall never be able to forgive myself.'

'But I don't want to go without you.'

'There will be other operas, Effie,' Angelica said, 'and we shall see them all together, I promise, but you must see this one without me. I'm sure I shall feel much better when you return. We'll have a wonderful evening together.' Angelica opened her eyes and looked up at Effie. She found her hand and held it, squeezing it weakly. 'Please say you'll go. This was for you, after all. It would make me happy to know you had not missed it on my account.'

Effie sighed as the hint of a smile creased her lips, but it was not a happy smile, born more of

284

reluctant acceptance than pleasure. 'Very well,' she said, 'but only to make you happy.'

Angelica smiled back at her, and then her eyelids began to flutter. 'Good. Now let me rest, and when you return you can tell me all about it.'

'I will,' Effie said. She stood up and went to their adjoining doorway. 'I'd better get ready then,' she added. 'I'll look in on you before I go.'

Effie closed the door, and Angelica could do no more than lie there with her thoughts while she waited for Effie to leave for the theatre. She was anxious to go to the address she knew Hardy would be heading for, if she was right about his reasons for being in London, but she had to be patient. Hardy also had to check in to his hotel first, and to her knowledge he did not know London well, and neither did he know the precise whereabouts of the address in question. He would have to enquire as to where it was, and he would then have to find it, so she had a little time.

She began to wonder whether anyone from her old neighbourhood would recognise her after so long—Angelica Wren née Chastain, the woman who had supposedly drowned with her son in the Thames. For the most part, she doubted it, but she would have to be careful. There was one man in particular who most definitely would recognise her if he ever saw her again, and under no circumstances could she afford to let that happen.

CHAPTER TWENTY-THREE

The house Angelica had gone to stood beside a crooked old barber shop on Bull Lane, Stepney, in East London. It had never been a very nice house to look at, and from where she was now standing, on the opposite side of the street, trying her best to blend into the shadows, she could see that time had done nothing to improve it. If anything, it was even more dilapidated than it had been when she was last there. The dark green paint was peeling from the window frames, and most of the windows themselves were cracked and filthy with grime. Its poor condition, however, did not stand out; it looked just like every other house on Bull Lane. This was not somewhere Angelica wished to live ever again.

It was cold in the shadows. The lane was narrow, which made the wind that periodically howled along it all the more ferocious. She raised the collar of her coat and pulled her fur-lined hat further down over her ears to meet it, until she could barely see out from beneath the brim. She thought that no bad thing. Should anyone who had once known her see her standing there with her back to the wall, as if waiting for someone, they would not be able to see enough of her face to draw any recognition.

That much no longer worried her. Now she worried that she had arrived too late. Had Jack Hardy already been and gone? It was a possibility. She had been forced to stay in her room at the Savoy longer than she had hoped to, because of Effie's insistence on looking in on her before she went to the opera. Had Hardy already heard what he had come to London to hear? Perhaps he was still inside the house now, talking to the man from her nightmares while she stood out in the cold, powerless to stop him. The notion worried her. It worried her a great deal, because she knew the only way she could find out whether Hardy was there was to knock and see if anyone was home.

But what if *he* was home?

Angelica could not bring herself to knock and find out. After all, she could be wrong about everything. Hardy may very well have come to London for other reasons. He might not know about this house at all, and in knocking she risked the chance of coming face-to-face with her past. She would have succeeded in doing Hardy's work for him by bringing her world tumbling down around her. There was still a chance, however, that Hardy had learned of this address but had not yet arrived, so she decided to wait.

The lane was relatively quiet given its proximity to the High Street. A group of children in need of a wash and a meal were sitting in the gutter further along, no doubt crafting some new mischief with which to occupy themselves. Someone had not long left the barbershop, and while several people had passed her since her arrival, there was not so much activity that Hardy's approach could be missed. She would see him coming in plenty of time, and if he were already inside the house, then she would see him leave, and would know without a doubt that he was leaving with every means to destroy her.

As it was, Angelica did not have to wait very long.

No more than five minutes had passed when the door to the house she was watching opened and a young, blonde woman with a pale complexion and a small baby wrapped in her arms stepped out and began tapping dirt from a dustpan into the street. Angelica did not recognise her. She wondered who she was and how she came to be living there. Had the man from her nightmares taken up with this woman, or had he moved on? There was only one way to find out. A quick glance to her left and then to her right told Angelica that Jack Hardy was nowhere to be seen, although she still could not be sure that he was not already inside the house. A horse and cart carrying beer barrels was approaching along the street, but she did not wait for it to pass before crossing. She stepped out from the shadows at a pace.

'Excuse me!' she called when she was halfway across.

The young woman had stepped back inside the house and had almost closed the door. She opened it again and looked Angelica up and down with a bemused expression, as if wondering what such a finely dressed woman was doing on her doorstep.

'I'm sorry to trouble you,' Angelica said, glancing along the street again. 'I'm looking for a Mr. Wren. I was told he lived here.'

The baby in the young woman's arms began to cry, prompting the woman to bounce the child in her arms. She shook her head. 'Not no more, he don't. We took over the rent from him two years ago.'

'He moved away? Do you know where he went?'

'I should say I do, and I'll tell you the same thing I told the gentleman what called before you. He's moved up the West End with his wife and daughter—that's what my Jimmy said.'

'His wife?'

Angelica had not considered that he might have remarried, but why not? She had apparently drowned in the Thames, after all, leaving him legally free to marry again.

'That's right,' the woman answered. 'Got a fancy shop in Regent Street now, they have. What's all this interest in Mr. Wren about, anyway?'

Angelica barely heard the question, her mind suddenly focused on questions of her own. 'How long ago did the gentleman you just mentioned call?'

'Only half an hour or so, and before you ask, I'll tell you what I told him. I don't exactly know the number of the shop in Regent Street, just that he makes and sells leather stuff—cases and whatnot.'

Angelica already knew his business. She had not lied to Effie when she told her that it had been his obsession, to the detriment of everything and everyone around him. It was true that he had never made any more money at it than to pay the rent while she had been living there. A roof over their heads was all he needed to be able to fashion his fine leather cases, his head full of fancy dreams, while their bellies were as empty as their coal buckets. She had suffered because of him, only turning to prostitution behind his back so that William would not, mixing with all the wrong kinds of people—brutal people like Reggie Price and Tom Blanchard. William's father, Jonathan Wren, was not dead, as she had told everyone. The man from her nightmares, her first husband, was still very much alive.

Angelica did not thank the woman for her help. She simply turned and walked briskly away, desperate to get to Regent Street, to stop Jack

291

Hardy from proving that her life was a lie—that she was a bigamist with no legal right to have married Stanley Hampton. The repercussions, should the truth be known, were unthinkable.

The hansom cab Angelica was quick to hire sped across London at a bone-jarring pace, weaving between the other carriages, carts and omnibuses, which at times made the main thoroughfares so congested that other routes had to be sought. She had told the driver that haste was of the utmost importance, a matter of life or death, and perhaps for her it was, or at the very least the death of the life she had become accustomed to. She had offered to pay four times the usual fare if they arrived in Regent Street in good time.

'Slowly now!' she called to the driver as they left Piccadilly Circus, not that he had much choice as the area was so busy.

Regent Street, regarded as the centre of fashion, was a long, crescent-shaped road lined with shops selling all manner of niche items to the more discerning customer. Rather than look for the case-maker's shop on foot, jostling with the Saturday-afternoon shoppers and the many street vendors and advertisement conveyancers, Angelica thought it would be quicker to look for it in the cab, but even that was not easy, especially as her view was often blocked by one of the many double-deck omnibuses going the other way. The combined noise of so many people and horses was deafening, and she quickly found herself wishing she were back in Edgbaston with this unwelcome part of her old life behind her once and for all.

The afternoon was still bright enough to warrant the many awnings that extended out over the pavement on one side of the street, making it difficult from her elevated position to see the shop windows fully, and all but impossible to read the signs painted on the fascias above them. Thankfully, though, every awning that was out had its business, or the name of the proprietor, emblazoned on it. But which one was it? Angelica's neck began to ache from continually looking to her left one minute and then to her right, turning back and forth as the cab made its slow progress, and all the while she feared she was too late to prevent Hardy from making the discovery she knew would destroy her. She was a bigamist, after all. If Hardy could prove as much then it would nullify her marriage to Stanley Hampton. What then of Stanley's estate? What then for William? It upset her to think that her son could be left with nothing after all she had done, but it was the thought of William discovering her lies that scared her the most.

It absolutely terrified her.

They were about a third of the way along the crescent, heading in the direction of Oxford

Street, when she thought she saw what she was looking for. She caught her breath and rose out of her seat to better see it, and now there was no mistake. One of the shops to her left had the name 'J. Wren' written in gold lettering above the window. It was on the shaded side of the street where no awnings were out, although an omnibus carrying advertisements for Hudson's soap had stopped adjacent to it, preventing her from being able to read anything more.

'Stop here!' she called to the driver, thumping her hand against the roof. 'Pull over across the street there, by that large awning where it says London Stereoscopic Company.' She did not wish to stop right outside Wren's shop in case he saw her, and she thought the shade from the awning would provide good cover.

The cab slowed further, waiting for another that was travelling in the opposite direction before crossing to the other side of the road. Once it had passed, the driver pulled up outside the photographic studio Angelica had indicated. The driver smiled toothily as Angelica handed him his generous fare, then as he pulled out into the traffic again, she stood back beneath the shade of the awning to take a better look at the shop across the street. The omnibus had moved on by now. There was no doubt that she had found the right place.

'J. Wren. Case-maker. Purveyor of fine leather

goods,' she said under her breath as she read the sign in full.

She stepped closer, almost to the edge of the pavement, so that her view was not hindered by all the people coming and going on the pavement in front of her. She had no fear of anyone but her husband or Jack Hardy recognising her in such a fine area of London as this, but it was still no use. Through the gaps between the horses and the carriages, the bicycles and the pedestrians on the other side of the street, she could make out the shapes of the many leather cases in the display window, but little more. She quickly realised she was too distant to see inside the shaded shop and would have to move closer.

Angelica crossed the street with great apprehension, all the while looking out for Hardy. When she arrived outside the shop, she stood with her head bowed low, feigning interest in a silver saddle flask and case that was sitting on top of a long gun case with heavy brass locks. She waited a moment, taking everything in, thinking that her husband's workmanship really was very fine, and a part of her was glad to see that his dreams had come to fruition at last. It had simply taken far too long to do so for her.

Gingerly, she lifted her head enough to see inside the shop, and even now she had to squint because the interior was so dark against the otherwise bright street, making the glass act like a mirror, reflecting her own image and that of the sunlit buildings behind her. She could make out a man standing at the counter with his back to the door, and there was a woman behind the counter with whom the customer was talking. There was no sign of the proprietor, so she thought she would wait and watch, and when the customer left, if Jonathan Wren had not yet appeared, she would venture inside to speak with the woman.

Who was she?

Angelica imagined she was her husband's new wife. She looked about the right age for him, of similar age perhaps to her own, though she thought her rather overweight and plain-looking. Then again, she supposed the woman could simply be someone Jonathan had hired to serve in the shop. As she continued to watch the woman serve the customer, she saw the man stoop and lean over the counter suddenly, drawing her attention. It looked as if he were writing something—a cheque perhaps, meaning he was close to leaving.

She felt a flutter in her chest and took a deep breath, bracing herself before she went inside, but a moment later the man turned around and Angelica froze. It was Jack Hardy, right there in front her, and now he was heading straight for her. She turned sharply away as he reached the shop door and came out, then she looked at the window again, but this time she was watching Hardy in the reflection, watching him stride right past her with a very satisfied look on his face. In a matter of seconds he was gone again, lost to the crowded street.

Angelica swallowed hard and made straight for the shop door, confident now that her first husband was not there. If he was, Hardy would surely have been speaking with him rather than his wife, or whoever she was. But what had Hardy written down? He had certainly not written a cheque. He had not gone there to make a purchase. She had to know what Hardy had said, too, and whether he was now on his way to some other location to meet with Jonathan Wren. She opened the door and went inside, dreading that Hardy had already said enough to destroy her. Her eager eyes quickly found the corners of the room where another person might be standing in the shadows, out of view from the window, but there was no one else there.

'Good afternoon, madam,' the woman behind the counter said as Angelica approached. She was well spoken, if plainly so, and smiling kindly. There was a genuine warmth to her that Angelica instantly despised.

She forced a smile of her own. 'Good afternoon,' she said, trying to glimpse what was written on the piece of paper she could see was still on the counter.

'Is there something I can show you?' the woman asked. 'Whatever it is, I'm sure you'll find my husband's craftsmanship to be of exemplary quality.'

'I'm sure I would,' Angelica said, her smile suddenly turning to a frown at hearing confirmation that this woman was indeed her replacement as Jonathan's wife. 'I'm afraid I've not come to make a purchase,' she added. She paused and began to study the woman intently, as if overcome by a sudden need to understand what Jonathan saw in her. They were nothing alike, she and her—a peacock to a sparrow, and a fat, unremarkable sparrow at that.

'Madam?' Mrs Wren said, pulling Angelica from her thoughts.

'I'm sorry,' Angelica said, feigning her smile again as she thought hard on what story she would spin for the woman. A moment later she said, 'I'm looking for my brother. He told me he was calling at your shop on a personal matter. We've been shopping all day, you see. My feet grew tired, so he left me in a coffee house. I wonder if he's called in yet. His name is Mr. Hardy—Mr. Jack Hardy.'

Behind the counter, Mrs Wren's features became excited. 'Why, yes,' she said, pointing to the front of the shop. 'You've only just missed him. I'm sure if you run after him, you'll soon catch up with him.'

'My dear, I can barely take another step on these poor feet,' Angelica said. 'I'm afraid that running anywhere is entirely out of the question. My brother told me he had to speak with the proprietor on an urgent matter. Do you know if my brother was able to speak with your husband?'

Mrs Wren shook her head. 'As I told the gentleman, Mr. Wren is away on business.'

'What a pity. Do you expect him back soon?'

'Yes, in a day or two.'

Mrs Wren picked up the piece of paper from the counter. 'Your brother wrote down the address of the hotel where he's staying.' She showed it to Angelica briefly, and Angelica saw the hotel name, but not the address. It was, however, of no matter. While there were undoubtedly other hotels in London called the Victoria Hotel, she knew which of them Hardy, as unfamiliar with London as he surely was, would have chosen. He would be staying at the Victoria Hotel at Euston Square, on the west side of the arch that led to and from the very train station he had arrived at.

'Your brother told me it concerned my husband's first wife and their son,' Mrs Wren said, her features now twisting into a puzzled expression. 'I heard they drowned, poor things. I can't imagine what your brother has to say about the matter.'

'I have no idea,' Angelica said, sensing that Mrs Wren was fishing for more information. 'I try not to trouble myself with my brother's affairs.'

'Well, I'm sure Mr. Wren will be most keen to speak with your brother on his return,' Mrs Wren said. 'I'll pass the message on, don't you worry.'

Angelica tried to raise another smile, but it felt awkward at best. 'Thank you,' she said, thinking that worrying was all she would be capable of unless she could find a way to stop Hardy from seeing Jonathan Wren. As she left the shop, she knew she would have to give the matter a great deal of thought, but she did not have long. If she were to prevent Hardy from proving her bigamy, and her first husband from discovering that she and William were still alive, she would have to act quickly.

CHAPTER TWENTY-FOUR

It took Angelica the remainder of the afternoon
to hatch the plan she hoped would safeguard her
and William's futures, and all the while she had
been acting against the clock, conscious of the
curtain falling on the opera Effie had gone to see.
It had heightened her anxiety to know that she
had to be back at the Savoy, tucked up in her bed,
by the time it did, or it would only lead to more
lies, and she hated lying to Effie almost as much
as she hated lying to William, even when it was
for their own sakes. Had she not made it back to
her bed in time, she would have had to tell Effie
that she had felt much better and had gone out
for a stroll, and that would have raised questions
about where she had been that afternoon, which
wouldn't do at all. Should she require an alibi
for her activities in London that weekend, it was
imperative that Effie fully believed she had been
asleep in her hotel bed all afternoon. All she
had to do now was take care of the evening, for
which she supposed a further alibi could prove
all the more important if her plan played out as
intended.

They had been down to the lavish new American
Bar, which had opened earlier that year, drinking
champagne cocktails before dinner and listening

to the piano as they talked about the opera. It was all Effie had talked about since she'd come back to Angelica's room and gently stirred her from her feigned sleep. It was as if Effie felt so sorry for Angelica having missed the performance that she wanted to cover every detail, missing nothing out. Drinks before dinner had been the idea, but after two cocktails it quickly became apparent that they would not make it to the restaurant that evening.

'I'm so sorry,' Effie said as they made their way back up to their rooms. 'I really don't know what's come over me. I can't recall the last time I felt this sleepy, and it's barely half past seven.'

'I expect you've overexcited yourself, that's all,' Angelica offered, 'and travelling can certainly make one weary. Did you manage to get any sleep last night, or were you too excited?'

'I was rather excited,' Effie said. 'I didn't sleep much.'

'Well then, that's what it is.'

Effie sighed. 'Yes, I expect so, and those cocktails,' she added with a giggle. 'I'd like another one.'

'I thought you were sleepy.'

'I am, but I don't want the evening to end so soon. Shall we order room service? It could be rather romantic.'

Angelica was feeling anything but romantic.

Frustration had begun to rise within her, but she tried not to show it. Effie was still far too lively, and that would not do at all. That afternoon she'd visited the Victoria Hotel and had left a note for Jack Hardy, saying that she knew why he was in London and that she wished to meet with him. At nine o'clock that evening she would be waiting at the Town of Ramsgate public house in Wapping, in the East End—somewhere she knew from her old life. Long before then, however, Effie had to be fast asleep in her bed. Another drink was certainly required, this time laced with a little more laudanum than she had slipped into her cocktails at the bar.

'How about a glass of Madeira and an early night,' she said. 'I noticed there was a small decanter in each of our rooms.'

Effie sighed again, and as if she had not heard Angelica, she said, 'I was so looking forward to dinner. I've heard such good things about the *chef de cuisine*, Auguste Escoffier.'

'We have tomorrow night, Effie. We can sample Escoffier's menu then, after a good night's sleep.'

Effie yawned as they reached their rooms. 'Excuse me,' she said, opening her door. She turned back to Angelica with a furrowed brow. 'Did I tell you about the opera band—the James Clinton Clarinet Company? They were marvellous, too.'

'Yes,' Angelica said, 'you told me all about

them as soon as you woke me earlier. You showed me their name on the opera programme.'

'Silly me—yes, I remember. My room or yours?'

'Yours,' Angelica said, opening her door, thinking that she didn't want to have to drag Effie through the adjoining doors to her bed when she finally fell asleep. 'Give me a few minutes and I'll bring that glass of Madeira through.'

Effie winked at her. 'Sleep with me in my room tonight,' she said. 'I don't like being by myself in unfamiliar places. Please say you will.'

'Of course,' Angelica said, winking back at her. She thought it could only strengthen her alibi, should one be needed. If she was lying next to Effie when they woke up in the morning, how could Effie suspect she had been anywhere other than beside her all night.

They each went into their rooms, and as soon as Angelica closed her door behind her she went to the side table for the bottle of Madeira. The glasses that were neatly laid out on the little silver tray beside the decanter were disappointingly small, but the sweet Madeira would easily hide the laudanum's bitter taste, and she had to be mindful not to overdo things. The laudanum she used had been blended with a greater quantity of morphine than was usual. Heaven forbid, she did not want to risk killing Effie by giving her too much. She had already had two small doses that evening. Still, it had clearly not been enough and time was not on Angelica's side. As much as she hated herself for treating Effie like this, more drastic measures were required.

As Angelica opened her reticule and removed her little bottle of laudanum, she told herself that it was all for the best, and that Effie would want this if she knew it was the only way they could be together. If she did not do this, if Hardy had his way, she really could not see how there could be any future for them. She set the bottle down beside the drinks tray and removed the cork stopper, then she poured as much laudanum into one of the Madeira glasses as she thought the fortified wine could disguise, roughly equal to as much as Effie had already consumed that evening. It was sure to send her straight to sleep. She poured the Madeira then, first raising her own glass to her nose and then the glass containing the laudanum. She could just about tell the difference, but she doubted Effie would be any the wiser.

Still, she despised herself for doing it, and she loathed Jack Hardy all the more for making her do it. Again she told herself that she meant no harm by it—only good, as far as Effie was concerned. It was not at all like the time she had slipped arsenic into Violet's afternoon tea each week when she visited Priory House. Then she had meant harm. She had wanted Violet out of the way because she seemed too wise a woman to have in her new circle of friends, and far too nosy. Such a sharp, inquisitive mind as hers might have seen through her plans and threatened them. But the arsenic had worked wonders, and it was no surprise to her that Violet began to feel so much better when she moved to Brighton, far from the poison that would eventually have killed her had she not.

Angelica put her laudanum away again and quickly laid out her travelling clothes and boots. She removed her earrings and her pearls, understanding from her time living in East London that to venture out alone at night in such finery would only invite more trouble than she cared for. With that done, she collected the drinks tray, keeping an eye on the glass that contained the laudanum, and went through the adjoining doors to send Effie to sleep.

She hoped it would act fast and that she would not be late for her meeting with Jack Hardy, if he was there. She had no idea whether he would take her bait, but she imagined his curiosity to hear what she had to say would be enough. By now Hardy must have thought he had won their little game and would no doubt wish to revel in his triumph, but the game was not over yet.

CHAPTER TWENTY-FIVE

The Town of Ramsgate was a watermen's pub on Wapping High Street, with leaded-light windows and welcoming gas lamps that cast a warm amber glow on to its brick walls and the advertisements for Charrington's ales and stout. It sat dwarfed between the tall buildings that fronted Gun Dock and the River Thames, adjacent to Wapping Old Stairs, which was a narrow passageway alongside which most of the pub's interior ran. Angelica arrived by hansom cab with little time to spare, thankful that she no longer had to walk these streets, fearful of the shadows and the eyes of desperate men who would think nothing of beating her senseless for a few coppers if she strayed too far from the lamplight. She had thought to have the cab driver stop a short distance away, not wanting anyone to know she had been to the Town of Ramsgate that evening, but if her plan played out as intended it would not matter. It was also not worth the personal risk, however much she felt she knew these streets and the people who inhabited them.

The cheery din coming from within the pub as Angelica stepped down from the cab and paid the driver seemed welcoming enough, but even now she was mindful that the Wapping docks were no place for a lady, and certainly not a lady alone at night. The only women she would find here were prostitutes and toothless old gin soaks who would equally try to rob her blind if she was not on her guard. As she approached the pub's entrance, she noticed two men in the passageway, smoking pipes and talking together in hushed voices by the low light that spilled from the pub windows. One of them caught her eye and nodded to the other. He stepped away from the wall, as if to approach her, but she did not linger. Instead, she averted her eyes and hurried inside the pub to the sound of an accordion playing unfamiliar music somewhere at the far end of the bar, the player—no doubt a Russian Jew trying to earn his supper—out of sight for now.

It took few patrons to make such a narrow pub appear busy. The bar divided the room in two along at least half its length, rendering the walkway narrower still. It made it difficult to know whether Hardy was there. She saw several men in dingy, loose-fitting suits and flat caps leaning over the bar with their pints. Others were seated at the tables beneath the windows in similar fashion, talking loudly among themselves. In the corner to her left sat an expressionless old woman sucking a pipe, and she knew there were other women further in, because although they, like the accordionist, were obscured for now, she could hear their laughter.

But where was Jack Hardy?

Angelica moved further in, looking from one face to the next, paying particular attention to anyone wearing a bowler hat in case Hardy was still wearing his. She found that almost everyone she looked at was already staring back at her, no doubt curious to know why she was there. Her long coat, though black as the night and relatively plain, was clearly of too fine a cloth; her hat and the hair beneath it too neat and tidy to mark her out as someone who had gone there to sell her pleasures for a shilling. The higher-class prostitute did not ply her trade on the streets or in places such as this. They did so from their own lodgings, or were in the employ of a single wealthy client.

'Can I help you with something, miss?' one of the men standing at the bar said. He was already smiling at her when she looked at him, and she imagined he had been doing so since she walked in. 'Or maybe you could help me,' he added with a wink as she drew closer, continuing towards the sound of the accordion and the laughter. 'Like a drink, would you?'

'You couldn't afford her,' the older man standing next to him said, laughing as he spoke. 'Perhaps we could both chip in, eh? What do you say to that, my dear?'

Angelica said nothing. She turned away from them and kept walking, still taking in the faces around her, caring nothing for their stares and their leering. She began to convince herself that Hardy was not there, that he did not wish to meet with her, but as she reached the end of the bar she saw him. He was sitting on an oak settle against the wall with a pint of Toby on the table before him, a young rosy-cheeked woman perched beside him, clearly to his annoyance judging by his perturbed expression. Angelica approached, drawing his attention, and although he was no doubt glad she had arrived, bringing with her his salvation from the persistent harlot beside him, he offered her no smile in greeting.

The prostitute did give Angelica a smile, but it was not well meant. 'This gentleman's with me, deary,' she said. 'Plenty more pickings at the bar.'

Hardy opened his mouth as if to protest, but Angelica quickly threw a shilling down on to the table. 'That's the easiest money you'll make tonight,' she said. 'Now, if you don't mind, this gentleman and I have business to discuss.'

'What if I do mind?' the woman said, sitting up and straightening her tatty hat as she did so.

Angelica stood over her and picked up the coin.

' 'Ere,' the woman said, 'no need to be hasty.' She stood up, offering out her hand for the coin, and Angelica pressed it into her palm. Then she stepped back to let the woman pass.

Hardy removed his hat and set it down on the seat beside him where the prostitute had been perched. 'I don't much care for your choice of meeting place,' he said as he watched the woman go. 'I've been propositioned four times already this evening, and been met with more unsavoury glances while I've been sitting here waiting for you than my nerves are fit for. Besides that, the place positively reeks.'

Angelica sat in the Windsor chair opposite him. 'No one will mind our conversation in a place like this,' she said, unbuttoning her coat.

Hardy laughed dryly. 'No one will hear it over this din! I swear this must be the only tune that bearded old fool in the corner knows.'

'Then that is all the more reason to have chosen such a place,' Angelica countered. 'Now, are you going to sit there complaining all evening, or do you wish to hear what I have to say?'

Hardy's eyes narrowed on her. 'I very much wish to hear what you have to say, madam, but if you've called me here to deny the things I already know to be true, you're wasting your time and mine.'

'I can assure you, Mr. Hardy, this meeting will not be a waste of my time. Whether or not it proves to be a waste of yours will be entirely up to you.'

'And just how did you know where to find me?' Hardy protested, apparently too caught up with his own questions to give Angelica's words any thought. 'I suppose you've been following me,' he added. 'I take great umbrage at that, or would you have me believe that your presence in London at this time is purely coincidental?'

'It is no coincidence,' Angelica said. 'I've had someone following you since our last conversation outside the assize courts after Alexander's trial.'

Hardy's cheeks, still slightly flushed from his encounter with the persistent prostitute, reddened further. 'Then you'll know I went to see an eminent genealogist by the name of Mathias Pool in Hurst Street,' he said. 'That was time very well spent, I can tell you. You see, I now have in my possession a copy of your certificate of marriage to one Jonathan Wren, whom I shall be meeting on his return to London in a day or two. Pool connected you both via your maiden name, and I fully expect Mr. Wren to confirm Pool's findings when I see him—confirm to me that he is your husband, and is not as dead as you would have everyone of your acquaintance believe.' Hardy gave a snort. 'I am sure, madam, that I need not spell out the implications of such a discovery. I also have a copy of your death certificate, and your son's, too, issued here in London, while all the while you were both alive and well in Birmingham. Do you mean to deny any of this?'

Angelica shook her head. 'I deny none of it. Everything you say is completely true, and so much more. I faked my death, and that of my son,

to escape our impoverished lives in London—
to save us both. Jonathan Wren is my husband,
and by all accounts is indeed very much alive
and well. You have uncovered my deceit and
proved my marriage to Stanley Hampton to be
bigamous and therefore illegal.'

'But, if you do not deny any of this,' Hardy
said, 'why then are we here? What more of the
matter is there to discuss?'

Hardy's right hand was resting beside his pint.
Angelica reached across the table, meaning to
place her hand gently on his, but he snatched it
away, his eyes suddenly full of alarm.

'What's your game?' he said, studying her
warily.

Angelica smiled at him. 'We don't have to be
enemies,' she said, speaking softly. 'Quite the
opposite, if it pleases you.'

'It doesn't please me, madam,' Hardy said. 'It
doesn't please me at all. Now, I'll ask again, why
have you called me here?'

Angelica withdrew her hand. 'I thought we
could discuss a mutual arrangement,' she said.
'One that would make you a wealthy man.'

Hardy laughed. He slapped the table. 'Is that
so?' He shook his head. 'I'm afraid my silence
cannot be bought.'

'But you have not yet heard my offer.'

'It would make no difference, madam,' Hardy
said. 'Stanley Hampton was a very good friend

to me, and I shall never forget his kindness. Now that he's dead, my duty is to his family— his proper family—to Alexander.' He paused and sipped his ale. 'You confirmed a moment ago that what I've told you is true, but you also said there was more to it. What more do you refer to? Was Alexander right all along? Did you turn Stanley's will to your own advantage, meaning to exclude Alexander from his rightful inheritance?'

'If I were to tell you all I have done since first meeting the Hamptons, Mr. Hardy, I'm afraid your silence would cost me everything I have.'

Hardy leaned in. 'Perhaps that is the price you must pay for your lies and your secrets,' he said. 'If you wish the authorities, and Jonathan Wren in particular, to remain oblivious to the fact that both you and his son are still alive, that is.'

'I see you're a very shrewd man, Mr. Hardy. You appear to have turned the tables on me, but you set a very high price. For your silence, you wish to know the truth of all I have done, and would take everything I have gained from it?'

'Not a penny less,' Hardy said. 'I want nothing for myself, you understand. It all belongs to Alexander, and I aim to see that he gets it. Tell me what you've done, hand over everything that doesn't rightfully belong to you, and then take your son far away from Priory House and never return.'

Angelica said nothing for several seconds.

She simply fixed her eyes on Hardy, pretending to think the matter through. Give it all up? The idea was as preposterous as the thought of telling this man what she had done to obtain it. Still, there he sat, looking rather smug in his apparent victory. But this was not over. To the contrary, she thought their little game was playing out very well. She had not gone there to flirt with him, or to offer him payment for his silence.

'It seems you leave me no choice, Mr. Hardy,' she said, going along with him, trying to sound as meek as she could manage. 'I'll tell you everything, but not here. The music may be loud, but I must be careful. After you have bled my purse dry, I should not be able to buy my way out of trouble again should anyone else hear a word of what I have to tell you.'

'What do you propose?'

'There's a passageway outside. We can continue our conversation there.'

With that, Angelica stood up and turned to leave.

Hardy rose with her. 'Before we go,' he said with some haste, drawing her attention back to him. 'Soon after you sat down, two men came and sat at the bar, not far from us. I've noticed they keep looking over at you.'

'Are they still there now?'

Hardy gave a nod.

'Does one of them have bushy black sideburns and a flat nose?'

'He does. Do you know them?'

'No, thankfully. They were outside when I came in. It seems they've taken an interest in me. I shall have to watch my back when we leave.'

'I'll see you safely to a cab,' Hardy said. 'Don't you worry. I may appear mercenary in my pursuit of what I believe to be right, but I wish you no harm.'

'Thank you, Mr. Hardy. I feel so much better for knowing that. Now, let's get this over with, shall we?'

'After you, madam,' Hardy said, and then he followed Angelica outside.

The passageway that was Wapping Old Stairs was initially not as quiet as Angelica had anticipated. A few prostitutes had gathered beneath the lamp post outside the pub, touting for trade. In the shadows further along, between the pools of light spilling from the pub windows, one of the women had a punter against the wall of the adjacent wharf building, but once they had passed beyond the pub windows, and the amber lamplight was replaced by the silver-blue hues of the moon, they were entirely alone.

They went to the very end of the passageway, to the stone steps that at low tide ran down to a small beach where once pirates and smugglers were hanged and then chained to wooden posts for three tides, until their bodies became blackened and bloated. But there was no sign of the beach or the posts now. It was close to high tide, the greenish-brown Thames water lapping at the steps partway down, hiding all trace of the area's bloody history.

Angelica gazed out across the water momentarily, towards the sufferance wharves and Bermondsey beyond, thinking of Effie, hoping she was still sound asleep in her bed and had not yet missed her. She turned around to face Hardy, her back to the Thames, and felt her pulse quicken with anticipation, knowing this would soon be over.

'Do I have your word as a gentleman that what I tell you here tonight will go no further, however much it horrifies you?'

Hardy gave a sombre nod. 'Provided you adhere to our agreement, my lips will remain sealed.'

'Very well,' Angelica began. She drew in the cool night air and gazed absently past Hardy, along the passageway. They were still alone. 'My life here in London was not to my liking,' she said. 'When William was born I felt so ashamed of myself, so guilty to think that I had brought this innocent child into a world of filth and starvation. This new life I held in my arms resolved me to find a better future for both of us. You can understand that, can't you?'

'I can understand it,' Hardy said, 'but I cannot condone the bigamous manner in which you've attained it. Your husband, Mr. Wren, has done very well for himself, by all accounts. You need only have stood by him.'

'I needed a more certain future for William,' Angelica said, her eyes suddenly appealing for Hardy's sympathy. 'I tried to raise what money I could. I debased myself and became no better than these women in the passageway behind you. I fell in with the wrong kind of people. They were cruel to William. Then one day William took a beating and I snapped, as any mother might. I killed the man who beat him, which is why I had to leave London, faking my death so the authorities wouldn't come after me, faking William's death so I could take him with me without fear of his father pursuing us and taking him back.'

'All for William, eh?'

'Yes,' Angelica said with conviction, suddenly wide-eyed. 'Everything I have done has been for my son—for the future I promised him when he was born.'

'Why Birmingham?' Hardy asked.

'I had to flee. Birmingham was as good as anywhere, and while not then a city, it was a town large enough to hide in—a town full of

318

opportunity. Once there I sought to make the acquaintance of well-to-do ladies, hoping to strike up a friendship with one of them.'

'Mrs Hampton,' Hardy said.

'Yes, Georgina took to William and me instantly, particularly to William. At first, I thought to obtain a position with the family—a roof over our heads and food in our bellies, but once I saw how the Hamptons lived, and how their friends lived, I knew that was the life I wanted for William, so I hatched a plan to get it, starting with Georgina.'

'Mrs Hampton died in an accident,' Hardy said in a matter-of-fact tone, challenging the suggestion that it could have been anything else.

Angelica raised her eyebrows at him. 'Did she? I was with her, and my recollection is quite different. We were out shopping with the two boys, Georgina and I. We were on the High Street and the boys had been told to hold on to their hoops, not to roll them in case they spooked the horses. Even so, William would give his a little roll now and then and it was on one such occasion, when Georgina's back was to me, taking in one of the shop display windows, that I gave his hoop a firm push. I held him back, hoping that Alexander would go after it, which of course he did. I had timed it well, waiting for the right moment. I had seen the carriage across the street that Alexander was now running towards,

319

and I had seen the fast carriage turn the corner behind us. I raised the alarm, knowing that any mother would see the danger her son was in and run out after him, which Georgina did, oblivious to the fast carriage coming the other way.'

Hardy's face reddened with anger. 'Then you as good as murdered her! She was carrying Stanley Hampton's child!'

'Yes,' Angelica said, showing no remorse. 'I told you what I had to say would horrify you, Mr. Hardy. If your stomach is too weak for our conversation, perhaps I had better not go on, because I'm afraid the rest of what I have to tell you will not fall any easier on your ears.'

Hardy drew a deep breath, trying to calm himself.

'Georgina stood in the way of my plans,' Angelica continued. 'How could I marry Stanley otherwise? He was a good man. He would not have entertained anything more than the idea of me while Georgina was alive. It took longer than I imagined, but I had to be patient. Stanley was such a long time in mourning, but very gradually I began to notice the way he looked at me. I pretended not to of course, teasing him, although it was soon obvious to everyone else who saw us together.' Angelica smiled to herself. 'Yes, I teased him all the way to the aisle.'

'You're a monster!' Hardy said, seething.

'I do what I must,' Angelica replied, 'and I can

see the extent to which it already pains you, so I will say no more. It was never my intention to make you suffer like this.'

'But you must tell me,' Hardy insisted. 'Our deal, remember? I want to know everything you've done, or I shan't hesitate to go to both the authorities and to your husband. Whatever would your precious William think of you then?'

Angelica scowled at the thought. It had always been her greatest fear that William might someday learn the truth about his father, and of the terrible things she had done, but Hardy was no threat to her tonight. She had seen to that.

She laughed at him. 'You poor fool. I never intended to tell you everything. I just wanted you out here where we could be alone.'

With that, she reached beneath her coat and drew out her reticule, which was hanging from a cord around her neck. She opened it and reached inside, and it was only then that Hardy seemed to realise the full extent of what Angelica was capable of. His eyes widened. He appeared to be in fear of his life at last. He grabbed her arm, squeezing it tight, restraining her movement.

'What are you doing?' he said, his tone suddenly full of alarm. 'What have you got in there? A pistol? Show me, and do it slowly.'

Hardy relaxed his grip a little, and Angelica pulled out a small drawstring purse. She shook it up and down and the coins inside began to clink and clank together.

Hardy's brow set into a deep furrow. 'Money?' he said, incredulous.

It was money, and yet it might as well have been a gun, for it would prove just as deadly. Over Hardy's shoulder Angelica saw that the passageway was no longer empty. Two men had emerged into the moonlight and were striding briskly towards them—the same two men who had been waiting for her outside the pub when she arrived, and had followed her inside. Now they had followed her out again, waiting to hear the jangle of her money purse—their signal to act. It had not been difficult to find such men, who would do anything for a price and ask no questions. She had once known such people better than she had liked, and little had changed in London since then.

Hardy seemed at a loss to understand Angelica's actions. 'What is this madness?' he said. 'Whatever are you doing, woman?'

Angelica did not answer his question. She continued to shake her purse, and slowly she began to smile at him, holding his stare and his attention so that he would not turn around. It was a sympathetic smile, but one that offered no apology. As far as Angelica was concerned, this had to be done. Hardy had given her no other choice. He had pursued her, intent on ruining her one way or another. Now the matter would be settled.

'Goodbye, Mr. Hardy,' she said as both of the men she had hired that afternoon arrived together and began to strike their blows. She flinched as the vicious assault began, but she stood her ground, watching as the points of their knives continued to stab, stab, stab into Jack Hardy's sides. His jaw dropped, his eyes began to bulge, and his face contorted and shook with terror in the pale blue light of the moon. He did not cry out; perhaps the knife blows had instantly taken the wind from his lungs. There was no sound other than the repeated thudding of the men's fists against Hardy's coat as they forced their knives into him over and over again until his eyes fluttered and his body at last went limp.

Angelica stood back as the men went through Hardy's clothing, like hungry hyenas over a fresh carcass, taking everything they found on him: his money, his pocket watch, anything that could identify him. They then dragged his body to the steps, lifted him by his hands and feet and threw him down into the Thames to wash up somewhere, anywhere away from the place of his murder. Angelica did not linger in her moment of triumph. She knew the Thames well enough to know that the strong current would quickly carry Hardy's body away, perhaps to be discovered in a day or two, or never at all. As the two men let go of him, she simply tossed her purse to the ground beside them and calmly walked away, content that her secret was once again safe.

CHAPTER TWENTY-SIX

Winson Green, Birmingham
1896

What a fool I've been.

But doesn't love make fools of us all at one time or another? I have asked myself over and over again whether I would have done anything differently had I known then why Angelica was really in London. If she had confided in me, would I have tried to talk her out of having poor Mr. Hardy murdered, knowing that to do so would likely spell the end of our relationship? Could I truly surrender that much for a man I never really knew? I have searched my soul long and hard since Angelica came to me and told me what she had done, but I do not know the answer. Does that make me a monster, too? I know only that my conscience will be at war with my heart over the matter until I draw my dying breath.

Of course, as with so many of these terrible things that transpired during my acquaintance with Angelica, I knew nothing of it at the time. I was so full of joy at being with her that it was easy to overlook the brooding, contemplative moods into which she soon began to descend, which seemed to haunt our stay in Brighton.

I had thought it merely due to the events of the past year catching up with her as she began to relax and unwind while we took the fresh, seaside air, but the real cause of her worry and anxiety is now plain to see. For myself, I had a wonderful time visiting our friend Violet, despite Angelica's dark moods and her frequent absence from our company, entirely oblivious as I was to the terrible realities that troubled her mind.

Her unusual disposition, however, did not last long.

We returned to Birmingham to the best news Angelica could hope to hear. While we had been away, William had proposed to Louisa, and to Angelica's delight, Louisa had accepted. It was enough to make Angelica forget everything that had happened in London, or so it seemed to me, because as the weeks and months slipped by I had never seen her more contented. William and Louisa were married in the spring of the following year.

Even then, there was more wonderful news to come.

A little more than two years after our return from Brighton, in the March of 1896, William turned twenty-one, and there was a very special gift in store for him. With it, I even dared to imagine that my hopes of Angelica and me someday moving away together were one step closer to becoming a reality. But it was not to be. Although I could not have foreseen it, all our darkest days were yet to come.

Birmingham 1896

It was late afternoon, the skies over the Jewellery Quarter still clear and bright, the gas lamps not yet lit inside the pen factory on Legge Lane. The multitude of machines and presses had stopped over an hour ago, the factory workers' tools laid down early for the day, although none of the workers had left—not on this day. On this most special day for the pen factory, there was great cause for celebration. Drinks and canapés had been circulating among the workers and guests alike, from the lowest-paid cleaner to members of the press and the most prominent of the city's dignitaries, which included the Lord Mayor of Birmingham himself, Sir James Smith.

Angelica could not have been happier.

She was standing beside William and Louisa, high up on the walkway at the top of the ironwork stairs that led up to the main office. From there she looked down over the gathering at a sea of bright faces, all gazing expectantly upwards as they waited for Alfred Moore to begin his speech and make his announcements. Her eyes found Effie, who was below with her parents. They exchanged smiles, and then Angelica's eyes drifted across to Alfred, who was standing proudly beside the Lord Mayor and his wife. Given Angelica's inauspicious beginnings, she could hardly have believed it possible to be standing amidst such fine company. A tear formed in the corner of her eye and she dabbed it with the back of her lace-gloved forefinger, the lace no longer black, but white. Her dress not dark, but bright, shimmering blue.

Alfred puffed his chest out and raised his bearded chin as he tapped his hand against the top of the railings. The rings on his fingers reverberated against the metal and the sound rang out over the gathering, ensuring he had everyone's attention before he began. He may have been a short man, but as he spoke his voice was that of a giant.

'Thank you all for coming,' he bellowed, peering down from beneath the bottom of his glasses. 'As most of you will know, young William here beside me, whom I'm proud to call my son-in-law, has today turned twenty-one years of age. So, while I've said it before, I'll say it again. Happy birthday, William!'

There were cheers from below as Alfred turned to William and beckoned him closer. 'Come along, young man. This is all for you.'

William stepped closer to Alfred, and Alfred pulled him closer still, until their shoulders were touching. 'That's it,' Alfred said. 'You stay right by my side. I have something else for you, too.'

William smiled and the gathering kept cheering. Angelica had a lump in her throat. She knew exactly what Alfred was going to give William, even though William did not.

Alfred raised his hand and the gathering fell quiet again. 'Now, as I'm sure none of you yet know, I have decided to retire from business.'

That announcement was met with a number of low groans from many of the people below, and Angelica understood why: just as Stanley Hampton's death had been deeply mourned by the factory employees, so too would Alfred Moore be greatly missed.

'I thank you for that,' Alfred said, earnestly, 'but as much as I've enjoyed being a part of this business, I'm not getting any younger. My health isn't what it used to be, either. It was always my hope to someday have a son of my own with my lovely wife Dorothy—someone to step into my shoes, so to speak—but as you're all no doubt well aware, that was sadly not to be. Fortunately, the good Lord has chosen to bless me nonetheless with a young man any father would be proud to call his son.'

Alfred turned to William, his face beaming. At that moment, the Lord Mayor produced a small mahogany box and handed it to Alfred.

'This is for you, son,' he said to William, and

Angelica held her breath as William took it from him.

'Well, open it, won't you?' Alfred said after William had stared at it far too long.

As William lifted the lid, Angelica stepped closer. She saw his eyes grow wide with delight when he saw what was inside, and her heart could have burst. She had never felt more proud, more complete, than she did at that moment. William turned to her now with a look of disbelief on his face, and Angelica nodded back at him, confirming his thoughts.

Alfred puffed his chest out again. 'I give to you, William Chastain, the keys to this factory. I do so in the knowledge that between you and my daughter Louisa, they are in the safest of hands.'

The gathering began to clap and cheer again, but Alfred had not finished. He raised his hand for silence. 'Furthermore,' he bellowed, 'the company shall no longer be called Hampton and Moore, but simply Chastain Fine Pens, after its new owners, William and Louisa Chastain.'

Alfred shook William's hand, and with the other, William held up the keys for everyone to see. Now the gathering erupted as cheers rang out and hats were tossed in the air.

'And perhaps,' Alfred continued, more quietly now as he paused and looked at his daughter, focusing on the sizeable bump protruding from her dress, despite her maternity corset, 'perhaps there will soon be occasion to change the company name to Chastain and Son Fine Pens.'

'I very much hope so, sir,' William said, his eyes on Louisa's as he spoke.

'Good, good,' Alfred said. 'Now, where's my brandy? I think it's your turn to say a few words, William. I'm parched.'

'Of course,' William said. He turned to the gathering and leaned over the railings. 'Thank you!' he called, raising his hand as Alfred had to quieten everyone down again. 'Thank you, Alfred. Thank you, Lord Mayor.' He looked at his mother, her hands clasped together in joy, and he returned her smile. Then he turned to Louisa again, and still addressing the gathering, he said, 'Mr. Moore has already given me so much. As if his daughter's hand in marriage wasn't enough, he has now given me the keys to the pen manufactory business both he and my late stepfather built, and my own name over the door.'

He turned back to Alfred. 'Sir, it is my most humble privilege to accept these keys, and I give you my solemn promise to uphold the time-honoured traditions of Hampton and Moore as the business moves into a new era under the Chastain name.' To the gathering, he added, 'Thank you all once again for your attendance this evening. I promise to work hard for you, as I hope you will for me, and for your fellow workers.'

Hats were flying again as soon as William

stepped back from the railing. Angelica rushed to his side. 'Bravo, William!' she said, kissing his cheeks. 'You speak so beautifully, and look, they all love you, just as I love you.'

William gave an embarrassed laugh. 'Thank you, Mother,' he said. 'I really had no idea this was coming.'

'We wanted it to be a surprise for your birthday,' Angelica said. 'It's all for you, William. It was always for you.'

'You did well to keep it from me. How long have you known?'

'Since we heard Louisa was pregnant. I merely had to suggest to Alfred that with your twenty-first birthday coming up it was the perfect time for him to step down and enjoy his garden. He was all for it.'

'Well, thank you. You're the best mother any son could wish for. I have so many ideas for the company. It really is the most perfect gift.'

Yes, it was, Angelica thought. It was the fruition of everything she had hoped for when she held her then five-year-old son in her arms and leapt from London Bridge into the filthy River Thames. The uncertainty of both their fates had hung in the balance from that moment on, but she had triumphed. The life she had sought for William was now his, and her duty as his mother, as she saw it, was complete.

CHAPTER TWENTY-SEVEN

Two days after William's twenty-first birthday celebrations, Angelica was home at Priory House, sitting in the drawing room before dinner, going over the old newspapers from the day before. She had a copy of the *Birmingham Daily Gazette* open on the low table in front of her by the fireplace and was reading all about William again. The story had been covered by all the major news publications in the area, and even some further afield. She had seen to it that William's rise to fortune was as widely reported as possible, and she could never tire of reading about it. It filled her heart with such joy that it made her impatient for his return from the pen factory so she could hold him and kiss his cheeks again, and tell him just how proud of him she was.

She picked up another of the many newspapers from the pile, the *Birmingham Daily Mail*, and as she opened the pages to find the article about William and the renaming of the pen factory, her mood suddenly darkened. It came without warning, but she knew at once what had triggered it. It was the newspapers, or rather, it was the fact that she was sitting there poring over them, just as she had when she returned from Brighton with Effie. She turned away to the windows, which were aglow with the day's last vestiges of sunlight, and tried to block those dark thoughts out.

But she could not.

Then, as now, she had gathered all the newspapers she could lay her hands on. For weeks she had secretly studied them, looking for any connection to Jack Hardy. She had even arranged for newspapers to be sent to her at Priory House from London—especially from London—where she at least expected to read about the discovery of a body in the Thames, and the brutal stabbing of an unidentified man. For the first week, she had found nothing, but then . . .

'Horrible murder! Read all about it!'

She could still hear the cries of the newspaper sellers in her nightmares as they repeated the headline over and over again from the corners of every street in London. Following that, she had read only that the victim was believed to be someone called Jack Hardy from Birmingham after staff at the Victoria Hotel in Euston Square reported that one of their guests had not paid his bill, and had absconded in an apparent hurry because he had left what few belongings he had arrived with in his room.

Believed to be Jack Hardy, Angelica reminded herself. Clearly after being pulled from the Thames, bloated and colourless, no one had been able to identify him with any great certainty. She imagined the police would have searched his rented accommodation on Navigation Street, but what could they hope to find? Certainly nothing that would incriminate her, or anyone else for that matter. If there was anything, she would have been questioned about it long before now. She was glad that Hardy's employment at the pen factory had been terminated before his demise. The police, uncertain as to whether they even had the right name and address for their victim, had likely taken their investigation no further than his lodgings. Three years had passed. The case was surely closed.

So why did Jack Hardy still haunt her?

The only answer she could ever think of was Alexander Hampton. He was safely locked away in prison, yes, but had Hardy visited him? Gentleman John had reported no such visits in all the time he was following Hardy, while Hardy had been unearthing her past with the help of Mathias Pool. There were, however, two days unaccounted for. The last time she had seen Gentleman John was on a Wednesday. He had told her that Hardy was taking a train to London that coming Saturday. After that she had, perhaps foolishly, discontinued his services, leaving Hardy entirely unobserved on the Thursday and Friday of that week.

Had Hardy been to see Alexander during that time? Had he told him everything he had uncovered about her, and what he planned to do about it? Did Alexander know that Hardy was going to London? It was not knowing the answers to these questions that tormented Angelica, and she knew her torment would not abate until she worked through her usual rationale, and in doing so brought peace to her mind again. She told herself that Alexander would have missed Hardy's visits long before now. If he knew what Hardy knew, he would have suspected foul play as the likely reason Hardy had never once gone back to see him after his trip to London. If Alexander suspected foul play on her part, he would surely have told the authorities, and yet here she was, years later, without having had so much as a polite conversation with the police about her association with Jack Hardy.

No, Alexander did not know what Hardy had discovered—she was certain of that. She had no doubt that there would be a confrontation between them in the years ahead, but she was ready for him. He would wonder what had happened to his friend, Mr. Hardy, and it was possible that if he looked hard enough for the answer then he would find it in London. But that was all Alexander would find. Any accusations levied at her would only be laughed at. After all, Alexander Hampton had every reason to seek retribution, as he saw it, against her, disgruntled as he would be at his new position in life as a penniless ex-convict, at the very least seeking to besmirch the good name of the woman he blamed for his pathetic situation. She thought Alexander was most likely to wind up in a lunatic asylum for the remainder of his days if he tried to take her on.

And she would see to it.

She took a deep breath, her eyes still on the light at the windows, which was now fading. Where was William? He was due home from the factory soon, but she imagined all manner of situations could have arisen to keep him there. She went to the windows to look for his carriage, making knots with her fists as she went. Why was she still so anxious? She had gone through everything again, hadn't she, just as she always did? She hadn't missed anything, had she? So why hadn't it helped to lighten her mood again this time? She needed William, just the sight of him would be enough to calm her down. She looked out, but there was no carriage on the drive.

She returned to the settee, thinking that her son should be in a greater hurry to return home, if not to his mother, then to his pregnant wife, who had largely taken to her bed with a maid on standby outside her room night and day since the celebrations at the factory, which Angelica imagined must have been too much for the girl. They had planned to find a home for themselves soon after the baby was born, but Angelica had other ideas.

'Why don't you and Louisa live here?' she had said one morning soon after she heard that Louisa was pregnant.

Since their marriage, they had been living with Louisa's father part of the time, and at other times with Angelica at Priory House, sharing themselves between parents. It was an entirely unsatisfactory arrangement, and it would become more so once the baby was born.

'That's very kind,' William had replied, 'but we aim to find somewhere of our own as soon as possible—somewhere in town, closer to the factory.'

Angelica had wanted to tell William that they could soon have Priory House all to themselves if they wished, that she was going away with Effie, perhaps in a year or two, but she did not say it. She could see his heart was set on living in the city, and she thought it would raise awkward questions about why she and Effie wanted to move away together. She wished she could tell him how she felt about Effie. She wished he would understand and not judge her as she knew others would, but she was certain that he would think less of her for it.

Effie . . .

They had been out shopping all day, trying to find a new hat for Effie to wear to her parents' golden wedding anniversary, which was only a few weeks away. Heaven knew she had enough hats already, but she was so insistent on wearing something no one had seen on her before that she had worn herself out trying to find one she liked. She was staying at Priory House for the night and was now upstairs taking a nap in the hope that she would recover her strength before dinner.

Angelica began to crave her company.

She went to the drinks table and poured herself some Madeira. Then, from her reticule, she withdrew her little bottle of laudanum and added a few drops to her glass to help calm herself. Her hand was shaking as she held the neck of the bottle over her drink, being careful not to add so much that it would make her sleepy. She put the bottle away again, and before she had taken a sip of her drink, she heard a sound that instantly lifted her spirits. It was a carriage. She heard a horse whinny and went to the window to see the carriage drawing up outside, and she sighed with relief to know that William was home at last to ease her pain. She quickly went back to the table and folded the newspapers away. Then she drank half the Madeira and tried to relax so that when William came in to kiss her, as he always did before going up to change for dinner, he would not sense her anxiety.

When the door opened, however, it was Missus Redmond who entered, red-faced and flustered. With her was not William, but a man Angelica recognised equally well, despite not having seen him in more than fifteen years. She stood up, catching her breath at the sight of him as all her nightmares, all her deepest fears, caught up with her at once.

'I'm sorry, madam,' Missus Redmond said as the man pushed into the room ahead of her. 'The gentleman invited himself in as soon as I opened the door—wouldn't even give his name. He's most insistent to see you.'

'Angelica!' the man said, breathless and pale, his eyes staring wildly at her in apparent disbelief. 'I knew it had to be you.'

Angelica met his stare blindly, wondering how this man came to be there, in her home of all places. The man from her nightmares, Jonathan Wren, had at last found her. But how? Why was he even looking for her after all this time?

'Shall I call for Mr. Rutherford?' Missus Redmond asked, breaking the spell Wren seemed to have over Angelica.

Angelica's eyes snapped to Missus Redmond. 'No, that won't be necessary. I know who he is. You can leave us.'

CHAPTER TWENTY-EIGHT

Jonathan Wren was a tall, well-built man, smartly dressed with short, dark hair and a few days' stubble on his face. It made him look roguish, although Angelica knew he was not. At least, he was not when she had known him. Then, he had been a kind and genteel man, but she supposed time could have changed that. She tried to assess his intentions, studying him, thinking him as undeniably handsome now as he had ever been. She held his eyes in hers for several long seconds, neither one of them saying a word. She sensed no hostility or hatred, despite the immense wrong she had done him in leading him to believe that both she and his son were dead. Instead, his eyes were full of questions.

'Why?' he said, stepping closer.

'You know why,' Angelica said. 'I wanted more—for William.'

'I could have given him a good life.'

Angelica laughed. 'You neglected us.'

Wren was already shaking his head. 'I worked my fingers to the bone for both of you.'

'Yes, you did. But it wasn't enough.'

'Could it ever have been enough?' Wren asked, looking around at all the finery in the room, as if to suggest that, try as he might, he could never have given her all this, or that she would ever have been truly satisfied.

'I suppose we'll never know, will we?' Angelica said. 'I did what I had to do, for William.'

Wren's tone darkened. 'By denying him his father?'

'I found him a better father!' Angelica said, spitting the words back in his face. She turned away and paced towards the window. 'But how did you find me? Surely you believed us to be dead. Why were you even looking?'

'I never supposed you to be dead,' Wren said, his voice suddenly close behind her. 'The day you disappeared, all my savings disappeared with you. I figured you must have taken it, and why would you do so if you planned to kill yourself? When no bodies were found, I was certain, although I was worried for William. I would not have been surprised to hear that his body had been found in the Thames. I half expected you had drowned him for one less mouth to feed.'

Angelica spun around and their faces met. 'How dare you!' she said, her tone seething. 'I could never harm my son. I've devoted my life to his happiness.'

'And I'm glad to hear it,' Wren said. 'Where is he? I demand to see him.'

The thought sent an icy chill down Angelica's spine. They could not meet. William could not know that she had lied to him all those years ago when she told him his father was dead. Before Jack Hardy died, he had asked her what William would think of her if he knew. Now his words were replaying in her mind. Whatever would William think of her indeed? She looked out of the window for his carriage, making out little but shadows in the half-light. There was no sign of it. That was good. She needed time to think.

'You have not yet told me how you found me,' she said. 'I suppose it was the newspapers, wasn't it? But what led you to look for me here in Birmingham? The story of William's success was not reported by the London press.'

'I have been looking for you here, on and off, for the past three years,' Wren said, 'ever since a man came to my shop in Regent Street and told my wife that his visit concerned you and my son. My son!' he added, his eyes flaring as he spoke. 'Imagine hearing that, so many years after I'd given William up for dead.'

'That doesn't explain what led you to Birmingham.'

Wren gave a frustrated sigh. 'Don't play the innocent fool with me, Angelica. I understand you too well. You know it was this man, Mr. Hardy, who led me here to Birmingham, where the police say he was from. Do not try to deny it.'

Angelica bit her lip, saying nothing, knowing that to admit it would be to incriminate herself in Hardy's murder.

'I went to see Mr. Hardy at the Victoria Hotel,' Wren said, his narrowing eyes suddenly filled with accusation. 'He wasn't there, of course. No one knew where he was, but you did, didn't you?'

'Don't be absurd,' Angelica said, knowing Wren could have no proof against her.

'My wife also told me that Mr. Hardy's sister came into the shop looking for him soon after he left. The odd thing is, Mr. Hardy had no sister. The police found that very curious, as did I. They didn't know what to make of it, of course, but I did. It was you, wasn't it?'

Angelica began to shake her head, but Wren put his hand up to stop her. 'It doesn't matter. I know it was you, and your motive is plain to see. Among other things, I'm sure, Mr. Hardy was going to tell me where you were. You couldn't have that, could you?'

'You're clutching at straws,' Angelica said. 'What evidence do you have?'

'None, I'll grant you, but after taking one look at you, my wife will swear that you were in my shop that day pretending to be Mr. Hardy's sister. I knew it was you from her description alone. Your lie implicates you. The police will find the evidence they need.'

Angelica could feel her heart racing inside her chest. She wanted to run and hide from this man, just like in her nightmares, but this was no dream. She could not run from it. If she did not think of some way to escape the reality that now confronted her, it would never end. At least, it would not end well.

Wren continued. 'I'm also equally sure that the police will be very interested to speak to you now that I have proof that you and William did not drown in the Thames all those years ago— that, to the contrary, you're both very much alive and well.'

Angelica could take no more of his threats. He had more than enough to ruin her and William, regardless of whether or not the police would be able to prove her involvement in Jack Hardy's murder.

'I see there are no police with you today,' she said. 'Are they coming for me? Have you told them about me already?'

Wren shook his head. 'Not yet.'

'Then what do you want from me? Do you need money, is that it?'

Wren laughed at her.

'I want no charity from you, woman. I want my son back, that's all. My silence for my son.'

Angelica drew a long and bitter breath. She had feared as much. She would have given anything in her power to make this man go away, but she could not give up her beloved William. She quickly became lost to her thoughts, dark thoughts of how she was going to turn this situation around. She had always managed to before, but now . . .

She was not prepared. There was no time for her machinations. No time to think.

A sound startled her, snapping her from her thoughts, prompting her to look out of the window again. It was the unmistakeable sound of another carriage approaching the house. It had to be William this time, and the thought of him arriving to find his father there with her in the drawing room filled her with utter dread. Her thoughts grew darker still, until a familiar cloud began to fog her brain, blinding her to all sense of right and wrong. They ceased to exist. Now there was only survival—her survival, and above all, William's. She heard the carriage draw up outside, and as William's faint voice reached her ears, she took one step away from Wren, reached into her reticule and pulled out the Derringer pistol Effie had given her from her father's gun collection.

'Move away!' she told Wren, thrusting the pistol towards him, taking a firm aim at his chest.

Wren drew a sharp breath, his eyes suddenly wide with fear at what Angelica might be about to do. He staggered back towards the fireplace, his hands held out in front of him. 'What are you doing, Angelica? This is madness. I want my son back, that's all.'

'That's all?' Angelica repeated, her twisted features mocking him. 'Do you think so little of my love for William that I could give him up so easily? Or perhaps you think me incapable of loving anyone, is that it?'

She stalked up to Wren until the pistol was so close to his chest that she could not miss. She knew what she had to do, and she gave no rational thought to the consequences. She was far beyond that now, possessed by the singular need to keep this man's identity from her son. Her arm stiffened as she strengthened her grip, ready to pull the trigger, but at the same moment, seeing his opportunity now that Angelica was so close, Wren lunged at her and knocked the pistol violently from her hand. She felt a spasm of pain shoot along her arm, but she paid it no attention. Her eyes were on the pistol as it fell on to the settee beside them. She went after it at once, but Wren seized her by her wrists, his coarse skin like leather straps, constraining her. She struggled and kicked, but it did her no good.

'I see now that there can be no bargaining with you,' Wren said, his eyes conveying nothing but pity for her. 'The authorities will hear of you. Mark my words.'

Angelica wanted none of his pity. She spat in his eyes and kicked him harder, prompting him to throw her from him, away from the settee towards the door. He went for the pistol then, but Angelica had no fear of him using it on her. His back was to her only for a second as he stooped to pick it up, and at that moment she leapt at him, clawing her nails across his forehead for want of something sharper. She wished she had a pen in her hair, as she had on the day she had gone to kill that unfortunate wretch Hector Perlman, but she did not. She was not prepared for this.

Her nails, however, had given her the upper hand. Wren winced at the pain and covered his face. Angelica went for the pistol, but Wren recovered quickly. He turned on her, blood now running from his wounds, but even now he did not lash out. He sought only to stop Angelica from reaching the pistol, and to protect himself from her blows as she struck him again and again with her clenched fists until he caught her wrists again. Now they turned and twisted against the back of the settee and suddenly he was on top of her, restraining her every movement.

'Stop this!' he demanded, and just then, Angelica heard the door open.

Wren was suddenly pulled off her. William was there. She saw him throw a punch at Wren, no doubt fearing for his mother's safety. What a brave young man he was. Wren staggered back from the blow, but as before, he gave no fight. He put his hands up in front of him and just stood there, staring at William as William's frightened eyes stared back. Wren smiled at him, and Angelica knew he was about to tell William who he was. She had to act fast and she didn't hesitate for a moment. She reached down to the settee and grabbed the pistol. Then she turned with it, took aim and pulled the trigger.

The bullet ripped through Wren's jacket with a thump, straight into his chest. His body jerked from the impact and he swayed momentarily before steadying himself, just long enough to look down at the blood that was rapidly seeping into the fabric of his clothes. He touched it and looked at his bloody hand in wide-eyed disbelief. Angelica was about to fire the bullet from the second barrel, but there was no need. A moment later, Wren fell.

'Mother! What have you done?'

She could hear William's voice, but it seemed somehow distant, despite the fact that he was standing right in front of her. She was so focused on what she knew she now had to do that she blocked out all else. Everything that followed the sound of the bullet being fired happened so fast that Angelica had no time to think. She acted on instinct alone, and her instinct reminded her that no one must know who this man, who had practically forced his way into Priory House, was.

As soon as Wren's body hit the floor she was on her knees beside him. She went through his clothing, frantically searching for anything that could be used to identify him, just as the two men who had stabbed Jack Hardy to death had done.

William dropped to his knees to the other side of Wren. 'What are you doing?'

Angelica gave no answer. She quickly found Wren's wallet, and not knowing what it contained, she removed it, taking no chances. In one of his pockets there was a train ticket stub that would tell the police he had travelled from London—clues to his identity she would rather no one know about.

William leaned in over Wren to see if he was still breathing, and at that moment Wren coughed. Blood spattered and dribbled from the corners of his mouth, and with what must have been the last of his strength, he grabbed William and pulled him closer.

'William,' he said, his voice so weak and faint that it was barely audible. 'I—I'm your father.'

His words immediately drew Angelica's attention. 'Don't listen to him, William,' she said, fear causing her voice to tremble. 'He's delusional.'

William looked confused. 'My father?' he said, turning back to him, but Jonathan Wren was dead.

At that moment the door opened and Angelica's head snapped around to see Effie walk in. Angelica looked down at the pistol, which she had placed beside Wren's body, and then back at Effie as she came further into the room. Then, without the slightest thought for Effie, driven solely by her own instinct to survive, she slid the pistol—Effie's father's pistol—across the parquet floor to her feet.

'Effie!' Angelica screamed. 'No! What have you done?'

Effie's brow furrowed. She began to shake her head. Her mouth opened as if to speak, but she seemed momentarily dumbstruck. She looked suddenly pale, clearly shocked by what she saw, and by what she had just heard Angelica say. No one moved or spoke again for several seconds. They were all still frozen in place as Missus Redmond burst into the room, closely followed by Mr. Rutherford.

'Did I hear a gunshot?' Rutherford said, almost before he had entered the room. 'Oh, good Lord!' he added when he saw the body. 'What's happened here then?'

Missus Redmond just stood to one side with her hand over her mouth.

'Effie, you've killed him!' Angelica said, feigning a look of horror.

Effie was still shaking her head. 'No,' she said at last, her voice little more than a whimper.

'Is it true?' Rutherford asked, looking at William.

William looked slowly up at his mother before answering, and Angelica had never seen such a look of bitter contempt from her son before. His cold eyes never left her as he said, 'Yes. There was a struggle. Effie came in and she shot him.'

CHAPTER TWENTY-NINE

Winson Green, Birmingham
1896

I have been betrayed in the cruellest manner imaginable. I know now that Angelica's heart is as black as the ink that flows from the penmaker's nib, yet why do I still love her so? I should hate her, and believe me when I say that I have tried to, but I cannot close my eyes without seeing her face and recalling the happiness she brought into my life—the happiness we shared. How can I hate something so beautiful?

When William condemned me in front of Missus Redmond and Mr. Rutherford, bearing false witness against me, I understood why. I considered at first that the same black heart beat inside his chest—like mother, like son—but I do not believe that. When it came down to it, he could not hate Angelica either, not enough to tell the truth and condemn her instead of me. And what son would not choose to protect his own mother, whatever the circumstances? No, I do not blame William. His hand was forced, manipulated perhaps, as Angelica manipulated everyone.

We were all very calm as we waited for the police to arrive, no one saying much. I was lost in my thoughts, above all too shocked by Angelica's wicked betrayal to speak. As the hour wore on, I became keen to hear her explanation of who this man I was supposed to have killed was, and why I would do such a thing. Of course, Angelica had plenty of time to think of a plausible story. She was good at that, and so very clever.

It was Sergeant Beauford who attended, the same policeman who had arrested Alexander for attacking William after Stanley was murdered—yes, murdered, but I'll come to that. Angelica told the sergeant that the dead man's name was Blanchard—the same name she had given to the man she previously told me she killed when she first arrived in Birmingham. She offered no first name and no other particulars about him, saying that she knew him only as Blanchard, ensuring it would be impossible to fully identify him from that alone. No papers were found on the body, but then of course Angelica had seen to that, too.

She said that she and William had fallen in with Blanchard soon after arriving from London, seeking work and shelter, and that he took them in, but that in time he meant to put both her and the young William to prostitution, to pay back his kindness and earn their keep. It was the same story she told me, to a point, altered now to suit her explanation. The story of Angelica's rise from poverty to fortune is widely known. She made it all seem very believable.

She went on to say that she managed to escape with William, and that Blanchard had been looking for them ever since. Now he had found them through the newspaper articles about the pen factory and had come to collect what he felt he was owed. Angelica said that Blanchard turned on her when she refused him, and that when William came home he was unable to stop him. She told the sergeant that I then entered the room, and at seeing the danger she was in, took out my father's pistol and shot the man dead, to protect the woman I loved.

Yes, our love for one another was laid bare.

I suppose Angelica was trying to throw me a lifeline, or so I like to think. By revealing the love we shared, she was providing just cause, as she saw it. She knew the shooting would not be considered a matter of self-defence—I was not being attacked, after all—but I believe her admission of our love for one another only served to condemn me further. I saw the disdain on everyone's face as soon as Angelica spoke out, and I could not fail to notice the distasteful tone of Sergeant Beauford's voice during his questioning thereafter. I believe he condemned me of the crime there and then, and I received no better judgement at the assizes. William's testimony sealed my fate, but as God is my witness, I did not shoot that man.

Angelica visited me here in my dark little cell two days ago. She sat at the table opposite me, where you are sitting now, Father. She told me she was going away and wanted to see me one last time, to explain everything. We should have been going away together someday, but as I have already said, that was not to be. Now you understand why. Perhaps confessing her wrongdoings to me helped to clear what little conscience she has, as it has eased my mind telling all this to you.

I was shocked to hear that Angelica had been poisoning Violet to get rid of her, and that she had killed her dog. Yes, it was Angelica who killed Captain Sammy. She told me she had done so to spite Violet for all her cruel remarks, particularly for those directed at William. She said she had gone up to the suite after Stanley and the boys left for the aquarium, having no intention of going to look for me and Violet. She wrapped the dog in a bathing towel and dropped him off the West Pier as one might discard a bundle of old rags. William hadn't left the suite door open, but how could he be sure? The dog was gone, the door found ajar, and there was no other explanation for it. I think it shocked me most to know that Angelica could stand by and allow William to take the blame for what she had done, and suffer the guilt he felt for so long afterwards because of it. She told me she only did so because she knew how Violet would react, and that it would turn Stanley against her. I suppose she thought it would be better for William in the long run if Stanley wanted nothing more to do with Violet, and perhaps she was right.

If only Angelica had stopped there, but there was far worse to come.

She went on to tell me that she had orchestrated the seemingly accidental death of my other good friend, Georgina Hampton, and her unborn child, paving the way for her marriage to Stanley, but not before taking care of the wretched Hector Perlman. I sat here feeling horrified at everything she told me as she went on to say how she had manipulated Stanley's will, and had later begun to poison him, too. She wanted to weaken him, you see, to make his death appear natural, due to some unfathomable illness. She thought killing him outright would have drawn too much suspicion.

Once Stanley took to his bed, Angelica said she purposely called on Doctor Grosvenor, knowing full well that his methods were outdated. She knew he would bring his leeches to effect Stanley's cure, and that in doing so would weaken him further. She had sent no telegram to London for another doctor, as she had told Alexander. It was all a lie. Angelica suffocated Stanley that night with a pillow, while he was in too weak a condition to resist her.

It was not the same pillowcase that Angelica had been seen leaving William's room with. That was nothing more than a ruse, and of all the terrible things Angelica has done, I think this shocks me the most. She wanted Alexander to beat William that day, and the harder the better, to deliberately shatter the close bond that existed between them. Perhaps she felt she was being cruel to be kind as far as her son was concerned, because it was all for William in the long run. He would take a vicious beating and in return win Louisa's hand and inherit everything.

She made sure that the maid, Sarah, saw her leaving William's room with one of Stanley's pillowcases. In pointing out the blood on it, she knew Sarah would take it straight to Alexander, whose suspicious and fragile state of mind at the time saw to the rest. She played them both, but she could hardly have killed Alexander so soon after his father's death. She had to settle for a long prison sentence for Alexander instead, which ostracised him, turning Louisa Moore and her father against him. It also gave Angelica every reason to cut Alexander from his inheritance. Then there was just the matter of poor Mr. Hardy to deal with, which I have already explained.

Angelica told me all this knowing that no one would believe me if I ever repeated any of it, but you are a man of God. How could I lie to you? What purpose would it serve me now? No, do not answer, Father. I do not expect you to do anything with this information. I can offer no proof of what I say, and I am sure none could be found, but I thank you for listening. Now there is no more time. I hear my jailer's key rattling in the lock. Oh, Lord, give me strength. They have come for me.

The gallows await.

CHAPTER THIRTY

Angelica's eyes were fixed on the hands of the carriage clock that sat above the mantelpiece in her hotel room. It was ten minutes to eleven in the morning, and she was alone with her thoughts, standing before the clock. Waiting. In her hand, she held a well-thumbed letter. It was from William, and yet it was not from William, not directly. William would no longer speak to her or write to her, other than through the family solicitor. The letter had arrived soon after William and Louisa had left her alone at Priory House with the servants, to live solely with Louisa's father. Angelica must have read it a hundred times or more.

The letter informed her that she was to stay away from William, and from Louisa and their child, and if she did not, she knew what would come of it. The letter did not spell it out, but Angelica understood well enough. If she tried to see William or his family again, he would go to the authorities and tell them what she had done. She had no idea whether he would actually go through with it, incriminating himself at the same time, but what was the use in testing his resolve now? Her son had made his position very clear:

he had disowned her and wanted nothing more to do with her.

She supposed it was largely because of Effie, and the fact that she had forced him to choose between them—to lie for her and condemn the innocent. It was also because of Jonathan Wren. She could not bring herself to tell William that she had lied to him all those years ago about his father being dead, or that it had been his father whom she had shot in front of him in her attempt to keep the truth from him. But William had believed the dying man's last words, and why would he not? Her own silence over the matter only served to confirm what William knew to be true.

The hands on the clock seemed to mesmerise Angelica. Her face conveyed no expression as her eyes followed their slow, relentless movement. She felt numb to everything she had done, and she had no regrets. After all, her work had not been in vain. William would have the life she sought for him, and she would have hers, albeit apart from him.

And from Effie.

As the clock chimed eleven, Angelica felt her body stiffen. She drew a long breath and a single tear fell on to her cheek, although it was accompanied by no other show of emotion. In her mind she saw the drop as Effie fell from the gallows. She imagined the rope snapping taut

362

around her delicate neck, and hoped her death came swiftly. Then she turned away and made for the door, putting all thoughts of William and Effie behind her. She was thinking of herself again now. She had an important loose end to attend to at a certain leather-case maker's shop on Regent Street, and it would not wait a moment longer.

ACKNOWLEDGMENTS

My thanks to Laura Deacon and the team at Amazon Publishing, to Katie Green for her expertise in helping to develop this story, to my copyeditor, Laura Gerrard, to Gemma Wain and all the proofreaders who have helped to make this book as error-free as possible. Further thanks to my eagle-eyed friend, Kath Middleton, for picking up the things that my eyes fail to see, and to my wife, Karen, who has contributed so much more to the pages of my books than she knows. I would also like to thank you for taking the time to read *The Penmaker's Wife*. I hope you enjoyed it.

ABOUT THE AUTHOR

Steve Robinson is a London-based crime writer. He was sixteen when his first magazine article was published and he's been writing ever since. A love for genealogy inspired his first bestselling series, the Jefferson Tayte Genealogical Mysteries, and he is now expanding his writing to historical crime, another area he is passionate about. He can be contacted via his website, www.steve-robinson.me, or his Facebook page, www.facebook.com/SteveRobinsonAuthor, where you can also keep up to date with his latest news.

Center Point Large Print
600 Brooks Road / PO Box 1
Thorndike, ME 04986-0001 USA

(207) 568-3717

US & Canada:
1 800 929-9108
www.centerpointlargeprint.com